THE

WOEFIELD

POULTRY

COLLECTIVE

THE WOEFIELD POULTRY COLLECTIVE

SUSAN JUBY

HARPERCOLLINS PUBLISHERS LTD

The Woefield Poultry Collective
Copyright © 2011 by Susan Juby.
All rights reserved.

Published by HarperCollins Publishers Ltd.

First Canadian edition

HarperCollins books may be purchased for educational,
business, or sales promotional use through
our Special Markets Department.

HarperCollins Publishers Ltd
2 Bloor Street East, 20th Floor
Toronto, Ontario, Canada
M4W 1A8

www.harpercollins.ca

Library and Archives Canada Cataloguing in Publication
Juby, Susan, 1969–
The Woefield Poultry Collective / Susan Juby.

ISBN 978-1-55468-744-2 (trade paperback)
ISBN 978-1-55468-743-5 (library hardcover)

I. Title.
PS8569.U324W64 2011   C813'.6   C2010-906987-0

Printed and bound in the United States

RRD 9 8 7 6 5 4 3 2 1

For James

Human nature will not flourish, any more than a potato, if it be planted and replanted, for too long a series of generations, in the same worn-out soil. My children have had other birthplaces, and, so far as their fortunes may be within my control, shall strike their roots into unaccustomed earth.
        —Nathaniel Hawthorne, "The Custom-House"

Remember, God doesn't want anyone to be left behind!
        —Leftbehind.com

PRUDENCE

I don't know about you, but for me there came that moment during every visit to the farmers' market when I wanted more. I wanted to be the one standing behind the folding table, a truck of organic produce at my back, displaying my heirloom tomatoes and baby potatoes. I want to be the one handing over glossy sheaves of swiss chard at a reasonable price and talking knowledgably about my mushroom patch. The one looking cold and somewhat chapped about the face and hands, yet more alive than anyone else in unfashionable rubber boots and dirty pants. Obviously, I had no desire to be the one in the lace-edged bonnet accompanied by a stern-faced, black-hatted man and a brood of six children. I want to be that *other* person at the farmers' market. The one with ideals and produce to sell.

It's a bit difficult to become truly productive when one lives in a six-hundred-square-foot apartment on Roebling Street in Williamsburg, Brooklyn, no matter how strong your ideals, but I did my best. I raised herbs year-round in my hydroponic grow box (powered with solar panels mounted on the fire escape). I collected yeast and hand-milled my own organic ancient grains to make bread. I used the car share service to drive out to the country with other local foodies to buy sustainably raised chickens. I didn't kill the birds myself; I offered once and the farmer said he thought he'd like to spare them that, at least. Still, I saw the buckets of guts and was left with no illusions.

The other thing I did was worm composting. It's hardly a radical concept, but it turned out to be the precipitating factor in the

1

destruction of my relationship and perhaps the thing that made all this possible.

You see, my ex never felt as strongly about sustainability as I did. He used to object when I restricted our diet based on local availability.

"For god's sake, Prudence," he would say. "We live in the greatest city on earth. Must we really eat your lumpy homemade bloody cheese with everything? I've heard Stilton makes a nice change of pace."

Leo had that English quality of being very sarcastic.

We went away to visit some friends of his in the Hamptons the same weekend New York experienced a brutal heat wave, and when we got back, it became obvious that the oppressive temperature had killed my red wigglers. I'd left my neighbor Kimi in charge and she'd overwatered them, probably in an attempt to keep them cool. The poor things drowned *and* cooked, leaving a sort of warmed-over red wriggler soup. Leo overreacted. He'd been increasingly testy since Kimi and I tried canning our own preserves and asked him to be our taster. He became violently ill because Kimi had misread the temperature gauge and the preserves were a bit poisoned. He was also still feeling bitter and sore after the fall he took when he was helping put up the solar panels and the chair Kimi was holding slipped after she became distracted by an unusual bird call, which I'm fairly sure was actually a problem with the building's plumbing.

Things came to a head over those worms. I guessed that Kimi had been doing a marathon session at her art studio. She sleeps there sometimes when the stuffed animal sculptures are really going well. Leo and I walked into the wall of dead worm smell and Leo immediately began to complain. "For god's sake, what is that smell?" and "Dear god, this is intolerable." And so forth. I found the source of the problem almost immediately and took a moment to decide where to dispose of the bodies. I wondered aloud whether any of our neighbors had a cone composter I could put them in. A cone composter allows you to compost meat and other things you can't put in a regular composter. They're really fantastic. Leo went wild. Well, wild might be an exaggeration. His voice took on an even more unpleasant tone and he went on about rats and flies. He refused to listen to my explanation of the advances being made in composting and talked right over me as I tried to tell him about the breakdown of different kinds of organic matter. He wasn't acting rationally, so I chose not to respond. I just took the worms outside onto the fire escape and left them in a biodegradable garbage bag until I decided where to take them. Brooklyn might *smell* like people are leaving piles of rotten worms all over, but that isn't the truth.

The fight wasn't over. Later that afternoon I caught Leo throwing out the recycling. He stood in the small kitchen shoving paper and cans from my recycling bin into a garbage bag in an angry and furtive manner.

"What are you doing?" I asked.

I apparently surprised him because he froze with a clean tin can in his hand.

When he finally spoke his voice was hoarse, as though he'd been yelling for hours. Perhaps in his head he had been.

"Putting out the trash," he croaked. His eyes bulged unpleasantly, and I reflected, not for the first time, that the Lasik hadn't been such a great idea.

"Why are you putting recyclables in the garbage?"

"Because you think everything is recyclable and it's not. Sometimes a person just wants to throw things away."

This was completely unacceptable, and when I told him so he began pulling papers and cans out of the bag and letting them fall onto the kitchen floor.

I hated to see that. If there's one thing I can't tolerate, it's a mess.

"Just because you're feeling a bit disposable yourself doesn't mean you have to project your rage onto household objects," I said. Leo had been an emerging manager at one of the shakier hedge funds until it went broke during the financial meltdown and he was let go.

He gave a strangled shriek and began shoveling the paper and cans back into the garbage bag. Then he started putting everything he could reach into the bag, including dishes, the toaster, a bag of steel-cut Irish oatmeal and some expensive pumpkinseed oil.

It's so sad to see someone lose control.

I waited for his tantrum to wind down a bit and then told him that when he was done, it was probably time for him to go home. That meant his cousin's place in Teaneck. He'd had to sell his co-op in Manhattan at a huge loss to cover his credit card debts, and he didn't want to return to London and tell his parents that he'd lost his job.

At that he picked up the overflowing garbage bag and stormed out the door to the fire escape. As he went to sweep down the iron stairs, he grabbed for the bag full of worms, informing me that he was going to throw them out, too. Unfortunately, I hadn't knotted it at the top, thinking that I might be able to reuse it somehow. The stinking mass spilled down his Bastian khaki shorts and bare legs, and onto his leather sandals.

Another shriek. Much use of British swear words.

I persuaded him to put the bags down and take a shower. When he got out, he put the recycling back in its place and washed and dried the dishes and foodstuff containers. He even took the worm bag with him, saying he was passing a park with a community garden. He was sweet about returning my key.

That evening, a few friends came over to cheer me up.

"Well, Pru, what will you do?" asked Jeanine. Jeanine and Ruth are young adult writers, which is what I used to be. The difference is, Jeanine and Ruth are successful. So is Kimi, at least in the field of stuffed animal art installations. Jeanine has won several major awards and is revered by teacher-librarians. She was working on a novel in verse about date rape, and the rhyming was creeping into all of her conversation.

"I don't know," I said.

"A date with fate, for that you wait," said Jeanine, musingly.

"You should write another book," said Ruth. She writes comedies about girls with relatable hair and makes a small fortune doing it.

"No, I don't think I will."

Jeanine and Ruthie had encouraged me to write a teen novel when I was trying to figure out what to do after we graduated. At the time it seemed like half the English Lit graduates of our liberal arts college were publishing YA novels, so I gave it a try. I wrote *The Sun Doesn't Forgive* in two months. It was a parable about the ramifications of global warming and the need for personal responsibility. Jeanine even found me a publisher, a small press located on the third floor of a near-derelict building in Queens. They specialized in slender volumes of poetry about drug and alcohol addiction by authors who wrote from experience. The publisher, Dan Mullin, was a decrepit, sparsely bearded twenty-four-year-old. He wore the same green polyester cardigan every time I saw him.

My book deal was largely a matter of timing. He'd met Jeanine at a party, and she'd told him that publishing for teens was like printing money and that she had a friend whose new book was a sure thing. Dan believed her. It was a poetry conference and Jeanine was the only one in attendance who had sold more than two hundred copies of anything.

Jeanine led me to believe that Mama Said Press was a children's publishing company and told me to send them my manuscript. Dan responded almost immediately with a contract and a low-three-figure advance. I was pleased, even after I realized that I was their only teen fiction author. Dan decided that the market for my book would be ten-to-fourteen-year-old boys. I'm not sure how he decided this. I doubt it was on the advice of any actual ten-to-fourteen-year-old boys. My expectations were modest. I knew that first novels published by small presses are usually quiet affairs. But I hadn't counted on Dan's sister, Sherry. She was the publicist for Mama Said Press and she had a raging case of OCD, which she brought to work with her.

Once Sherry realized that, unlike the rest of the Mama Said authors, I would actually show up for readings and other events, I became her sole focus. She booked me to speak at nearly every middle and high school in the state.

Although the teachers weren't very interested in the subject (there was a glut of global warming books at that moment), they were enthusiasm personified compared to the kids, who were often actively hostile. I was chum in the shark tank at my readings.

I decided the writing life did not appeal. Really, it had just been a way for me to talk about issues that mattered to me: sustainability, local food security, climate change and so forth.

"Your book wasn't that bad," said Ruth. "I think you were building."

I gave her a look and sipped my organic wine.

My book was, according to the lone blogger who reviewed it as part of one of those roundups about what is wrong with young adult literature, "anxiety-saturated but surprisingly dull." I couldn't, in good conscience, argue with that assessment.

"So if you aren't going to be a writer and you aren't going to marry a hedge fund manager, what's the plan?" asked Ruth. "You can't exist on dead worms and flickering solar-powered appliances."

"You'll need to come up with other reliances," added Jeanine, straining to find a suitable rhyme.

They were referring to the fact that the solar panels hadn't moved me off the grid quite as much as I'd hoped, probably because Leo broke one of them when he fell.

"There's my allowance," I said.

"Which is barely enough to pay rent on this place." The apartment was rent stabilized, which made me an object of envy among my friends. Other tenants in the building were paying between twenty-two and twenty-six hundred. A young Hasidic man had taken a shine to me and rented me the place for five hundred dollars a month, much to his parents' dismay. That modest rent took up nearly half the monthly allowance I get from my parents' estate. They died in a car accident on a Florida turnpike when I was twelve. I didn't know them particularly well because they were addicted to golf vacations and I'd been at a boarding school since I was eight.

"Maybe I'll move," I told my friends.

They gasped in unison, their wine glasses frozen in midair.

"Leave New York?"

"Leave this apartment?"

"It's been done."

"What will you do?" Jeanine's hair, which looked like an enormous and unruly swarm of bees departing from her head, expanded with alarm.

"Maybe I'll get a job on a farm. Or out in the woods doing something with nature. Maybe I can hire on as a cook at one of those penguin research stations out on the South Pole."

"Please," said Jeanine. "You can't even handle winter in New York."

"A job doing what?" Ruth asked, her tone as shocked as though I'd suggested getting a job turning tricks in the bathrooms of a family restaurant chain.

"I don't know. You two have found your callings. It's only a matter of time until I find mine. Something will work out. It always does."

"Oh, Prudence," said Jeanine and Ruth together.

Here's the great thing. Not even twenty-four hours later, the lawyer called and told me I'd inherited the farm from my only remaining relative, Great-Uncle Harold. Life is funny. One day you're struggling to make ends meet in Brooklyn, the next you discover that you're headed to an island off the coast of Canada to make a new life for yourself and the children you would have if you weren't concerned about overpopulation. It's the journey that my ancestors made, only in reverse. At least I assume they made a journey like that. My parents were always reluctant to discuss relatives.

I'm just sorry that Uncle Harold had to die for my dream of moving to the country to come true.

SETH

It might interest you to know that I've lived across from the place my whole life. Let me paint a picture for you in words. People don't take my skills seriously, but there's an art to it. There really is. When I was on a roll, I used to update my blogs eight, sometimes twelve hours a day. That's eight or twelve hours of *writing*. Stephen King is probably one of the only other guys who writes that much. Him and James Patterson, although King's the only one of those two worth reading. I wasn't creating books, but there was definitely some storytelling happening. My mother used to call my blogging mental diarrhea, and my former father, Prince of Pubs, used to ask me if I was some kind of pervert because I was on the computer so much.

But back to the part where I unleash my descriptive powers. Now, our house is a dump. I'm the first one to say it. Shaped like a box of Kleenex, vinyl sided, Mom's old craft projects everywhere, like the boots she painted and stuffed with flowers and then forgot so now there are boots full of dead twigs all over the place. Like the twig furniture she made, thinking it was going to make us rich, only she's shit with a hammer and nails and the stuff ended up being deadly. You were practically begging for a colonoscopy if you sat on it. My aunt Elsie, a bigger lady, tried out a stick couch Mom made and the thing collapsed and she nearly got a splinter in her no-no hole. She was drunk at the time, so she barely noticed, but I was well and truly traumatized. I can still remember her lying in the pile of sticks, giant white underpants showing because her caftan ended up around her waist. That image is seared into my brain.

In addition to my mom's artistry, we have the year-round, extra-tacky Christmas ornaments and lights and the puddles of deflated Santa and Frosty next to the Prince's inevitable fixer-up Firebird. When he moved out, not long after the thing with the drama teacher, my mother took her ball-peen hammer to its windshield. She whacked at the glass for about forty minutes, but all she did was make pock-marks all over the glass and tire herself out. Not quite the effect she'd been hoping for. My mom isn't in the greatest physical condition. The point is that we aren't Trump Tower over here.

So keep that in mind when I tell you that our place always, always looked better than Misery Acres, the scaliest scab on the ass of Vancouver Island. I'll tell you what they had over there. Nothing. Well, almost nothing. You know those movies where Sissy Spacek works her skinny ass off in a dried-up garden while wearing a thin cotton shift with the pattern washed out of it? You know the ramshackle farmhouse she lives in? The one that tilts to the side and has a big verandah and peeling paint and wide stairs and basically reeks of despair and poverty and everything people associate with the poor-ass countryside? Yeah, that was what Woefield Farm was. The house was painted this color that was really more of an *anti-color*. If I had to guess, I'd say it used to be something in the yellowish-gray family. When I was in about fifth grade, they put a big piece of blue tarp up on the roof to stop a leak. The year I would have graduated from high school if I hadn't dropped out, which is about four years ago now, they put *another* tarp on top of that one, probably because the first one started to leak.

There used to be a barn made of random boards and corrugated tin and whatnot, but that burned down not long before she showed up. The finishing touch was the poor sheep over there that had been living in a lean-to since the barn burned. And that was it, except for the cabin, way down at the edge of the property, which looks over at the house and the field beyond.

The field, at least the part of it we could see, was maybe thirty acres of rocks and scrub grass. The trees at the edges of the property looked like they were hanging on by their last root. Keep in mind that this is

Vancouver Island, for Christ's sake, not Easter Island. We're supposed to be a temperate rain forest not a barren moonscape. The property was huge and everything on it seemed half dead no matter what the season. Like it was a nuclear dump site.

I used to look over there and think that I wouldn't be surprised if the whole thing turned to dust and fell into a sinkhole.

I hardly ever saw the other guy who used to live there. I knew he was old and that he watched a shitload of TV. The nicest thing on the property was the satellite dish on the side of the house. The satellite company came and repossessed it about a week after he died. He seemed friendly enough, I guess. Once, I was drunk and depressed and sitting by the side of the road just outside our house, and he drove by in his old-man car, a New Yorker or a Pontiac or something. That was back when I was still making the effort to go outside. He asked if I wanted a ride home. That was kind of funny because I was only about twenty yards from our house.

I said no. I was fine. But I was obviously impaired, I guess. The guy, Harold Burns, could probably see that I was a bit shittered, but there was no judgment in his eyes. Most people are pretty quick with the condemning look. He told me to take care of myself and drove his big old car a few feet down the road and then turned up his driveway.

That was about the extent of my interaction with him: He once offered to drive me a few feet to my front door.

Anyway, as you can probably tell, everything changed when she showed up. She really got the ball rolling, so to speak.

EARL

She showed up the first of April, I guess it was. I'd been out there think-ing about getting to work on Bertie's shed. I was going to use some scrap lumber I been keeping dry under the last tarp. It was just dumb luck them boards wasn't stacked in the barn when it burned. The old man had a few one night and went out to inspect the "grounds," as he liked to call it. I usually followed him, just to make sure he didn't fall in a goddamn hole. But this time I was watching a show about Canada geese and let him go by himself. He must have dropped a cigarette because half hour later the old barn went up like Satan himself lit her on fire.

There wasn't nothing in there except a few bales of hay, but the old man bawled like a heifer. Maybe that was what finally did it to his ticker.

Like I said, I was thinking I'd get to work on a new shed for Bertie because that poor old sheep didn't barely fit in the old shelter we been using since the barn burned. Also, I figure she probably gets cold on the one side because the old man left her half sheared when he passed. He'd decided it was cruel to shear both sides of a sheep at once. He said they liked to get their haircuts in stages. He had a lot of funny ideas like that.

I was coming around the side of the big house with my tools in my belt, heading for the lumber pile, when the taxicab pulled up. I took one look around the corner and right away I thought of the *Antiques Road-show*. There's nothing some people like better than digging around in other people's stuff. I wondered if somebody from the show heard that the old man left something valuable behind. I didn't reckon anything on the place was worth a goddamn wooden nickel, but I'm not up on the antiques, so how the hell do I know?

I stayed back and waited to hear her say something. If she was *Antiques Roadshow* I thought I might head back to my cabin and put my town shirt on. Not that I give a shit what people in show business think of me.

Now I seen some things in my day, but I ain't never seen nothing like her, getting out of that cab, looking like she just landed on the moon and forgot her space suit. Bewiddled, if you catch my meaning. She had on some little shirt and shorts and then these big bloody green gum boots up to her knees like she didn't know if it was summer or winter.

She was a skinny little thing. Hardly nothing to her, but she was pretty enough. Shiny hair reminded me of a mink, only a little lighter in color.

The cab driver got to pulling suitcases and bags and boxes out of the trunk of the car. He kept looking up at the house and asking if she was sure this was the place. Only he had one of them foreign accents, so he said it kind of funny. She told him the address was right and he asked her if she was sure and she said she was.

The cab driver kept shaking his head and looking at the house.

By this time I was pretty sure she wasn't *Antiques Roadshow*. No, I figured she'd be some greedy goddamn relative. The old man'd mentioned a few but I never paid no attention to him when he talked. Sure as shit she'd run me off. It was time I left anyway. Never meant to stay so long.

I come around to see what she wanted and straightaway she started talking a mile a goddamn minute. Uncle Harold this and Uncle Harold that.

She was just a little bit in them big green boots. Next thing I know she had a hold of me. I damn near fell over from the shock of it. She reminded me of one of those feral hogs I seen once on the Nature Channel, the ones so fearless they'll take a run at a grown man.

This bitty girl got me in a clinch and she hung on. The cab driver feller was right behind her, and he had a hold of a suitcase damn near the size of Bertie's lean-to. He was staring at me like he was about to lose his lunch so I started to feel offended.

I asked her if she was done, and she finally let go.

She told me it must be so hard and it was hard for her, too.

So I said, Yeah? Because I didn't know what the hell she was talking about and I was starting to get the feeling that she might not be the brightest bulb in the lamp.

She said she was sorry, she should have introduced herself. She's Prudence, Harold's niece, and she's come to stay.

I'm not surprised the old man never mentioned her specific. People never like to talk about their slower relatives. I got a cousin, twice removed, got webs between his toes, ain't said one word his whole life. You never hear about him in the family newsletter that goes around every Christmas. Hell, nobody mentions me, either, if it comes to that. Families is funny about who they advertise. A lot of the time, the people worth knowing in a family is the ones that don't get mentioned in the newsletter. That's my opinion.

The girl was still talking, saying how I must be devastated because of how Harold and I worked together for so many years and it must have been so special.

It's true that I've been living in the cabin down at the edge of the far field for going on thirty-five years, ever since the old man hired me.

So I said, Oh yeah. Like that.

And the cabbie feller leaned over to her and whispered, Are you sure this is right?

And she whispered back, Yes. This is Earl, my uncle's right-hand man. His partner, really. Earl keeps the place going. My uncle was very lucky to have him.

I was starting to feel not right. I'm not saying I didn't help the old man, because I did. But I wasn't ready for all that right-hand stuff.

I told her I worked the farm, such as it is, and got paid every month for my trouble and how it was never any kind a partnership, less'n it was one of those 98–2 deals.

She said, Oh, like she was disappointed.

We stood there for a while. Finally, the girl says, Well, maybe we should go inside? It kind of smells out here.

Like a poo, said the cabbie.

I told them that was the rendering plant down the road. It can get a little ripe in the afternoons. And since I didn't know what else to do, I let her in and that cab driver come in right behind her, still hanging onto that goddamn suitcase. Once she was inside, I didn't know what in hell to do with her. I don't do a lot of entertaining, you want to know the truth, especially not young girls.

She told the cab driver he could leave the suitcase in the "four year." Whatever the hell that meant.

He said, You sure Miss?

And she told him it would be fine.

And he asked about the rest of her bags. He wanted to know if he could bring them in for her too, like it was a goddamn special treat. And she says, That would be incredibly nice of you. And he started grinning like she just gave him a thousand bucks.

The cabbie left and she followed me into the kitchen. She looked around like she was from the health inspector and asked me if I lived in here. I told her I got my own place. Little cabin out back.

Then she asked what's happening on the farm and I was about to tell her to mind her own damned business when we got interrupted by the cabbie. He was huffing and puffing like a workhorse with the heaves and he had hold of a suitcase even bigger than the last one.

He says, You want here?

And she says, Yes, Hugh, that's fine.

So off he went again.

She asked again what we were producing and normally that might have seemed like a pretty goddamn snotty question, only the way she said it, it was hard to tell what kind of question it was.

Before I could tell her the place was producing nothing but bad luck and trouble the cabbie was back again. This time he had a big canvas bag like a hockey bag and a couple more of them suitcases, all of it kind of hooked together. This time he couldn't even talk, the damn things was so heavy. He was fighting for air.

The girl, she just smiled at him and right away he's smiling back, even though the poor bugger's half dead.

Off he went again and before we could start talking the girl turned to me and she's got the tears in her eyes. Her voice was kind of sniffly and hell if she didn't have the waterworks going. Anyway, the girl cried for a while and the cabbie came and went with a few more bags and every time he saw she was still crying he give me a look like I just shit on the floor. Then she got calmed down and asked me how her uncle died and I told her he was watching TV.

And she says, What?

I said I didn't know what he was watching because I was back at my cabin.

She said she meant *of* what?

I got it, so I told her what the paramedic doctors said, that his ticker probably give out.

And she says, Heart attack, and starts up with the crying again. The cabbie was still standing beside her staring at me like I was the biggest bastard who ever lived.

Nobody said nothing for a couple of minutes and she asked him, Is that all the bags?

He said yes, but he didn't move.

And so she said, Thank you, Hugh. You've been terrific. He asked about four more times if there was anything else he could do for her and he shot me a few more of them suspicious-type looks before he buggered off.

Then the girl saw the pile of mail on the table and asked if it was her uncle's.

I nodded, but didn't say nothing else. I knew what those letters was full of. People asking to get paid. It was happening even before the old man died. Between you and me, I knew his financials wasn't in order. I'd just been waiting for someone from the bank to come along and close the whole shitteree down. Put a padlock on her. When that happened, I was going to put the camper on the back of the truck and head south, like I'd always planned. To hell with waiting until I had the money for a new camper. The old one would do fine if I took it down south where it never rains. I'd give that damn sheep to the neighbors and get the hell out. I never did much around the place anyway, 'cept let the old man listen when I played.

The girl flipped through the letters, looking at the addresses. Real snoopy. She said that even though she never got to know Harold, she knew about him because he was the last of her family and he lived in Canada, which she says she respected, especially during the Bush era, and she couldn't believe he'd left her everything.

It took a minute for what she said to sink in. The old man left this little girl the farm. Jesus, Jesus.

I didn't know what the hell to say to that. All I know is that I got the hell out of there before I said something I'd regret.

Prudence

For me, the first priority was building a sense of community. I don't think many people would argue that whether you live in the city or on a farmstead, you need your neighbors. Of course, the type of community will vary.

In rural communities church is very important, as are farmers' cooperatives and so forth. In cities, it's more about . . . well, I'm not sure. I went to a square dancing club on the Upper East Side for a while. I also belonged to an interesting rooftop gardening group. Plus, I hung out with my friends from college. Things are a bit more fragmented in the city. I wanted to be open to every possibility here. Joining a church. Volunteering at the Ladies' Auxiliary. Having coffee at the local café. All of it. My first order of business was to establish myself as a new and valuable resident of the area.

I thought I'd get to know people by hosting a memorial in honor of my uncle so locals wouldn't think I'd just swooped in and taken this prime piece of property out from under them. For all they knew, I could have been a developer, looking to put up condos or mini-malls or something. I wanted to allay their fears and get to know them.

Next on the To Do list was tackling the house and land. The property was spectacular. So rugged and untouched. All that wonderful grass. The beauty of stray stones in a field! It just needed to be cultivated and enriched. There was even more work to be done around the house. Consistency is a thing that matters to me and there was a severe lack of it in the paint scheme, which varied radically from room to room: eleven rooms in the house painted thirteen, non-complementary colors. For the first little while, I had to pause between rooms for a moment to let my eyes adjust to the different shades. There were eight different flooring materials, including five types of linoleum, two species of hardwood and one bathroom done entirely (floors, walls and even the ceiling) in chipped one-inch tiles. The porch sagged and the roof was sheathed in several layers of tarps. But the house had good bones. My guess was that once I'd made an effort to meet people in the community, offers to help would come pouring in. After all, Hugh the taxi driver had already volunteered to assist in any way he could.

I thought of all these things that first night in my uncle's house. It was cold and the blankets and sheets were threadbare. I could feel wind slipping into the room through gaps around the window frames. Also, the silence was strange after so many years in Brooklyn. To deal with the cold I wore warm-up pants over my pajamas and two pairs of socks. I slept soundly and woke with the birds. I think they might have been crows, rather than songbirds, but still!

When I was dressed I went outside and found Earl feeding a sheep, which was just so great, even though the sheep didn't look quite right. It appeared to have a skin disease that had caused it to lose its wool on one side, but Earl appeared to be fond of it so I didn't comment. He seemed a bit sensitive about the farm in general. I made a mental note to put calling a vet on the To Do list along with adding weather stripping to the windows once I was settled in and Earl trusted me more.

I asked Earl to join me in the house for coffee so we could discuss our plan of attack, but when I went to make coffee I found only a plastic tub full of instant crystals in the cupboard. The door of the cupboard was sticky to the touch and missing a handle. It was another thing to add to the list! I wasn't about to make instant coffee, so I pulled the four-pound bag of Mayan organic beans and a grinder from one of my bags and brought them downstairs and got to work.

Earl had come in and was taking off his work boots on the rag rug in the kitchen doorway when his head came up and he sniffed the air. He asked what was burning.

"Oh, that's coffee," I told him. "I think you're really going to enjoy it."

He winced and crinkled his brow like I'd just told him the most outrageous lie. Such a character!

When he was seated at the kitchen table, I poured him a cup of coffee and put the jar of sugar on the table and apologized that there was no light cream.

"Where's the Coffee-Mate?" he asked.

"Coffee-Mate? Oh, you mean the powdered stuff. You don't want that. It's full of chemicals. We'll keep cream on hand from now on."

He took a sip of the coffee and scrunched his face even harder, making him basically indistinguishable from a raisin.

"Too strong?" I asked.

"Jesus Christ Almighty," he said.

I could see that he wanted to spit it out.

"I'll add some water." I took his cup and added a splash of hot water from the kitchen faucet. The water smelled lightly of sulfur and I made a mental note to find out why.

When I set his mug down in front of him he stared at it like it was a coiled rattler.

I took a seat across the table from him.

"So Earl, you mentioned yesterday that the barn burned down recently," I said.

He grunted.

"That's really too bad. A barn seems like an essential thing on a farm. Do rural people still enjoy barn raising?"

He transferred his suspicious glare from the coffee cup to me.

"You know, one of those parties where everyone comes together to help out a neighbor who has had a misfortune," I added, in case he wasn't familiar with the custom.

He grumbled something about not being "goddamn Mennonites." I think he may have meant Amish. I gathered from his reaction that barn raisings are not as common as they once were. Or maybe they belong to a bygone era, perhaps due to worker's compensation considerations. In any case, I didn't have the money for building supplies, so our barn raisers would have had to bring the materials, which is probably considered above and beyond even among the Amish and the Mennonites.

I thought for a moment and sipped my coffee. It was good, but the rotten-egg smell was persistent.

"How about a strawberry social. Those are still extant, aren't they?"

Earl just stared at me.

Considering that he was hired help, I couldn't avoid noticing that he wasn't very helpful. I wondered when he'd last been paid. Perhaps a raise would improve his morale.

When he still hadn't spoken after three long minutes, I made up my mind. You can't wait around for other people to make decisions or nothing will get done.

"Yes, I think we'll have a strawberry social tea in honor of my uncle's memory. I just need to know who to invite."

"Don't have a goddamn clue," said Earl.

The man is wonderfully fierce. A classic type. I'd been reading about people like him for years but never met one in the flesh. I knew as soon as I saw his wide orange suspenders that he was going to be an important source of local knowledge if I could just get him to open up. When I pressed, Earl went over to the bulletin board by the phone and copied down a few names and numbers on the back of an envelope, which he handed to me, and then went to the back door and started pulling on his boots.

The list was very short, which was probably just as well because the supplies for entertaining around the house were limited. I'd surveyed the kitchen and found only two cheap pots, one frying pan, four bent forks, two butter knives, three mismatched spoons, a large collection of lethal-looking but dull knives stuck in a dirty wooden block and a can opener. None of it appeared to have been used for a very long time. Everything was sticky with old food residue and grease and dust. Uncle Harold must have eaten out a lot, which probably helps to explain his premature death.

I asked Earl if he'd mind calling the people on the list and asking them to come over on Saturday at three. He grabbed the hammer that he'd leaned against the wall when he came in, and for a disconcerting second I thought he was going to swing it at me. Then he said he had business to attend to and walked out.

Mr. Blandings, the lawyer handling the estate, had told me over the phone that the will stipulated that Earl remain at Woefield for the remainder of his days. If I sold the farm, Earl was to receive ten percent of the proceeds. This had led me to believe that Earl was crucial to the operation of the farm, but there didn't seem to be a lot of farming going on. So what did he do? Clearly he hadn't helped my uncle arrange his social calendar.

When I called the people on the list, they were all extremely pleasant and immediately agreed to come. Country people are so polite. Well, except for the one man who said he wouldn't cross the road for my uncle if he was on fire and my uncle was standing there with a bucket of water and a fire extinguisher. Fortunately, his wife took the phone from him and was really gracious. Perhaps her husband has suffered through a crop failure recently.

SETH

It was lucky that I was sober when my mother kicked me out of the house. Things might have turned out different if I'd gone over there drunk that first time.

Let me back up. My mother didn't exactly kick me out. She came in and told me she needed my room. I was just writing a post on a certain actor's freakout on the craft services staff on the set of *The Indivisible Man.* Apparently, he asked for an oatmeal muffin and someone at craft services gave him bran and he had a fit, screaming about did they want him to shit his pants and why did everyone always fucking defy him. One of the grips got the whole thing on his iPhone, sold it to TMZ, and now the studio is in full damage control mode. I don't care what anyone says. He is one of the few actors I actually respect, even if he does have a rage disorder that causes him to menace the shit out of his crew and members of the public at large.

I seriously considered menacing my mother when she came in with her little piece of news. I'm basically a peaceful guy, even if I do listen to heavy music, which is the other prong of my media empire. In addition to writing Celebutard.com, which some people have called Hollywood's vilest gossip blog, I write RagingMetal.com. It's a heavy metal gossip site. You might have heard of it.

Anyway, my mother told me to turn my music down around ten times. I heard her the second time, but I like to get her blood pressure going. My mother doesn't get anywhere near enough exercise. Yelling at me was basically her only activity, besides her crafts, which were getting less and less physically demanding. At least with her stick furniture she had to swing the hammer. At the time I'm talking about she'd gone balls deep for scrapbooking. How much cardio does a person get putting stickers on a page? It's no activity for a grown woman.

When I finally turned down the volume on the tunes, she was still screaming. You know how I said my aunt is a bigger lady? Well, my mom's always been the opposite. There's nothing to her. She's basically an angry bit of gristle covered in leathery smoker's skin. A steady diet of cigs and rye and Cokes will do that to a person.

"Seth!" she screamed.

"I'm trying to work here," I told her.

My mother didn't fully appreciate my writing. She was always going on about how I never left the house and it was so unhealthy, even though she knew perfectly well why I didn't go out. I *tried* going out and it was a total shit show.

She stood in the doorway of my room with her highball glass in her hand, but she wasn't plastered. Truth is, my mother never gets too drunk. She nurses her cocktails. I get my drinking habits from my old man, who never nursed anything but his hangover and a grudge.

"Seth," she said, quieter, "Bobby's moving in."

That stopped me. Bobby was this guy she met at bingo the month before. He's a good ten years younger than her. Hell, he's not much older than me, probably. It doesn't matter since people with mustaches all look basically the same.

"Why?" I said.

She didn't answer.

"I hope you'll be very fucking happy together," I told her.

"And Bobby and I have decided that he's going to need your room."

"Are you serious?"

"You're a grown man. It's time for you to move out. You're twenty-one years old. It's not healthy for you to live at home anymore."

"I'll tell you what's not healthy for me. Going out. I can't believe you're doing this after everything I've been through."

"Bobby says I'm enabling you."

"The fuck he says," I said, which made no sense. "Where am I supposed to go?"

"Don't you have any friends on your Internet?" she asked.

"Yeah, that's right Mom. I'm going to message one of the freaks who
comments on my blogs and ask if I can move in with them. Jesus."

"I'm sorry, Seth. But Bobby needs the space."

"I can't believe this. You two are shacking up, right? Why do you
have to drag my room into it?"

"Bobby has helicopters," she said.

"Bullshit. The guy drives an '86 Cavalier. No way he has even one
helicopter, never mind a whole fleet."

"Models," she said, totally unconcerned that she was destroying my
life. Ruining my security. Taking away not only my home but also my
home office. "Bobby's going to start a parts shop for remote-controlled
model helicopters. He says it's a great business."

"And he has to do it in my room? Jesus. This is such a load. What
about the garage?"

"You know perfectly well my recycling and crafts are in there."

My mother is a low-level hoarder. Our house would probably have
room for three or four Bobbys if there wasn't so much *debris* everywhere. Her mind was made up. I recognized the signs. It was like when
she dropped papier-mâché for decoupage. Once my mother decides
something, it's all fucking over. She's like Mussolini or Stalin or one of
those guys.

"So where am I supposed to go?" I asked her. A reasonable question
for a son to ask of his mother.

"Why don't you try across the street? There's someone new moved
in there. It's a girl and from what I hear, she's all alone. Maybe she's
looking for a roommate."

"I'm sure she wants the reclusive long-haired stranger from across
the street to move in with her. That's definitely going to be top of her
agenda."

"Doesn't hurt to ask," she said. Then she went back to watching
Ellen while she finished up her scrapbook documenting the life of

Aunt Elsie's dachshund, Vlad the Destroyer, who is now hooked up to one of those little carts because his hind legs don't move.

I'll show her, I thought. I put on my Iron Maiden hat and headed over there. I'd ask whoever was living at the place if they were renting rooms and that person would chase me off the property and maybe call the cops and I'd tell my mother and Bobby that I'd tried but unfortunately they were going to have to go fuck themselves. Or I'd just move all my shit onto the front porch. See how they felt about that.

Bobby. Jesus. The guy's not even interesting. Half the time there's food in his mustache.

Earl

Well, first he come wandering over to where I was going to get working on that new shed for Bertie. He was a scrubby-looking bastard. He had that long, greasy hair some of them guys like and a hat with a skeleton on it pulled down almost to his nose and white shoes hanging open like he was too goddamn tired to tie them up. He was skinny everywhere but his belly. No color in his face. Like I said, a scrubby-looking bastard.

Seemed kind of nervous, too. Twitchy. Like maybe he was on drugs or something. A lot of young guys are now. On drugs, I mean. I saw it on TV.

He muttered something about a room and I told him I don't know nothing about no room. I told him to try up at the house.

He started walking over there, bent nearly double like he was packing a bag of cement on his back. I got to thinking, maybe I shouldn't let him visit her alone. She might be nosy, but she was a woman and she was from the city and didn't know her ass from her knee, as far as I could tell.

I followed him around the house. He stood in front of the porch steps for a good minute or two, still hunched over. Then he pulled his hat down even further so I don't know how he could see where he was going and dragged himself up the stairs and knocked on the door.

Feeblest goddamn knock I ever heard. The old house was going to hell but it still had solid doors.

Nothing happened, so I spoke up. I told him that the front door is oak, so you got to put some force into a knock to get yourself heard.

26

I must've surprised him because he jumped a good foot and a half. Good to know he had some life in him.

He gave the door another little knuckle rap and I knew that unless the girl was standing on the other side of it with a glass to her ear she didn't have a hope of hearing him.

Goddamn it, I said, and climbed the stairs, pushed him out of the way and pounded out a couple of good ones. Ten seconds later she opened the door. She was wearing an apron and rubber gloves and smiling to beat all hell, not the least bit suspicious of the guy, which made up my mind that she needed some looking after.

The longhair mumbled something else that I couldn't hear. He was staring at the front doormat.

Speak up, I told him. I wanted to hear what he had to say.

He told her he was looking to rent a room in exchange for work and that he lived across the street, at least he used to until the helicopters came. Like I said, I was pretty sure he was into the drugs.

I snorted. I'd never seen him before and I could tell from that soft little fish belly he'd never worked a day in his life.

The girl, Prudence, she cocked her head like a little bird. Then she give him another big smile.

She asked him if he was afraid of hard work and he said yes. She laughed like that was a hell of a good joke. She asked him when he wanted to move and he said right away.

Neat as you please.

Twenty minutes later, that sad-sack bastard started carrying things up the driveway. Turned out he did live across the street in that god-damn slag heap with all the junk in the yard. He moved like he was wading through a swamp. I still hadn't seen his eyes. He could have been a goddamn ax murderer, for all she knew. And she moved him right into the house.

I asked her if she knew what she was doing and she said that great results demand great risks and that when she needs help she trusts in Providence and Prudence.

Shithouse luck is more like it.

Prudence

I'd been trying to scrub the bathroom. It's one thing to have a house in the rustic style. It's another thing entirely to have a filthy bathroom. As in many farm homes, there was only the one, and my uncle's looked as though it hadn't been cleaned properly since the house was built. There was a coating of mineral deposits and I hate to think what else in the crusty sink basin and toilet bowl. There were at least three empty, uncapped tubes of toothpaste glued to the counter with petrified gel.

After an hour I'd just finished removing the rusty razors, unused cleaning solutions and slivers of desiccated, hair-covered soap, and had taken down the moldy, rust-stained shower curtain. I was bracing myself to begin scrubbing the sink, and it occurred to me that in order to get ready for the party, I was going to need more assistance. Earl seemed to prefer working outside. Perhaps, I thought, I could barter with a cleaning service. It was too bad we had no livestock or produce to barter with. One could probably go far trading eggs.

Just as that thought was tumbling around in my head, I heard a knock downstairs.

When I opened the door, the young man standing on the porch appeared as uncomfortable as it's possible for a clothed person to be. At first I wasn't sure what he was saying because he mumbled. He reminded me of some of the boys I used to see outside the heavy metal club down the block from my old apartment. They would come in from New Jersey to see bands. They were so picturesque, with their long hair and jean jackets and high-tops. They really added something to the neighborhood. Leo used to say it was a smell, but he never appreciated the importance of nurturing subcultures.

Just the sight of the young man on the porch gave me a warm, slightly homesick feeling. Maybe it was just the lingering aftereffects of staring into the toilet for so long. When he asked if he could work in exchange for room and board, I knew it was meant to be.

Earl, who stood off to the side of the porch listening to our conversation, kept shaking his wattled neck and giving me outraged looks. From outside, my decision probably looked hasty, but I believe that things unfold as they are meant to.

Seth informed me that he was twenty-one, that he didn't have a high school diploma and had almost no skills. He looked younger than that, perhaps because he appeared never to have been exposed to sunlight. Also, he was not a landowner with responsibilities. I suspect that was aging me quickly, as was the task of cleaning Uncle Harold's toilet. At any rate, I felt twenty years older than him rather than the three I actually am.

When Seth showed up at the door again, not quite half an hour after we first spoke, he had a computer tower in his arms and a set of old computer speakers dangling around his neck. I told him he could have the bedroom upstairs.

"There's nothing on this floor?" he asked. "This stuff's kind of heavy."

"Afraid not."

Over the next few hours I watched him carry two or three items at a time, none confined to a box or a bag. At one point, he dropped a tall stack of VHS cassettes. They skittered all over the driveway and it took him a good ten minutes to gather and stack them all again. When he came into the house, his chin resting awkwardly atop the pile, I asked if it might be easier if he packed his things in boxes.

"They're all taken. My mom does crafts," he said.

Night had fallen by the time he finished moving into his room. I'd seen three trips worth of magazines, four trips to move a small aquarium with fish and accessories, a single trip for a canvas chair labeled

"Director of Rock," another for a laptop the size of a small coffin. On the last walk up the long, pitted driveway he pulled behind him a small rolling suitcase with one broken wheel. It zigzagged erratically like a disobedient scent hound. I could see a sleeve hanging out of it. He walked as though he were on the last leg of the Great March. When he made it into the house I asked if he wanted some of the salad I'd made for dinner.

"It's been a pretty tough day," he said. "No sense making it worse with salad."

Then he went upstairs, shut his door and I didn't see him again for the rest of the night. I decided to wait to share with him the To Do list for the party the next day.

Seth

Yeah, so the whole thing was surreal. I mean, the way she said yes. No girl, especially no decent-looking girl, had said yes to me about anything in about ten years. I'm not trying to be creepy or anything. But you can see where I was coming from. I didn't get out much and I was just trying to make a point to my mother and then all of a sudden this fairly hot, dark-haired girl with cool rubber boots was saying I could move in with her basically for free.

Sheer fucking surprise is probably what got me through the move, which was a full on shit show because I had to bring my stuff over one thing at a time. My mom wouldn't let me use any of her craft boxes and she already gave all the garbage bags to Bobby for his move.

Anyway, so I went back and forth about eight hundred times and no one offered to help. Not my mom, who was watching a *She's Crafty* marathon, or the old grumpy bastard who lives on the property with the girl, but not, thank fuck, in the same house. The girl's the only one I didn't blame for not helping. She was working the whole time I was moving. Scrubbing up a storm. She's pretty goddamned active and she has that cool name: Prudence. She's from New York, which is pretty cool in itself.

Normally, I'd have hit the sauce pretty good to deal with the stranger danger factor, but I was too exhausted from all the walking and carrying. I kept feeling grateful that I didn't have any *collections* of things like beer steins or Transformers or whatever. Something like that would be a bitch to move. I did have numerous books, movies and CDs, but I

31

left a lot of them at home. Books are heavy as hell, so I just brought my favorites, like the Ringworld series and the biographies of Mötley Crüe and Hendrix. The essentials. Maybe Bobby will learn to read from the books I left behind.

I even slept okay that first night, which was strange since I'd only ever slept away from home like a few times. There was the time when I was ten or so and Aunt Elsie tried to take me camping. We only made it half a night because she got a digestive upset. Christ, for an adult man I sure don't have much life experience.

Things went to full hell five the next day, though. First of all, the girl, Prudence, knocked on my door at six-thirty. *In the morning.*

It was like waking up on another planet or at least a part of the planet far away from where I'd always lived. All that sunshine blazing in. Prudence had told me the day before that she was washing the curtains. At home, I used Sabbath flags to black out my windows so I could see my computer screen better. I was used to living in total darkness, almost. Waking up in the new place made me feel sort of like a mushroom that someone just yanked out of a log.

I got out of bed in my underpants and a Floyd concert T-shirt, which I'd ordered off the Internet because I don't go to concerts. I looked around for something to cover myself. I don't own a bathrobe, so I wrapped one of the Sabbath flags around me. I took them from home because that prick Bobby doesn't deserve to look at them.

When I opened the door Prudence was basically beaming at me, bright as the sun outside.

"Good morning," she said. "I may have forgotten to mention that we're having an event here today."

I was hoping I didn't have any boogers in my eyes, but didn't want to feel around to check. "Event?" I said.

"A strawberry social," she said. "A memorial for my late uncle."

"Good luck with that," I said. Because seriously. The fuck? Strawberry social? Did I somehow move onto the set of the remake of *Little House on the Prairie*? I bet they didn't even have strawberry socials back when that shit was originally being filmed.

"I'm going to need quite a bit of help today with cooking and shopping. So as soon as you've showered, we'll get some breakfast into you and off we go!"

I couldn't even react. I never really thought about the work aspect of the room and board arrangement. I guess I thought maybe I'd, I don't know, take the garbage out here and there. Hang pictures. Maybe do a few dishes. But this crazy bitch wanted me to slave for her. This was bullshit, even if she was hot.

She handed me a towel. "See you downstairs in fifteen minutes. I made coconut and orange juice pancakes."

Then she turned and zipped down the stairs. Who the fuck moves like that at the crack of dawn?

Here's another thing. I don't shower every day or even every two days. I'm a once a week man. I was being coerced into showering before my time. But I did it and then went downstairs, which was also blazing with harsh sunlight and full of food smell. It was nice in a way, but it also kind of gave me sensory overload. My mom doesn't cook, especially breakfast. The only time our house smells like anything other than microwave dinners is when she does mulled apple cider at Christmas, but since she always gets a little hammered and forgets it, it starts to stink like apple moonshine after about four hours.

I ate a pancake and liked it, even though I normally never eat before one or two o'clock in the afternoon. Then Prudence started laying this *list* on me. After about item two, I realized that I was going to have to cart all my shit back across the road pronto. No way I was going to the grocery store and running around town doing errands. Fuck that noise.

"And I'm going to need strawberries," she said. "Not the kind from California. Local berries."

She turned to Earl, the old guy, who was gulping down pancakes like a starving dog, swallowing pieces so big you could practically see them going down his throat. "Earl, can you lend Seth the truck to go shopping?"

"It's my truck," said Earl.

"Doesn't the farm have a vehicle?"

"Old man took the insurance off the Buick after he drove it into a tree last winter."

"I see," said Prudence. "But I'm sure you're willing to lend your truck to Seth so he can get groceries for the party."

"I don't drive," I told her.

They both stared at me.

"Just not a driving man," I said and hoped that would be the end of it. "Maybe Earl should go to the store."

"Nope," he said, biting another pancake in half. "Too much goddamn traffic on the road on Saturdays."

"Is there a bike here?" asked Prudence.

And I was like, Why would she want to know that? Turns out she wanted me to ride a bike to the fucking store.

Earl started telling her how there was some busted relic out back, but he was going to have to pump up the tires before I could take it out.

That's when I excused myself and headed for home. It was time to call a halt to this absurd shit.

I found my mom and Bobby in her bed. They weren't sleeping. They each had a coffee mug and a couple of Eggo waffles on a tray on their lap. My mom made the trays out of kits she bought at Michaels. She's crackled the shit out of them so they look like they're covered in diseased rhino skins. Seeing Bobby and my mom like that made me feel even more like the world had turned upside down. I move and suddenly everyone starts having healthy breakfasts.

"I have to come home," I said.

"You are home," said my mom.

"I mean I need to move back in. Things aren't right over there."

Bobby just stared at me. There was already crumbs in his mustache and it was barely seven in the morning.

"They want me to ride a bike into town. And help with a party."

"That sounds nice," said my mother, like she'd ridden the Tour de France four times herself and went to parties nightly.

"A strawberry social," I said. "I can't be attending something like that. I'm the author of Raging Metal, heaviest blog on the web."

She didn't say anything.

"I tried moving. It didn't work out. I'll be moving back in now."

"There's no room," she said. Bobby nodded.

I walked down the hallway to my room. There was about one foot of floor space left that wasn't covered in boxes and garbage bags. Bobby had moved enough shit in there to equip a fleet of real, full-sized Apache helicopters.

"Fuck sakes!" I screamed. "Where am I supposed to go?"

In response, my mom just turned up the volume on the bedroom TV.

Earl

When Chubnuts came over to where I was working on the little shed, Bertie walked up to him and he started backing up and bellering and going on about how she was coming for him. I told him she just wanted to say hello and he tried to pretend like he knew that.

Then he asked if I would give him a ride into town so he wouldn't have to ride the bike. And I told him, hell no. I had things to do.

He said, Fine, and reached into his pants and pulled out one of them little phones, so small you could drop it down a drain. He hit a button or two and pretty soon he was saying, What do you mean, busy? There must be more than one cab in Cedar. Then he swore and closed the lid on the phone. He better hope he don't ever need a cab again. Old Mrs. Larson answers the phones for Cedar Cabs and she's a woman who can hang onto a grudge. Jacquie Peters, hairdresser over at the mini-mall, insulted Mrs. Larson one time by asking if there was anything that could be done about the BO smell in the backseat. Mrs. Larson never forgave her. When Jacquie called for a car one afternoon when she went into labor at home and her husband was working in the oil patch in Fort McMurray, Mrs. Larson told her she could have the kid on the walk into town as far as she was concerned.

I pointed over to where the bike was leaning up against the porch. Front tire was flat but I showed him where the pump was. I told him that the milk crates wired onto the front and back would let him carry quite a bit of stuff.

He said, Yeah, thanks, and, By the way, how long do you think it would take me to ride to the Liquor Depot?

I said I thought he was trying to get to the grocery store. He said since he was going out he might as well make a few stops.

Like hell, is what I thought. Then I told him he was looking at ten minutes in a car, forty on a bike. Maybe an hour on the bike he had.

His face under that hat of his was pale as dough when he put his leg over the bike. Said he hadn't been on one since he was a kid. Still looked like a goddamn kid, far as I could see. Acted like one, too.

He was none too steady on his way out. I thought he might take a tumble when he hit that first pothole on the way down the driveway but he made it. I figured a little exercise wouldn't hurt him. He was awful young to be that flabby. Not a bad-looking kid, though, if you cleaned him up and got him to look you in the eye.

Must have been two hours before he came back. Jimmy Samuels, from over at the reserve, pulled in and I wondered why he was coming to visit. Then Chubnuts got out the passenger side of Jimmy's pickup carrying a bunch of shopping bags. He reached into the back of the truck and grabbed two cases of beer. He said something to Jimmy and then dragged himself and his bags to the house.

Jimmy called out after him, Hey man, you want your bike?

He's a nice kid, that Jimmy. Works at the hatchery. I used to see him sometimes when I'd take the old man fishing up there. They'd get to bullshitting about hockey.

Chubnuts didn't even turn around. He just waved a hand, like he didn't care. Wasn't even his bike and he was ready to throw it away, which is typical of his generation.

I went over and Jimmy helped me get the bike out of the back. Both the tires were flat as boobs in the *National Geographic* magazine.

Jimmy said he found Chubnuts sitting outside the Co-op like he'd give up on life.

I said he was just too lazy to walk.

Jimmy laughed and said it was a pretty far ride, especially with flat tires, and I said it would do Chubnuts good. Jimmy said he always

thought Seth moved away after what happened at the school play. I
didn't know what the hell he was talking about, so I never said nothing.
Doesn't pay to ask questions about things that is none of your business. That's my experience. Everyone's entitled to their private selves.

Jimmy laughed again and said, Take care, Earl. Then he drove off.

I headed back to my cabin to get cleaned up for the party.

Prudence

Our energy affects the things we create. I suspect that some of the trouble I had with the food for the social was a direct result of the conversation I had with the woman at the bank right before I started cooking. She was a nice person and professional, but her comments about our financial situation took me by surprise.

I hadn't been aware that it was possible to inherit a negative asset. I realized that the farm's financial picture wasn't rosy. The bills my uncle had allowed to stack up were evidence of that. But the situation was much, much more dire than I initially thought.

We owed some taxes and had to pay back a home equity line of credit and there were mortgage payments. All of these things were seriously overdue. I decided not to get discouraged. A farm is nothing but limitless potential, waiting to be uncovered. If I was lucky, opportunities might even present themselves at the strawberry social. With that in mind, I decided it was best to focus on making food rather than fixing finances until after the party. I was so intent on scraping designs into the skins of the cucumbers that I barely even noticed when Seth returned.

When he put the bags down on the counter, I went over to look inside. He'd purchased two strawberry shortcakes. Obviously, they would be full of corn syrup and petroleum by-products, but my uncle's kitchen was not equipped for baking yet so that was fine. Home baking would come later. The cakes were in good shape, which was amazing considering that he'd driven them home on a bike. A quick survey of the bags and their contents revealed that he'd gotten everything else on my list.

Before I could thank him, he disappeared. I guess he wanted to get cleaned up before the guests arrived. A glance at the brass-trimmed, sun-shaped clock hanging on the kitchen wall told me I'd better hurry. I looked around the kitchen and living room. At least the house was clean. Old farmhouses are often eccentrically appointed, so the cheap furnishings and out-of-date colors could be excused. There were several problem areas, however, such as the large ragged-edged holes that had been cut into the drywall in the living room and kitchen for unspecified and mysterious reasons. The fridge made a strange squealing noise at five-minute intervals.

There was nothing I could do about those things before the party, so I returned to my preparations. I layered thin slices of fresh cucumber onto slices of crusty local bread and spread the aioli I'd made on top. I cut the sandwiches into quarters and stacked them onto the only two matching plates I could find. I arranged the cheese and fruit on a rustic board I'd found outside and washed and disinfected. The effect was simple and charming.

I hadn't had Seth purchase flowers because the flower industry is incredibly destructive, especially in Africa, but I gathered interesting Salal leaves and grasses and put them in water glasses. These I placed throughout the kitchen and living room. The effect was pretty and unpretentious.

The doorbell rang at 3:00 p.m. exactly. I pulled off the tea towel I'd tucked into my skirt and opened the door to find Earl standing on the porch.

He'd washed his face with extra ferocity so it was almost as red as his neck. The overall effect was reminiscent of an angry, underweight turkey. He had on an old-fashioned white button-down short-sleeved shirt and wide orange suspenders holding up clean green work pants. I tried to imagine what process of elimination he'd used to decide that this was the perfect outfit for a memorial social. Perhaps Earl had no other clothes. It's often that way with country people.

He gave me a single scornful glance and walked into the living room, sat down on the couch and turned on the TV.

"Can I get you a drink?" I asked.

"Love one!" boomed a voice behind me. A woman craned her head, atop which was balanced an enormous pile of bleached blonde hair, through the doorway.

She came in, followed by a man in a brown suit that strained too close around his middle. The hair that ringed his skull was cut into a sparse, Friar Tuck pageboy. It had been dyed the same mole-brown shade as his suit.

"You must be Prudence," said the woman. "It's so nice of you to invite us to your party. I'm sorry you couldn't come to the funeral."

"So sorry," added the man.

"I'm Doreen. I've known your uncle forever."

"Forever," said the man.

"This is my husband, Marshall," said Doreen. Marshall nodded, as though he couldn't agree with her more.

"We run the Sundowner's Memorial Gardens. Where your uncle is laid to rest."

"Oh, of course. Thank you. Please, come in."

I ushered them farther into the kitchen and only then did I notice the third person. He was thin and pasty and wore a dark, oversized suit and a mournful expression.

"Hello," I said.

"This is Ted," said Doreen, who looked around like a newly installed dictator sizing up a predecessor's palace. She didn't offer any further explanation of Ted's relationship to my uncle.

Ted had moved into position near the sandwiches. I could tell he wanted one.

"Please, help yourself."

He grabbed one and stuffed it into his mouth. Then he made a face and spit the bite into his free hand. He put the rest of the sandwich, bit section and all, back on the plate.

"I think that mayonnaise has gone off," he said.

"That's aioli," I explained. He nodded gravely, like he'd suspected as much.

As soon as he looked away, I removed the remains of his sandwich from the plate.

"I've got coffee and tea and homemade iced tea," I told them as I went to answer the door again. It was three minutes after three.

"Seth," I called upstairs. "Can you help me serve the drinks?"

There was no answer.

I opened the front door and found a plump lady with a round, pretty face standing there. "Hello," I said, "you must be . . ."

"Sally Spratt," she said. "And this is my husband, Dean."

Dean Spratt, who looked a bit like his namesake, Jack, made no effort to smile or say hello. He was tall and had mottled cheeks and a pinched expression.

"Please come in."

I pointed them toward the sandwiches and was about to start pouring drinks when the doorbell rang a third time.

This time I opened the door to a man with the spare, rawboned appearance of a person who works hard every day. A long mustache drooped beneath his nose and he had on a vivid Hawaiian shirt in shades of burnt orange and violent yellow. He was accompanied by a tall, broad-shouldered woman.

"I'm Brady," he said. "This is Yolanda, my sister."

"Brady's a writer too!" said Doreen, the funeral director's wife, coming up behind me.

"Writer, my ass," snorted Yolanda.

Brady seemed transfixed by Doreen's words. "You're a writer?" he asked me, eyes wide.

"I'm sure I remember Harold saying his niece was a writer," said Doreen.

"Well, I wouldn't say I was a—"

"What have you written?" interrupted Brady.

"She wrote a novel," said Doreen. "I'm sure Harold told me he had a niece who lived in New York City who wrote a novel."

"Been published?" Brady asked.

I was feeling rather on the spot.

"Sort of," I said, thinking of Mama Said's shabby offices.

I stepped back and walked right into the yielding expanse of Doreen's tremendous bosom.

"I'm sorry," I said.

"A published writer," said Brady, following me in. "Don't that beat all. What the hell are the odds?"

The fact that I'd had one young adult novel published by an obscure press had certainly never garnered this kind of attention in New York. It was actually sort of gratifying.

We walked into the kitchen, where everyone was standing around the table, staring suspiciously at the sandwiches.

"I don't know about that mayonnaise," Ted was telling everyone.

In the living room behind us the television flickered. Earl showed no signs of getting up to join us.

I set about getting the guests drinks and answered questions about the mayonnaise and my writing career.

"What kind of mayonnaise did you say this was?"

"You ever meet that Grisham guy?"

"It tastes kind of funny."

"She said it was called Yowly or something like that."

"Saw him interviewed on TV once. Seemed like a helluva nice guy. No swearing in his books."

"I think I heard about this once on the cooking channel."

"If you ask me, it's gone off."

Once each of the guests had a drink, I tried to change the subject.

"It's so nice of you all to come," I said. "I'd love to know how you all knew my uncle. I never did get to meet him, although we wrote letters back and forth for several years."

They all looked down at the floor, except Ted, who'd picked up another cucumber sandwich and held it a little way from his body, studying it as though afraid it would bite him if he let it go.

"I met the old man, I'm sorry, I mean your uncle, a couple of months ago when his toilet backed up. Made a hell, sorry, heck, of a mess," said Brady.

"I never met him. I just came because Brady's giving me a ride to the casino after," said Yolanda.

"We held services for Harold," said Doreen. She patted her trembling mound of hair and then stopped herself from reaching for a sandwich, making a little moue face as she did so.

"We followed his wishes to the letter," said Marshall.

"Your uncle used to come through my till," said Mrs. Spratt. "At the Price Mart."

"I came because the wife was worried no one would show," said Dean.

Sally Spratt ignored her husband and continued. "Your uncle came by the store all the time. He was a very nice man. We're going to miss him."

I looked at Ted. "And you?"

He shrugged.

"Ted comes to all our funerals," said Doreen. "Some families appreciate having extra mourners."

"So none of you really knew him?" I struggled to understand how a man could live in a community for so long and remain completely unknown.

"Hmmm," said Brady, nodding. They all swayed back and forth, like trees in a stiff wind. Well, all except Dean Spratt, who'd edged over to watch the TV.

There was a long moment of silence. Then Brady asked if I'd ever thought about teaching a writing workshop.

"Are we going to eat those?" asked Ted, pointing at the two strawberry shortcakes on the counter.

"Hell, yes," said Seth, stepping into the kitchen. He'd exchanged his hat for a bandana worn Axl Rose style, and his eyes were hidden behind mirrored wraparound sunglasses.

"Everyone, this is Seth. He's helping around the place," I said.

The ones who were listening nodded.

"It's too bad about . . . you know. Prudence's uncle. Kind of a fucking shock, eh?" said Seth.

There was something odd about him. I couldn't put my finger on it. Normally he was so contained. Nearly inert. And now he was expansive. I wondered if he was drunk and then told myself that he couldn't be. It was 3:00 on a beautiful Saturday afternoon.

Before I could speak to him, Sally Spratt came over and said how nice it had been to meet me.

"Are you sure you won't stay for some shortcake?"

"We need to get home. Our daughter's waiting." She hesitated for a moment, then seemed to make a decision. "I was wondering. Sara— our daughter—she belongs to a poultry fancier's club. But she can't keep her birds at home anymore. We live in a strata and a couple of neighbors have complained. I don't suppose you'd have room for them here?"

"Chickens?" I said.

"Stinky damn things," said Dean Spratt, without turning away from the TV.

"We don't really have any place to put them," I said.

"Sara will get things set up and teach you everything you need to know."

I told Mrs. Spratt to have her daughter drop by so we could discuss it.

"Oh, that's wonderful," said Mrs. Spratt. "Sara's been so worried about those birds. She's very involved in her club."

"Pain in the ass," said Dean Spratt.

When they were gone, I found Seth talking to Yolanda in the kitchen. This too seemed out of character. He hadn't struck me before as much of a talker. He was trying to get her to admit that she followed celebrity news.

"I don't give a shit about them people," she said, tucking the last of a piece of shortcake into her mouth, leaving a blob of cream at the corner.

"Yes you do," said Seth. "The truth is, everyone does. That's why what I do matters."

"What you do?"

"I cover celebrity gossip on my website. I also have a heavy metal blog."

"So you don't got a job," she said, quite reasonably.

"That's where you're wrong!" said Seth.

"How much do they pay, these websites of yours?" asked Yolanda, signaling to Brady to bring her another slice of cake.

"Numbers are so reductive, man," said Seth. "Ask me how much the sites have the *potential* to make. Especially the metal site."

"Maybe we'll see you at the farmers' market," said Doreen to me. "The Four Corners Market in downtown Cedar is quite famous. There are a lot of productive little farms around here."

My heart swelled with excitement. When I went to the local market I wasn't going to be buying—I'd be selling.

"Absolutely," I said.

"So what *are* your plans for this old place?" asked Marshall and Doreen together.

They held their coats over their arms, preparing to leave, and Ted the professional mourner stood behind them, nodding solemnly.

"I thought we'd start with a few chickens," I told them.

Sara

When my parents told me that I had to move my birds, I didn't say anything. In Jr. Poultry Fancier's Club they tell us that leaders are Even Tempered, which means they don't get mad even when everyone would understand if they were. The other thing leaders do is Take Action. I'm beginning to think I have some leadership qualities because even though I might feel mad, I try not to show it. Not like my dad. Since he lost his job he's mad all the time and he doesn't care who knows. He doesn't have very many leadership qualities. I think I must get mine from a distant relative.

I am also good at the Take Action part. Mr. Lymer, our Poultry Club Leader, said that I'm a "very forceful young lady," which is the same as saying I take action a lot.

When my parents told me I had to move my birds because some neighbors complained, I just got up and went to my room. I didn't tell them this was what we got for moving to Shady Woods Estates, where the houses are all packed together and there are rules about everything. I didn't tell them that my chickens are the nicest part of Shady Woods, which they are. I didn't mention that the word *Shady* is extremely ironic, which I learned about in English last semester, since there is no shade anywhere on our streets. You have to have trees to have shade and there are no trees left here. It's also kind of ironic that I'm only eleven and a half and even I know this. The bush my mom planted in front of our picture window is the biggest tree on the whole street.

By the time I got to my room my stomach was hurting a lot and I had to drink some of that stuff the doctor gave me. I think me being so brave about having to move my birds got my mom sort of worried, because a couple of days later she came to me and said she'd met someone who had a place where I could move them. Then she drove me over there and it turns out it's pretty close to my school. Shady Woods Estates is in the middle of a bunch of farms. It's the only subdivision in the neighborhood and my dad says it's the "shape of things to come," like that's a good thing. My dad used to work in a bank before he got in trouble for misappropriateness and he doesn't understand anything, especially not chickens.

My mom stayed in the car and told me to go and introduce myself to the lady who owns the farm and tell her about my birds and what they need. I think Mom just wanted to be alone in the car. Sometimes, when my dad and her aren't getting along, she goes outside and sits in the car in the driveway. She hasn't done it as much since we moved to Shady Woods because the neighbors stare, but when it's dark she sits out there all the time. I guess in some ways my mom is not much of a leader either. If she was, she'd do more than just sit in the car by herself.

So I had to show the lady at the farm and her friend my binder. She's pretty and young and smiles all the time. I told her what my chickens will need. We've been doing public speaking at Poultry Club, so I'm good at talking to adults. The lady, who had brown hair and eyes and no makeup, but was still kind of glowy, like people on TV, said she liked my binder, the one with the prize-winning Rhode Island Red picture glued on the cover, and she liked my hat, which I won in a poultry husbandry and knowledge competition. She said she could "accommodate" us, which I think meant that she would build a coop for my birds and do everything I asked. I gave her the plans I drew last winter. I got the highest mark of all the Division 3 juniors. Mr. Lymer said my drawings looked almost professional. That's because I did them over thirty times until I got one perfect. I didn't tell the lady, whose name is Prudence, that at home my chickens live in a garden shed. I didn't want her to think that I don't care about them. It's just that my dad didn't want me to have chickens in the first place. He says they're filthy. My mom let me get them after he got fired. She's the one who said I could keep them in the garden shed. Then my parents had a big fight about it. That was around the time my stomach started to hurt quite a bit.

I'm really looking forward to spending time on an actual farm. Prudence's farm doesn't seem to have anything on it other than the house, which is sort of old-fashioned, and a cabin way over at the end of the property and a sheep. Other than that it's just grass and some big rocks and a few bits of fence that are falling down. That means that anything is possible there! All the other kids in Poultry Club live on farms. Most of them take it for granted. If I lived on a farm, I'd be grateful every day.

SETH

Understandably, she had a few questions after the party. She wanted to know how often I drink and whether it's problem for me. She wasn't a bitch about it. It was more like she was curious. She sort of reminded me of her uncle and that time I mentioned when he asked if I needed a ride. Still, the fact that she had to ask made me feel like a prick.

I just had to take the edge off after I got forced into the public eye so abruptly like that. Also, there was the bike riding. I had to deal with the trauma of that shit somehow. So I bought a couple cases of beer and two bottles of Seagram's Five Star, and I had a few drinks before going downstairs.

I know my personality changes when I get loaded. That's actually the point. The personality I've got naturally is not your all-occasions variety. But I'm nowhere near as bad as my old man. He was a total Dr. Jekyll or Mr. Hyde, whichever one was a total ass licker, when he drank, which was basically two to four nights a week. He never got violent or anything. Lucky for him or my mom would have killed him in his sleep. But he was always trying to make cutting remarks, which he wasn't smart enough to pull off, and was severely emotionally incontinent, laughing and crying, neither of which looked good on him.

Anyway, so I explained to Prudence that I've been in like seclusion for a while and the party was a shock to my system. And she asked how long and I said, a while. She asked why and I told her no special reason. I told her that I wouldn't get drunk again. So yes, I lied to her.

She was pretty cool about it and I thought maybe that would be the right time to ask her about whether she was going to get an Internet hookup. There was no ADSL, so to get online I had to go and sit on the porch to catch unsecured wireless. But the signal was weak and I kept getting knocked off and I hated trying to update in public. Blogging should be a private activity, not that different from taking a crap.

Being at the farm I'd missed some good stuff, too. Like Angelina nearly started an international incident by trying to adopt triplets from North Korea, and Axl Rose tried to beat the shit out of another elderly fashion designer, only this one was a woman. I forget who. Coco Chanel? Is she still alive? Also, one of the contestants from Bret Michaels' *Rock of Love* got busted with more rock on her than Pablo Escobar and the Smoking Gun got hold of her mug shot and she looked so rough that you could see how much special effects makeup they do on TV.

I didn't get to blog any of it. In one sense, it was okay because I don't have as many readers as some of the other sites. Not to say I don't have any, but most of mine are creepy, to be perfectly honest. I'm always glad not to hear from them.

So I was going to ask Prudence about getting a high-speed connection on wireless when she unleashed this fucking To Do list on me that was as long as the Dead Sea Scrolls, if they were long. We were sitting at the kitchen table drinking coffee and I wasn't as hungover as I sometimes get, maybe because I was in a new environment. And I wasn't crawling all over with shame bugs, which sometimes happens. We were drinking Prudence's coffee, which was some New York type of powerhouse brew. Totally quality stuff, nearly took the top off my head. I was feeling okay. Human among the humans and all that. Then she turned this pad of paper around and showed it to me. It said "To Do List" and it was about seventy-five pages and three thousand items long. There was substantial shit on there, too. Like "plant crops" and "fix roof" and "build barn" and "put in composting toilet."

"Jesus," I said. "You gonna call in the National Guard to help you with that?"

She laughed. "You're it, Seth. You and me and Earl. Together we're going to whip this place into shape."

I didn't say anything, thinking I didn't want to be the one to go ruining her dreams all over the place. She'd figure out soon enough that it was hopeless.

"We are facing some financial issues. But in the meantime, we have to move forward. Today, I'd like to plan our approach for this growing season. I know it's April, and a bit late, but we have to make the most of the time we have. I'd like to have something to take to the farmers' market as soon as possible."

Next thing I knew, I was following her around the property with a notepad, pencil and camera.

In some not too noticeable ways, I'm a reasonably confident guy. Sure, I'm not into socializing and dating and whatnot, but I do write a couple of blogs. I form opinions and I write about them. I can decide between Old Style and Blue. That said, I'm a waffler of the highest order compared to Prudence. The girl is the fucking George C. Scott of decision making.

We walked every inch of the thirty acres of Woefield Farm and she made plans. Fierce plans. Raised beds here. Raspberry bushes there. Hay, pond, barn. She had me drawing diagrams and making notes.

Where I saw the least productive scrub farm in existence, she saw nothing but possibilities.

When she was snapping pictures, I tried to lighten things up by tossing out a few witty suggestions, like where to put the meth lab, pay parking lot or rock quarry, but she ignored me.

"The first bank payment is due next month," she said. "What's the best way to get money by then?" She was basically talking to herself. Obviously she wasn't asking me.

She kept bending down to feel the dirt, and I could tell from the way she did it she didn't know what the fuck she was supposed to be feeling when she touched it. She'd pick up a big dried-out clod and it would immediately crumble to dust in her hands.

"Hmmm," she'd say.

We'd walk a little farther and she'd bend down to pick up a rock the size of a cantaloupe.

"Mmmm," she'd say. Or she'd mutter something about turnips.

Goddamn Prudence is batshit, but in a nice way. If I was her, I'd have had the place on the market ten minutes after I first laid eyes on it. I mean, seriously. If not the first day, then definitely after she met her neighbors at that strawberry social. Those fuckers even made me feel normal. But she just smiled and chatted and acted like they were the most interesting people she'd ever talked to. She seems to like giving people the benefit of the doubt.

She was just starting to tell me about how grass was the key to productivity when this kid walked around the side of the house and came toward us.

She was a grim-looking child. Maybe grim is too harsh. Serious is better. She had on this fishing-slash-sun hat deal made out of canvas and it had pictures of chickens on it. I would have said she was dressed like a boy, but most young dudes wear more stylish threads. Her little face was all blank and unimpressed, like a Baptist minister running into the local whore at the bank.

"Hello?" said Prudence.

"My name is Sara Spratt. My mom said you said I could keep my chickens here."

"Oh, right. Your mom told me that you need to move your birds," said Prudence.

The kid nodded. Her jeans were too big and she was using binder twine as a belt, which I thought was a nice touch. She stared from me to Prudence.

"We're just planning new crops," Prudence said.

Nothing. The kid was Clint Eastwood in one of his less expressive roles.

"I'm open to the idea," said Prudence. "But at the moment we don't have anywhere to put them."

"I brought coop plans," said the kid and shrugged a little backpack off her shoulders, opened it, pulled out a small folder and handed it to Prudence. The cardboard cover was decorated with a magazine cutout of an enormous chicken. A piece of white paper glued to the front bore the hand-lettered words "Jr. Poultry Fancier's Club" and the girl's name, Sara Spratt. Each letter was a different color and outlined with glued-on sparkles.

She was seriously the coolest kid I'd ever seen. You could tell she really and truly did not give a fuck. I respect that.

"That's some chicken," I said.

"It's a rooster," she said, not easily swayed by compliments.

"Sorry."

"The plans for the coop are in there. I drew them up myself. I won for my division."

"You mean, you want us to build the chicken house?" asked Prudence.

"You designed it yourself?" I said. "Holy shit."

She ignored me and spoke to Prudence. "My mom will pay. She said to tell you that."

Prudence flipped through the plans for the chicken house. "This doesn't look too bad," she said. "I'm sure between Seth and Earl we can accommodate you."

I couldn't let that slide. The kid was cool but I didn't want to set up expectations.

"Building isn't really my thing. I'm more cerebral or whatever."

Prudence looked over at the old man's cabin. Smoke rose from the chimney and twisted up into the blue sky. "I'm sure Earl will be happy to teach you, Seth." She looked back at the plans. "I read somewhere that chicken manure is excellent fertilizer."

I mentioned the risk of avian flu, but they both ignored me.

Prudence's face broke into one of those big, sunny smiles of hers. "We'd be happy to host your chickens," she said.

"Okay," said the kid. Not bothering with a thank-you or anything. She picked up her pack, shouldered it and turned to go, leaving Prudence holding the plans for the chicken house.

"When are you planning to come back? With your chickens?" Prudence called after her.

"My dad said they have to be gone by the weekend," said the kid.

Prudence waved at her but she didn't look back.

EARL

The old man was a strange bugger. No doubt about that. One day he'd be reading some big book with small letters and the next he'd be deep in a soap opera. A goddamn pigmada, is what I think they call that kind of person who you can't figure out.

He used to say, Earl, everyone's family life has drama. I bet even you've got drama in your family life.

I'd just nod. Since we weren't hardly doing no farming, I figured it wouldn't hurt to try and get along. I let him listen when I played my banjo and he seemed to like that.

But he was right about the drama. Us Clementes had no shortage of that. I got reminded of it that morning when I turned on the country music channel. They were replaying some big country music award night. Giving out a prize for best bluegrass outfit. Before I could shut her off, there he was, big as you please. My brother Merle. All dressed up in a nice suit.

The woman giving the award had the big hair and boobs to match. She was wrapped up tighter than a Polish sausage in a red dress with shiny stuff on it. She was saying how she was just thrilled to be in the presence of a living legend.

Living legend, she said again, like once wasn't enough. It's what they call him now.

Merle ducked his head, real modest under that big gray hat.

I got one of them burning sensations in my chest. Thought it might be a heart attack. Then I thought no way am I going to let the goddamn reaper come for me while I'm watching Merle get a prize from a big-chested lady in a red dress.

Right then the girl came walking into my cabin without hardly knocking.

She got a look at the TV and said, Oh boy, it's Merle Clemente, like that's so exciting. Sweet Christ. That was all I needed. I used the clicker to shut the damn thing off before she could start asking questions. I wasn't fast enough.

You a bluegrass fan, she wanted to know.

I gave her a stare to let her know to mind her own business. I figured the sooner she quit yammering, the sooner I could get myself a hand-ful of Tums.

Then she started saying how she loves bluegrass and something about some eco fairs and coffee houses over there in New York City. She said she's into Flatt and Scruggs and Bill Monroe, like I'm sup-posed to be impressed.

I don't say nothing. Some types of people get like this about blue-grass. Her uncle sure did. He'd sit and listen all day if I'd keep playing. Then the girl got to yammering on about how she always wanted to see some big festival in Colorado.

I was wishing she'd get done talking. Forty-odd years on and the sight of my brother still felt like a railway spike to my goddamn chest.

She cleared her throat and apologized for busting in on me and told me she had what she called an exciting opportunity.

Then she told me about the goddamn chickens.

Far as I was concerned, that was the last straw. The old man, he was bad enough. Didn't know a goddamn thing about farming but at least he give up pretty quick and settled into watching TV and reading and let me do the same. This girl, she was a whole other story. She had that ambition you hear about.

Truth be told, I was too damn tired to think about trying to re-create the settler days on this old piece of land. I had some money put away. The old man used to pay me before he run low on cash, and I made money doing odd jobs for people. I didn't keep my money in the bank.

Christ no, I'm not that stupid. I had her tucked away safe. So I told the girl I was done and would be leaving as soon as I got organized.

Well, you'd of thought I'd told her I was going to cut off her right arm and take it with me when I went. The words wasn't barely out of my mouth before she started wailing and carrying on.

It was Oh, Earl, this and Won't you reconsider, that. Up starts the goddamn waterworks again.

I told her how there was nothing here for me and that was the goddamn truth.

That's when she told me I was in the will.

That stopped me short, I'll tell you.

Uncle Harold has given you a place to live in perpetuity, she says.

I didn't know what the hell she was talking about, who the hell would, and I told her so.

So she told me it means forever. She said I had a place to live for free as long as I stayed on the farm, and then she said I was on title for ten percent of the proceeds from the sale of the old place or any income it generates.

She told me she was sorry she didn't mention it earlier because she thought my uncle had told me, and I said I should goddamn hope so.

I figured with the way things was going, with so many of the farms selling to developers, the land had to be worth a pretty penny. Ten percent of this farm had to be more'n enough for a little place down south. Maybe even a new truck and camper, too. The place sure as shit wasn't going to make money any other way.

I asked her if she was going to sell.

She patted me on the shoulder and told me no, never. The farm was her legacy. Her heritage, she called it. Then she started talking about how someday, when there's no oil left, this old rock plantation may be our best hope for survival, and besides, it's heavily encucumbered because her uncle'd been living off the equity.

I couldn't follow all of what she said, but it seemed to me that she was saying that if she sold, she might even end up owing money and we had to figure out how to make a go of it.

That took the wind out of my sails.

She nodded and give me another pat and told me that together we could make the place a success and that the chicken house was just the beginning, and the first order of business was for me and Chubnuts to go shopping.

Goddamn it all.

Seth

People sometimes assume that people who live in the country can build stuff. It's not true. Remember I told you about my mom's adventures in stick furniture? Well, she was the fine woodworker in our family compared to the Prince of Pubs, my old man. He drove a truck for Rickert's Plumbing Supplies and he couldn't build a fucking résumé, much less a house, even one for chickens.

Same with his friends. They talked like they could slap additions onto their double-wides any time the mood struck, but it was all bullshit. A few of them had all the tools and never used them. There was the odd one who was competent and the rest of them would make sure that guy was around when they had to repair anything. It's like all the old skills have fallen away or something. I wasn't going to be the one to tell Prudence that. It would have ruined her whole life or at least her fantasy about farm life and competent country folk.

Other than the crib board I made in woodworking class, I have built almost nothing. Actually, I did help with the cross for our school's production of *Jesus Christ Superstar*. I didn't build the actual cross, which was made out of fancy plywood. The woodworking teacher did that. I just nailed a lot of boards near the base of it so it would stay upright until Jesus needed to carry it around and then pretend to get hung off it. Even doing that tested my skills. But I would have made the cross and the stage and the whole drama room from scratch for the drama teacher if she'd asked. Anyway, I don't want to get into that.

What I will tell you is that I'd never been in a hardware store before. I know. It's kind of fucked up. I'm a grown man from a rural area but I just never went before. Blogging about heavy metal and assholish actors doesn't call for trips to the hardware store. Still, I was pretty sure I knew what it would be like. The place would be teeming with people who'd been there the night of the big production.

Fuck that. I wasn't going to Home Depot with Earl. I even considered heading home to avoid it, but I looked across the street and saw my mom and Bobby sitting on the porch drinking beer. You know, I'd been at Woefield, basically within eyeshot of my mother, for like three days and she hadn't even come over to check on me. I know that doesn't sound very masculine or whatever, especially when combined with a story about how I've never been to a hardware store before, but too bad. When she saw me looking over at her and Bobby, my goddamned mother didn't even *wave*. How fucked is that?

It was so fucked that I decided I wouldn't give her the satisfaction of asking to come home again. I'd tough it out. Do the hardware store thing. Face all those pricks from high school. I knew at least half of them would be working at Home Depot.

To pull it off I'd need a little mellowing agent. The vodka didn't take effect immediately, so I had another couple of shots. Still, I was barely buzzing when I went out to the truck to wait for Earl. I was not in any way impaired. I just want to make that clear.

Earl didn't say one word to me on the drive to the store, which is way over on the other side of town. It didn't bother me. Certain types of manly men, especially old ones, are like that. This girl, at least I think she was a girl, used to write comments on Celebutard. She said she was once part of the craft services team on a Clint Eastwood movie. There's hardly any gossip about him because his people are pretty loyal. But this girl was lonely or on drugs or something and we started messaging back and forth. She said Clint would go entire days saying only what was necessary. I try to be like that when I'm sober. But when I'm drunk it seems necessary to say a lot of shit, such as how I'm feeling, whether my arm has a twinge, what I ate, what I'd like to drink, whether I took a shit recently and how weird it is that so many Hollywood people have such enormous heads. It feels completely necessary for me to say all that stuff and more.

This girl said that Clint pretty much only says please, thank you and good. When something's not good, he just grunts. Well, old Earl may be Clint Eastwood's long-lost brother or something. He wouldn't say shit if he stepped in it. At least not to me. But I didn't take it personally. I just tried to keep up a pleasant commentary.

When we got to Home Depot, which, as you probably know, is just basically a huge white and orange cube surrounded by about twenty acres of parking, the lot was packed. Earl's a prime candidate for that *Worst Driver* show, and I think he was scared to get hit or whatever, so he drove us way the fuck into some *other* big-box store's parking lot that was pretty empty because everyone was clogging up the Home Depot.

Earl was still doing his Clint Eastwood impression. I didn't point out that if he bought more than a box of nails we'd probably die of exposure trying to get it back to the truck. I kept my cool and acted like everything was good. Like I was enjoying my second trip to town in three days.

He headed to the store, walking in front of me. Guy stumps along at a pretty good pace. I mean, considering how wrecked he looks. He motored along, hunched over, leaving that funny wood smoke and old man BO trailing behind him. I didn't take it the wrong way that he didn't even wait for me. I just kept walking. Determined to be of service. That's what I was. I kept having to break into a run in order to catch up with him, which made me feel like an asshole.

Once we got in the store I figured I'd follow him around. Maybe push one of those big orange carts. I would be the steady helper guy. I bet Clint Eastwood is surrounded with steady helper guys, who all spend their free time cowboying on the open range and shit when they aren't on set. Anyone who recognized me would probably be scared off by Earl's hostile demeanor and not say anything. In truth, once we got there my worries eased some. Partly it was the drinks I'd had before heading out and partly it was the size of the place. Even if every single person from my high school worked there, there was a chance we'd never run into each other. After a minute or two, part of me started wondering if maybe some of the other contractor/manager-type guys would look at Earl and envy him for having someone like me on his crew. Someone reliable, a real up-and-comer.

But Earl fucked off down an aisle as soon as we got inside and I got sick of trotting after him. Screw this, I thought. Earl is no Clint Eastwood and I'm not his assistant.

Still, I was fascinated by the whole Home Depot experience. There was an aisle with nothing but brooms and Swiffers and mops. Another aisle with just rakes and shovels. One of drills and another that was just pieces of plywood. The lightbulb section was off the hook. I seriously had no idea how many types of bulb your average homeowner has to choose from. Between the cosmetic lights and the colored lights and the tubes and the weird ones that look like lollipops, I could have spent two hours in there. I was reading a pamphlet about the benefits of compact fluorescents when a clerk came up to me. She was eighteen or nineteen and pretty cute.

She looked like a girl you could talk to, you know, not all made up and hair done et cetera. She had on this semi-Western-looking checked shirt, not the affected kind, but more like maybe she actually rode around on her horse when she wasn't working at Home Depot. Her body was mostly obscured by the apron, but I liked what I could see. To be completely honest, I'm not exactly a masterful judge of woman flesh, as my personal history probably indicates.

She asked me if I was interested in CFLs.

Normally, I hate it when people use acronyms because they only do it to exclude you and show how smart they are, but I decided to let it go this time.

"Are people *into* CFLs?" I asked. She smiled. Her teeth were covered with those semi-invisible braces. That kind of sealed the deal for me.

"Some are. People who care about global warming and responsible energy use."

"Oh, those bastards," I said.

She laughed and pushed up one of the sleeves of her shirt. Her forearm wasn't tattooed, which was cool. Even in my darkest blackout hour I have never wanted to get a tattoo.

"You want to plug one in? Check the quality of the light?" asked the girl, waving one of the twisty bulbs at me. I realized we were flirting and that it was fucking excellent. I guess the drinks made me just relaxed enough that I could talk to her without being too self-conscious. I had this vision of the two of us holding hands or getting into some light petting behind shower curtains or up in the fencing aisle or some shit. They say the simple and clean-cut girls are the wildest. But I realized she wasn't being suggestive. She actually wanted to demonstrate the bulb. She screwed it into a small lamp that they had sitting on the shelf for that purpose, and flipped the switch. For a second, nothing happened. Then the light vibrated and a few seconds later it came all the way on.

"Oh. I get it. It's like a fluorescent tube. Only in a weird shape."

She nodded and I got the feeling she was checking me out. I was glad I'd worn my Iron Maiden hat because it's good luck.

"The light that it gives off isn't too flattering, is it? And it's kind of funky, the way it starts up all jerky like that. That flicker could give a person a headache," I said.

The girl's face fell. She looked so devastated, she might have personally invented CFLs and couldn't stand to hear them disrespected in any way.

"They've made a lot of improvements to the compact fluorescents," she said, very sincere. "You may be picking up some glare from the overheads."

The lights in the warehouse ceiling, far, far overhead, were banks of giant fluorescents. Nothing compact about them.

"Do they come in pink? Because that's really the only type of light you should have in your leisure areas," I told her. "Makes the skin glow. I saw that on *Colin and Justin's Home Heist* on HGTV." I was a flirting animal now.

"I'm sure they do," she said. "If they don't have them now, they will. Because pretty soon CFLs may be the only option."

"What do you mean?"

"Well, if we all use CFLs, a huge amount of energy will be saved."

"Yeah, but if we all look like crap and have to throw sheer pink scarves over everything, thereby causing increased risk of fires and other accidents, how much will really be saved? Think of the gas it takes to get all those fire trucks to all the scenes. Plus the oil products required to make all those flame-retardant outfits for the firemen."

The girl looked at me, confused. Not surprising. Even I didn't know what I was talking about. I was supposed to be flirting, but I was starting to *argue* with her now. I am truly a dipshit.

"This your department?" I asked, trying to change the subject to something less controversial than CFLs.

"No. Not really. I'm usually in Lamps. The bulb guy is out with a cold."

"Lazy bastard," I said and smiled at her. She returned my smile and I'm pretty sure the interest came back into her eyes. I sucked in my gut and shook my head a bit so she could see how long my hair was. I considered taking off my hat so she could see that it wasn't thinning or retreating. My hair, I mean. It's like Prudence says, you want to emphasize the positive.

The girl and I were smiling at each other, and I was thinking about asking her out. Not that I had any idea how people date.

Then all at once I realized that it had been a while since I'd seen Earl. A feeling came over me, and I said, "Hey, would you excuse me for a minute? I've just got to check on someone. Don't go anywhere."

She nodded and I walked across the front of the store, looking down each aisle as I passed it. He was nowhere to be seen. He wasn't in any of the checkouts, either. So I went running outside. I was kind of panting now, because I'd been racing all over the store, which is huge, in this increasingly panicky state, like Harrison Ford in *The Fugitive*, only not really, because I wasn't being chased, I was chasing.

I found him outside. He'd had an accident.

Earl

When he got in the truck he had on a pair of pants so tight it took him three tries to get his leg up into the cab. His T-shirt had a skull on it and the tongues in his big white shoes were hanging out like they belonged on a pair of dying dogs. He finally made her into the truck and right away he started talking this and that and never shutting up. Christ. I don't know how anyone could stand it. Soon as we got to the store, I buggered off. I figured he wouldn't stick around when there was work to be done and I was right on that.

I picked up the boards and the sheets of plywood and whatnot. I forgot the list the girl made for me, but I got an okay memory still. Jesus Christ if that wasn't the first useful thing I done around the old place in a long time. I like to watch the idiot box, same as the next guy, but it felt good to be out and doing something.

I'm not one of them real fine finishing craftsman like you see sometimes on the Home Network. But I built some things over the years. I can still remember the time I helped my brother Pride work on a bandstand at the old place. The High Lonesome Boys, which was just Pride and Merle at that time, was on a break and we were supposed to be getting the grounds organized so we could put on some shows during the summer. Merle wanted to start a High Lonesome Boys festival at our family homestead. He wanted a week-long deal with people coming from all over and camping out back and whatnot. But first we had to build a bandstand.

Merle didn't help of course. He was too busy playing the big rancher man with some little number he picked up in Dallas. She didn't know he had a wife and kids living in an apartment in Nashville. Merle was always picking up girls on the road. I couldn't tell you what they saw in him. So he was showing this girl the cows and the old farmhouse where me and Pride and our sister lived after our folks died and, I guess, the inside of his shorts. At least he wasn't telling me and Pride what to do.

We were making out okay. My brother Pride had a good sense of humor. And he was showing me a few things about building and talking about some of them gigs on the last tour. He was taking a few nips here and there, truth be told. Not like Merle, who never took a sip. Merle's vice was women.

Anyway, Merle come along and seen Pride with the flask and he give him shit right in front of me and the girl and everyone. Told him to get his butt in gear and get the bandstand up or he could forget about recording with Luellewan Norman, who was this big-shot producer who wanted to record with the High Lonesome Boys. Pride didn't take to threats. In a lot of ways he was named right. After Merle walked away Pride decided he was going to stage what he called a work stoppage. Sat down on the job and got himself drunk as a skunk, right there on the half-built bandstand.

When Merle came out later, he damn near blew a valve. That was the day he fired Pride, even though Pride was a fine mandolin player and some people said a better singer than Merle.

Come on, Merle said to me after he told Pride he was through. You're called up. Least you are once you get finished with this bandstand.

So that's how I ended up on the road with the High Lonesome Boys when I was just sixteen. And that's when things started to get bad for Pride.

As for the bandstand, well, that didn't work out so good. Collapsed during the second set by the Trifling Snakes. There were six of them and when they all got to stomping the way they did, it was too much for that old bandstand. Frank Cart, the singer, broke his ankle, threatened to sue. But that's a whole another story.

I hadn't thought about all that old history in years. Especially not about Pride.

Anyway, I set the building materials on one of them big flat carts they got at that store. It was a little shaky and the hefty gal at the only checkout that actually had someone on it said, Why don't you drive up front and we'll load your truck for you? I said, Hell, no, I don't need no help. Between you and me, I don't like squeezing the truck into these tight spaces no more. There have been incidents. I pushed the cart out into the parking lot. The goddamn place was full of trucks and cars and walking ways and concrete barriers. And damn it if the whole works on the cart didn't tip over when I got about ten feet from the truck.

It was too much trouble to load her up again and what was the point, so I started packing boards and sheets and the rest over to the truck, one at a time. Tell you the truth, by that time I completely forgot all about Chubnuts in his tight pants.

I had about half the stuff loaded and my nerves was getting a little testy from people driving around me, some of them honking until I give them the what-for finger. That's when Chubnuts came running out of the store, huffing and puffing like a fat man running for the dessert table.

He was yelling, Earl! What happened?

I didn't answer, because if he couldn't figure it out from looking that's too goddamn bad for him.

He said, Were you going to leave me here, man? And right then a blue Dodge half-ton come by and damn near drove over a sheet of plywood I was trying to lift. That just about did it for me and I told Chubnuts to stop his bellyaching and help.

He got a look on his face like I just took a shot at him. It kind of stopped me, tell you the truth. I don't know. It reminded me of something I guess, or someone. I didn't care to think about it, so I kept working the sheet of plywood until I got her upright and I started dragging her toward the truck. And do you know what that bastard did? Nothing. Not a goddamn thing.

He left everything where it was and got in the truck and stayed there while I finished loading it up.

And when we got back to the farm I called him a lazy bastard or something of that nature and he stomped off.

Funny how things go around and around. Maybe I was a little hard on him. But he's not a kid and somebody's got to tell him.

Prudence

The building of Sara Spratt's chicken coop took approximately the same amount of sweat, swearing and human sacrifice as the Pyramids. Possibly a little more.

The first mistake was to send Seth to help Earl get the building materials. The second mistake was to ask how it went.

"There are a shitload of lightbulbs at Home Depot," mumbled Seth. Then he stared into the middle distance. At least, I think he did. His ball cap was pulled so low I couldn't actually see his eyes.

Earl, carrying building supplies from the back of the truck to the site of the chicken house, muttered as he passed, "Useless waste of space."

I told Seth that Earl was probably talking about the merchandising techniques employed at the Home Depot, but Seth slumped his shoulders farther and said he was going to his room.

I looked at the pile of supplies lying in the yard and then at the long paper receipt Earl handed to me.

The materials for the chicken house cost over two hundred dollars. I hoped Sara's parents would pay me back right away. It wasn't a conversation I was particularly looking forward to, just as I wasn't eager to try and convince the bank to give me a grace period before I had to start paying down Uncle Harold's line of credit, which he hadn't insured, and making payments on the outstanding property taxes. Of course, the key is not to procrastinate. Face things head-on.

I realized that our projected income consisted of boarding a small flock of chickens and my modest allowance, but something would work out. It always does. Succeeding in life is a matter of making your own luck and taking advantage of all the opportunities around you. I told myself that before I knew it we'd have a table groaning with produce at the local farmers' market, just like the vendors I used to envy in Union Square.

But back to the chicken house.

I had assumed that because Earl was an old-timer and a country person and so forth that he'd be extremely handy and able to follow an eleven-year-old's building plans with no trouble whatsoever. This was an incorrect assumption.

After we'd finished unloading the building materials from the truck Earl found my list and realized all the things he'd forgotten.

"Where in hell are the goddamn nails?" he demanded. Then, "Who forgot the tar paper?" Followed by, "Where in Jesus Christ Almighty is the goddamn mesh?"

"Should we go back to the store?" I asked.

Earl stood in the middle of the bundle of plywood, boards, and bits and pieces looking like he wanted to kick something. "I knew that good-for-nothing little fart would forget half the supplies," he said.

From what had been said earlier, I'd gathered that Seth hadn't gone anywhere near the building supplies. He'd spent his time at Home Depot looking at lightbulbs. However, in the interests of keeping the peace, I didn't point out that Earl was the one who'd forgotten the list.

"How about you tell me what's missing and I'll go get it."

"Jesus, Jesus, Jesus," said Earl.

Ten minutes later I had a list of things and was reluctantly climbing into Earl's old truck for the return trip to Home Depot. I hated to drive such a gas-guzzler and looked forward to the day I could afford to buy us a hybrid truck or perhaps one of those vehicles that runs on old cooking oil.

I asked Earl to get started on the job while I was gone.

I'd just put the truck into gear when Seth lurched, zombie-like, into the driver's-side window.

"Prudence!" he shouted, smacking the window with the flats of his hands and pressing his nose into the window. "Prudence!"

This knocked his hat askew. His eyes were hidden behind his wraparound shades.

"What?" I asked, leaning way over to roll down the window. It took a bit of muscle power because the window was as creaky as the rest of the vehicle.

"Is that you?" he nearly shouted in my face. "Is it really you?"

There was a thin red crust at the edges of his lips and his teeth were stained, increasing the zombie effect.

"Have you been drinking?" I asked.

"Not much. I mean, I found some homemade wine in the attic when you asked me to clean it out. I think it may be what killed your uncle."

"You'll have to excuse me, Seth. I've got to go and get the rest of the chicken house supplies that you and Earl forgot." I realized with a sinking feeling that I was going to have to let him go. I couldn't have an employee, much less a live-in one, with a drinking problem.

"Can I come?" asked Seth, sagging slightly sideways. "I don't want to be alone with Earl."

I tried to get a handle on just how intoxicated he was. His sunglasses made it hard to tell.

I leaned farther out my window.

"Fine. But I'd like you to stay in the truck. You can help me load the supplies after I pick them up."

Next thing I knew he'd leapt into the passenger seat and was leaning forward with his hands tapping out a staccato drum solo on the dash.

"Can you stop at the liquor store? I can't drink any more of that homemade shit. I'm starting to feel like Helen Keller."

I ignored his request and drove straight to Home Depot. When we found a parking space, I reminded him to stay put.

"What if a cop comes by and thinks I'm driving? I could get an impaired."

"You'll probably be saved by the fact that the vehicle is parked and you don't have the keys."

"The rules are different in Canada," he said. "Loaded people here aren't allowed in vehicles unsupervised."

I was not looking forward to going shopping with him. He'd spilled a large quantity of homemade red wine down the front of his Judas Priest T-shirt. It looked like he'd been shot in the chest. For all I knew, all those metal guys I used to see at the club near my house looked like this at the end of the night. A fascinating subculture, but perhaps not one that stresses the sort of qualities one wants in an employee.

"Hey man!" he yelled after me when I walked ahead of him. "Wait for me!"

Seth lurched toward me, his skinny jeans making his legs look vaguely crustacean.

I turned and headed toward the big sliding doors of the store.

Behind me Seth kept up a stream of unintelligible comments. Every time I glanced back he seemed to be either in the process of falling or picking himself up. He stumbled over a speed bump and tripped over a yellow line painted on the flat pavement of the parking lot. It was really a bit embarrassing.

"This whole place is a liability suit waiting to happen," he said, after falling to one knee in the middle of the crosswalk and staying there for a long, painful moment. "Shit like this is why I never used to leave the house. Until you gave me my job. Which I fucking love, I just want you to know."

I went back, grabbed one of his arms and pulled him to his feet.

"Seth, this is unacceptable behavior. Please pull yourself together."

Once inside, he seemed to sober up. Perhaps it was the harsh lighting. I steered him over to a chair just inside of the entrance.

"I'm going to get a cart and find someone to help me so we can get out of here faster. Please don't move."

He nodded and looked so tired I almost believed him.

"Sit here and wait for me. Don't talk to anyone. You're drunk enough that you could get thrown in jail."

He said something about it being good enough for Lindsay and

Paris and those bitches, never mind the boys in the Crüe, so it was good enough for him. Then he lapsed into silence.

"Stay!" I repeated, and held up a hand.

I grabbed the first clerk I saw and asked for help. Unfortunately, she was from Plumbing and didn't know about Building Supplies. She walked me up to a front checkout and asked the cashier on the till to make an announcement over the PA.

"Building to number four. Building to number four!"

As I waited I watched customers try, unsuccessfully, to check themselves out using the self-checkout lane. They would hold up an item and thrust it at the scanner a few times, look around, embarrassed, then slink back into the lineup. The only time that lineup began to move was when one of the cashiers stood there and helped the customers through, just like a regular checkout, only both customer and cashier stood on the same side of the till.

I attempted to get the attention of the cashier who'd called for help.

"Excuse me? Is someone from Building Supplies coming?" I asked and got no reply.

I waited another few minutes and then headed off. Obviously I was going to have to take control of the situation. The store was the size of an aircraft hangar, lined with tall metal shelves that seemed to disappear into the atmosphere overhead. After what seemed like a ten-minute walk I finally came to an aisle marked "Building Supplies."

I consulted my list. Nails, tar paper, mesh.

A clerk in an orange apron stood at the far end of the aisle. I hurried toward him, but his head came up, he sniffed the air and he bolted.

"Damn," I said. I looked around the corner, but he was gone. I made a right-hand turn up the next aisle and passed stacks of lumber and formaldehyde-smelling plywood. No nails, no tar paper, no mesh. I was nearing the end of the aisle when another sales associate turned in and stopped dead at the sight of me. She began to back up as though she'd just spotted a bear.

"Excuse me!" I yelled. "Wait! I need some help here!"

She stopped.

"Just wait!" I found myself panting as I pushed my empty orange cart up the aisle as fast as I could.

"Mesh. Where is it?" I asked, as I pulled alongside.

"Aisle six," she said, edging away and glancing from side to side.

"Wait! Nails. Where are the nails?"

"Aisle four. Or five. I don't know. I don't work in Fasteners."

She was picking up speed in reverse. She was getting away!

"Tar paper?" I shouted. But she was gone, saying something about being busy with another customer.

I trudged back to aisle six, where I picked up a roll of wire mesh big enough to build a supermax chicken penitentiary. Then I headed over to aisle four, which turned out to be nail-free. On aisle five I hit the jackpot, nail-wise. There were hundreds in every shape and size.

A heavyset sales associate with a face like a bulldog walked by, deep in conversation with a couple, who clung to his shirtsleeve.

"Excuse me!" I said. "I'm looking for—"

"Back off," said the woman, moving protectively in front of her sales clerk. "We just found him."

I realized I'd just have to guess. I pulled a couple of large plastic tubs of nails off the shelf. Some about an inch long, some maybe two inches. They looked about right for building a chicken coop.

Then I walked each aisle in turn until I finally located tar paper, which was sold in rolls large enough to side an entire third world shantytown. I was just heading to the only checkout with an actual cashier when I heard the announcements.

"Manager to Lighting and Design. Manager to Lighting and Design."

"Security to Lighting and Design. Security to Lighting and Design."

A premonition came to me and I wheeled the cart around in a tight circle and rushed down the aisle, my shoes slapping against the concrete floors. I'd seen the sign for Lighting and Design when I came in. It was at the back of the store in the far left corner, near the Garden Center. I rounded aisle two, flushing out a couple of sales associates who'd been hiding in a blind spot just off Toilets. When I got to Lighting and Design I found Seth on his knees in front of a frightened-looking young girl who wore a cowboy shirt under her orange apron. His arms were stretched wide and he was making a high-pitched keening noise.

"Seth?" I asked.

"Dude, I thought we had a connection!" Seth said to the girl, who had backed up against a rack displaying fake Tiffany lamps.

She tried to smile but it came off as a sort of facial rictus.

"We talked about compact fluorescents," he said.

I moved closer to him, hoping to distract him before the security people arrived. If the length of time it had taken to summon a clerk from Building Supplies was any indication, I estimated that I had at least forty minutes.

"I wasn't aware that you were so passionate about compact fluorescents," I said in what I hoped was a calm, conversational tone.

He turned to me. His face was stricken. He'd somehow managed to break one of the arms of his wraparound sunglasses so they hung crookedly across one of his eyes and extended down his cheek.

"Truth is, I don't give a fuck about compact fluorescents. Don't even know what they are. I'm just trying to *meet* someone," he wailed. "Make a *connection* out here. I been home alone a long time, man. You have no idea."

The girl looked from me to Seth, her eyes wide.

"I don't think he's dangerous," I whispered.

I could tell she didn't believe me.

"Seth, Home Depot isn't the place to make a connection. At least not the kind you mean. But it's great that you realize that compact fluorescents are key to reducing our emissions," I said. "If we all switched to them the savings would be amazing."

"That's true. They might be mandatory in a few years," added the girl, in spite of herself. Her shiny brown hair was held off her face with a tortoiseshell headband. She really was very cute.

I put my arms out to pull Seth to his feet, but at the same instant he fell forward, flat onto his face. The girl leapt sideways, tipping over a fake Tiffany lamp, which toppled into a series of fake Craftsman-style lamps, which fell to the floor and shattered, Frey-like, into a million little pieces. At that moment the security detail swept in. They spoke rapidly into their radios, possibly to each other.

"Situation in aisle one," said the middle-aged man.

"Roger that," said the middle-aged woman.

The salesgirl stood among the wreckage of the lamps and gaped, horrified, at Seth, who had made it back to his knees. He'd cut open his chin and a trickle of blood ran down his neck and into his shirt, blending with the red wine stain on his chest to create a particularly gory effect. For some reason his hair appeared wet.

"Sorry," said Seth, to no one in particular.

I faced the security associates.

"That's right. He's really sorry. This was just a misunderstanding. He just wanted some information about compact fluorescents."

The security associates, a dim-looking man and matching woman, stared doubtfully at the mess on the floor.

"What's going on here?" the woman asked. "Was he bothering you?"

The girl looked from me to Seth. I could see she didn't know how much trouble to get him in.

"He keeps talking about his drama teacher," she said finally. "I tried to tell him I don't know her."

"I'm more than happy to pay for this," I said, gesturing at the mess of glass and wiring behind me. "Just let me get my employee to the car. He's not feeling well. He may be on medication."

Seth was crying silently, huge tears running down his face, joining the little trickle of blood from his chin.

The security people had been joined by a small crowd of shoppers.

I felt I had to keep explaining. "He's sensitive. In addition to working for me on the farm, he's in the entertainment business," I said, thinking of his blogs.

"Like Mel Gibson," said Seth, still crying, but now trying to focus on a woman in the crowd. She'd packed her chest into a very tight leather vest. "Hey, sugar tits!" he said, through his tears.

"I'll just get him outside and then I'll come back and pay for these things," I said, trying to ignore the thrilled look on the face of the woman who'd just been called sugar tits.

"Get him out of here or we'll call the cops?" said the woman security officer, who seemed to speak only in the interrogative.

"Absolutely," I said. I put my arm around Seth's shoulders and pushed him in front of me. The crowd parted for us, and the woman he'd called sugar tits winked at him. The security people followed at a safe distance.

"It wasn't my fault," muttered Seth.

"He's been under a lot of stress lately," I said to the crowd.

The security team nodded uncertainly, trying to look as though they dealt with weeping, bleeding drunk guys falling around the aisles every day.

"Me, too, actually. Just inherited this farm and I'm trying to get a chicken shed built."

People exchanged looks.

We made the long march out of the building and through the vast, bustling parking lot to the truck.

"Can I ask one of you to watch him while I go in and pay for the things he broke?" I asked, after I'd pushed and shoved and prodded the nearly comatose Seth into the truck.

Before they could answer, a flicker of movement in another corner of the parking lot caught their attention. A teenager, maybe thirteen or fourteen years old, was pushing two other teenagers in one of the carts. The kids were racing the cart toward an exit.

"Hey!" shouted the security man.

"Stop?" added the security woman.

They took off running after the kids.

I waited until they were halfway across the parking lot before leaping into the truck, turning the ignition and driving off, all in one violent motion.

"We'll get them next time," I said as much to myself as Seth, who'd passed out. His head lolled over and smacked against the passenger window with a satisfying thud as I made a sharp left onto the street.

Sara

There's this girl at Poultry Club, Bethany Blaine. She's kind of slow but not exactly retarded. It makes it hard because you don't know whether to encourage her to try to be smarter or be nice to her for trying, the way you would if she was definitely retarded. Earl, the man who works at Woefield, seems a little bit like Bethany.

He might not be handicapped but he doesn't seem totally normal either. My mom says you should always be extra nice to people with challenges, like mental or physical ones. She didn't say why. So I tried to be nice to Earl. Just in case.

When I saw what a bad job he was doing building the coop, I didn't let him know how disappointed I was or say anything mean. I just showed him what was wrong. Which I think is okay to do, even if a person has challenges. I mean, how else is he going to learn? I showed him that the coop didn't have any ventilation, except where the boards didn't fit together. I also told him he had to build a foundation and I reminded him about insulation. When he gets all that fixed, I'll show him where to put the nest boxes and the perches.

Bethany, the girl at Poultry Club, talks a lot. All the time, practically. That's part of how you know she's not quite right. But Earl is really old and hardly talks at all except to swear. That may be what happens to slow people when they get old. I'm not sure. Slow old people are kind of rare, I think. Him swearing in front of me made Prudence nervous at first. Every time he said a swear, she'd whisper "Earl!" and look at me. But my dad swears all the time so I'm used to it. It's probably not very good for me though.

Last Sunday I went to church with Bethany and her family. Bethany doesn't have many friends, and she and her mom have asked me about twenty times whether I wanted to go with them, especially after my dad lost his job and his name was in the paper. I feel kind of sorry for Bethany, so I said yes. It turns out that church was really great. The preacher or minister had an excellent message. It was all about being organized and prepared for the end and how there is evil just about everywhere and you have to guard against it. He also said you have to try hard to get ahead in this world so you can get ahead in the next one, too, by which I think he meant heaven. In that way, church was like Poultry Club. There is a strong emphasis on leadership. I think my parents could benefit from the Lord's message. I think they might suffer from apathy, which is another thing the minister warned us about.

Bethany's mom lent me some church literature to read and also this book called *Left Behind*. I'm looking forward to reading it. I read quite a few books, but mostly they are about chickens.

I can't decide whether going to church is making me more sensitive to swearing or less. Time will tell. Going to church with the Blaines is definitely making me more patient and kindhearted, although my stomach still hurts sometimes.

The truth is that if I didn't supervise him, I think Earl might try and get away with doing a halfhearted job. As a senior citizen, you'd think he'd try harder. He's only going to be around for so long and this chicken house may be one of the last chances he has to leave his mark on the world. I said that to him, but before he could thank me Prudence said it was probably time for me to go. She had been in a bad mood ever since she came home and had to put Seth to bed because she said he was feeling under the weather. She went across the street to tell Seth's mother that he was sick but I guess his mom didn't care. Prudence came back looking even grumpier.

The next day Seth was feeling better. He just sat on the porch and didn't move for almost two hours, except to smoke and check his watch a few times. He had on track pants and a shirt with no sleeves that looked American because it was made of a blue and red and white flag. His arms didn't have many muscles. When Earl saw him, he swore even more than usual.

Seth looked extremely tired and was a bit yellow, like he might have a disease or something. I thought I should probably be careful around him. I didn't want to end up getting abused. Guys who sit around and don't have jobs are more likely to be pedophiles. I saw that on one of those TV shows that comes on after eleven.

But to tell the truth, I kind of liked him. I think it was because when I talked he paid attention really hard, like he thought I might be interesting or worth listening to. Not many people listen to people who are eleven. I liked it when he sat outside and typed on his computer, which is quite big considering it's a laptop, or even when he just sat outside doing nothing.

My birds were moving to Woefield in two days and I could hardly wait. If Bethany didn't talk so much I'd have invited her, but I didn't want her bothering my birds.

Seth

I have this theory about hangovers. The theory is this: We are all born with a single hangover. It's located in our gut and when we drink, it wakes up. I had the bad luck to be born with an incredibly powerful hangover rather than any number of other attributes, such as an enormous cock or a fine head of blond, Bret Michaels–ish hair. The colon-shredding ferociousness of my hangover is one of the few things I can count on in my life.

I've even named my hangover. I call him Phil. Phil the Fucker. I think about him this way. Phil the Fucker lives deep inside me in the basement suite owned by Fear and Anxiety, whose '70s-style stucco home is located directly across the street from Shame and Resentment's rundown rancher. It's not a big neighborhood, but it has character. Then again, I may have gotten all this from an interview I read once with one of the guys in Van Halen.

A few times I thought Phil might kill me. The key to coping when Phil's awake is to do everything real slow. He seems to settle down if I feed him Chinese takeout. The greasier the better. I just thought I'd mention this. It seems relevant somehow.

Anyway, about the incident at the Home Depot. That was a shit show, I admit. When Prudence stopped by my room the next day I told her to go away and leave me to die in peace. That's what I used to say to my mother and she always listened. She was trained from living with my father. But Prudence didn't know any better and she walked right in.

She wrinkled her nose at the smell and then put a steaming mug on my bedside table and leaned forward and opened a window, letting in a blast of wind with a distinct Arctic bite to it.

"Please don't let the air in. I'm allergic," I said.

"I thought you wanted to die. That's what you said yesterday when I was trying to get you into the house."

"I do. But not of fresh air. I was thinking you could smother me or maybe I could overdose on something in the morphine family." As I spoke, Phil took a bite of my spleen.

I had to sit up to talk to her, but first I had to take a peek under the covers to make sure I had underpants on. I've been known to go commando. Also, I was never quite sure what might happen to my lower half when I was trying to sleep one off. Once I established that I was dressed I pulled myself up. God, it felt so bad to have a girl standing in my room looking at me when I felt so sick.

"So I guess I'm fired," I said. "Sorry about that. I'll get my stuff and head home as soon as I get my shit together. Thanks for giving me a chance and all that."

"That's not going to work," said Prudence.

"What? Me being fired? Dude, I've obviously crossed the line and I deserve it. I realize I'm not employee of the month and I'm ready to take the consequences."

"Your mother won't take you back."

"Did you tell her I was fired?"

"I told her I didn't think things were working out."

"So where does she expect me to go?"

Prudence just shook her head.

"This is such bullshit," I said, pulling the thin blankets higher.

Prudence sat down on a chair across from the bed, gingerly, like I was a very sick patient in a hospital.

"Hmmm," she said.

I couldn't even look at her. Her face was so clear and unfucked up. Looking at her, all healthy and everything, made me feel a hundred times worse about myself. My heart was slamming in my chest. I had nowhere to go.

"I brought you some chamomile tea," she said. "To help you rehydrate and calm your stomach."

She picked up the mug and I took it with a trembling hand.

Pushing through the pain, I leaned my back so it rested against the wall. I held tight to the cup with both hands and took a small sip. I could see Prudence notice the way my hands shook, even when I had them wrapped around the tea mug.

"Seth, you seem like a nice person. I hate for things to end this way."

I squeezed my eyes shut so Phil wouldn't push them out of my head.

"I'm sorry," I said. "I just can't seem to get it together."

"Have you ever thought about your drinking? How maybe it's becoming a problem?"

"It's kind of a family trait," I said. And as I spoke I knew how lame that sounded. "It's just sort of how I am."

"Or how you cope," she said.

Then she really floored me. "What happened with you and your drama teacher?"

"Nothing. It was just this thing that . . . I'd rather not talk about it."

She nodded.

"Seth, if you promise to do something about your drinking, you can stay here and keep working on the farm."

That surprised me so much that I looked at her.

"Many people have substance abuse issues. It's simply something you're going to have to tackle. Get in there and manage it."

She sounded so sure.

"As long as your drinking doesn't interfere with your work again, I will allow our arrangement to continue."

She reached out and put a hand on my forearm. Her fingers were cool and her touch was like that Noxzema cream my mom used to use.

"Seth, you are unlimited potential. I want you to remember that."

"I don't feel like unlimited anything, except maybe an unlimited disaster." There was this whiny note in my voice that I hated. When Keith Richards had to talk to the band about being a dope fiend and a drunk, I bet he didn't whine.

"Maybe you can look for an outpatient treatment program or get some counseling or something."

Fuck that, was my immediate response, but that would have sounded ungrateful.

"Maybe I could do treatment by correspondence," I said. "Like online with homework and stuff. You could supervise."

"Is there such a thing?" she asked.

"Probably. And anyway, people open treatment centers all the time. Like as businesses. Maybe you could do that in addition to your farming."

She smiled. Her teeth were extra white and probably not from bleaching but from inner purity or something.

"I don't think we need to go that far," she said. "I'm going to leave it to you to find a solution. In the meantime, there's plenty here to keep you busy."

I was going to tell her how grateful I was that she wasn't going to make me homeless, but before I could get any words out, Phil lunged for my throat and I had to scramble for the bathroom. I nearly knocked Prudence off her chair in my hurry. When I finished puking, she was gone. But I felt human enough to get dressed and lug my laptop outside, although I was too sick to actually turn it on. The thing is old as rocks, it weighs nearly as much as my tower, and the battery only lasts about twenty minutes and I didn't have the strength to get the extension cord organized.

As I sat there on the porch, random images from the day before floated into my mind. I couldn't remember much of what happened. I'm a pretty bad blackout drinker and even though it freaks me out to lose chunks of time, the reality is that a lot of my memories are better off forgotten or suppressed or erased or whatever it is that happens when a person blacks out. Sometimes I can't remember stuff that happened even before I started drinking. It's like my blackouts scrub memories on both sides of a drinking session.

I know I talked to the cute lightbulb clerk when I went to the store with Earl. And after I drank some of that rotgut homemade wine, I went back to Home Depot with Prudence. I think I wanted to try and talk to the girl again. I don't know why. I guess it was the way she looked at me and didn't know me or my story. It's nice, when someone looks at you like you might be cool or have something interesting to say and not like you're that guy who had that extremely fucked-up thing happen to him. That's where my memory starts to skip, like a scratched CD. A few images pop up: the look on the girl's face when I asked her some question. I hoped I didn't say anything dirty to her. I had this sense that Mel Gibson was there, which is doubtful, seeing as he lives in Malibu, where he's very active in his church and busy making ultraviolent religious movies with no English in them and saying horrendous shit on the phone. But there you go. After Mel Gibson, nothing. I woke up to find myself at home, in bed, with Phil playing in my guts like a pit-bull puppy with a rope toy.

Then I nearly got fired and kicked out and was only saved by Prudence's generosity.

Anyway, when I was sitting out there on the porch, I could see cars coming and going from my mom's house across the street. It looked like someone was dealing crystal over there, but it was just people coming to buy Bobby's remote-control helicopter parts. Dude was doing a booming business. Nobody ever stopped by when it was just me and my mom. The sight of so many cars going in and out of there made me feel left out, but not in a bad way. Like sometimes it's not so terrible to realize that things go on without you and that's totally the way it should be. I don't know what I'm trying to say.

Old Earl went by the porch and I could see that he was right overjoyed to see me. When he walked past, carrying a hammer, with his leather tool belt hanging off his nonexistent ass, he shook his head and muttered, but mercifully he was far enough away I couldn't hear what he said. He was doing something to the chicken house and the kid with the hat was out there with him, sort of supervising from what I could see.

She kept telling Earl what to do, pointing at stuff and never, ever cracking a smile.

If I hadn't had to concentrate on not vomiting up the lining of my stomach, I'd have laughed out loud about that kid. Not at her, but *because* of her. Watching her boss Earl around made me feel way better than I'd have imagined. If the whole world was full of stern little kids in chicken hats who carry clipboards and people buying parts for their model helicopters, there might be a reason to live.

Earl

I'd be the first one to tell you I don't know a whole hell of a lot about kids. Never had any. Barely even knew any. When you grow up in a musical family, 'specially a musical country family, there's a lot of working and playing music. Not too much being a kid. So for all I know, maybe all kids is bossy as hell. But I don't think any of them could come anywhere near that little Sara Sprout. Good goddamn name for her. Some ways, she reminded me of my middle sister, Luanne. Lu was opinionated too. Pride used to call her a wire-haired terror.

It's funny, because the whole time I been living here, and that's getting to be a hell of a long time now, nobody's been giving me orders. That's 'cause the old man didn't know nothing about how to work the land. Part of me figures that's because the place is mostly scrub. There are some nice parcels around here, but this isn't one of them. You'd need Jesus Christ himself to turn this into more than a bit of pasture for some goats or cows or what have you.

None of that mattered to little Sara. She was not afraid to dictate an order or two. I learned that after she looked at the chicken house. She walked around it a time or two and asked me if that was it.

So I asked her what the hell she meant by that.

She told me it looked wrong, and I was about to tell her to go to hell when Prudence comes rushing over and sticks her nose in, trying to smooth things out.

Prudence told the kid I been working on it all day and asked what the problem was. So the kid started to tell her. She said the frame wasn't plumb and she pointed to the tar paper poking out here and there and said there were no vents and how chickens need excellent ventilation.

God help me, she had a point there. But I didn't let on that I agreed. Truth is, I was getting a helluva kick out of her. Then the kid got down on her knees and looked inside and told me how none of the stuff she wanted was in there.

I acted like I didn't know what the hell she was talking about, even though I did. I just hate like hell to bend so I skipped it. Way I saw it, them chickens wouldn't last a week anyway. Some fox or raccoon'd get them and then the goddamn chicken house'd just be one more thing to trip over. Or burn down.

Prudence asked me about the roost and perches and I told her I forgot they had to go in first.

Kid reminded me that there was supposed to be a latch at the back of the nest boxes and a door there so she could get the eggs. I played dumb some more. The way she was getting steamed up was funny.

She told me she couldn't climb through the front door, which was a few inches square. Kid looked me up and down and said neither could I, obviously. Hell, I nearly laughed out loud at that one.

Had to maintain my sense of myself, so I told Prudence that I got better things to do than to be told my job by some little sprout.

Prudence told the kid I'd be happy to fix it and the kid said how at her junior poultry club they are taught that standards are important.

Standards. Can you beat that?

She told us that without standards you have nothing.

She had a point there. That kid's not much for smiling, but she sure as hell makes up for it on the giving directions side.

I spent another day fixing up that chicken house and when I finished it was slicker than snot, as far as henhouses go. That's when the kid got to looking at Bertie. The old sheep was the only livestock on the farm, 'less you include Chubnuts.

Bertie was hardly moving. I think it's because she had a dose of that depression you hear about. The old man started out with two sheep.

He got 'em from some guy down the road who didn't know what to do with them. There was Bertie and another one called Edie. Anyway, Edie and Bertie buggered off one night and Edie got herself run over on the road. Poor bastard who hit her was damn near hysterical. There was wool and blood and you don't want to know what all on the grill of his truck. He was near crying when he drove up with Edie's body in the back.

He told us he hit her and he was sorry.

I didn't say nothing, but the old man, he shook his head and said how Edie always had the wanderlust in her.

The poor bugger that ran her down didn't know what to say.

The old man kept going about how he could never keep her home, how she loved to roam. He said she should have been a sheep in the foothills of Scotland. Now if that wasn't a load of shit I don't know what is.

I'll tell you why that sheep roamed. The fences around here was held up with goddamn binder twine and half-assed prayers. That's why. You need good fences to keep sheep.

The old man got to moaning about poor old Edie and how he was going to miss her. That was another load. We only had them sheep for a couple of weeks and the old man hadn't barely looked at 'em. The young feller who hit her offered to pay for her. Nice enough kid. Drove a new Dodge pickup. Probably worked at the mill.

The old man told him no money could replace Edie. She was priceless.

That was a damn lie, too. That sheep cost forty dollars at the auction and the feller down the road gave her to us for free just to get rid of her.

Finally, I asked if there was another sheep with her. The old man plumb forgot about Bertie.

Now the kid with the Dodge was really starting to shit bricks, wondering if he hit two damn sheep. He said Edie walked right into him and at first he thought she was a plastic bag blowing across the road. A big one.

Now that I think of it, there's a chance that kid was on drugs. Sheeps can look like lots of things, but never plastic bags, as far as I know.

So the old man asked the kid to come in for a drink to calm his nerves, and while they were getting into the sauce I took the old truck and went to look for Bertie. I found her right about where Edie got hit. I could tell it was the place because there was wool and blood and skid marks on the road. Bertie was standing in the ditch, still as if she'd just come from the taxidermy.

I pulled over and got out. I had a piece of rope with me. Neither of those sheep was very good in a halter. No one ever took the time.

She didn't move when I walked up to her. I put the halter on her head and gave her a pat and under all that dirty old wool I could feel her body, near frozen with fear. I talked to her a bit and pulled on that lead rope and finally got her out of the ditch. She walked beside me all the way home and I put her in the barn to recover. She didn't eat a damn thing for two days. But on the third day, I brung her outside and kept her tied near the fresh grass. She finally took a few bites.

The night the barn burnt down Bertie's luck held again. She was still outside on the grass. By the time Prudence come, all Bertie did was lay out in the field. Like I said, I think she was too depressed to move. Didn't help that the old man left her half shaved. Even a sheep's got a sense of dignity.

He met some guy from New Zealand down at the pub. Guy told the old man that it's kinder to shear a sheep in two sessions. He said stage shearing was the way of the future. There was nothing the old man liked better than being part of the future, so he told Patty, the girl who always sheared Bertie, to do only the right side.

Patty's a stocky girl. I've seen her wrassle some damn big sheep. Got some pipes on her that would make one of them guys with all the tattoos who fight in their underpants stand up and take notice. She looked at the old man like he was crazy when he explained about the New Zealander he met down at the Grainery Pub and how they are doing sheep in stages now so they recover from the first haircut before they get the next one.

Patty told him she'd never heard of that and was he sure. The old man told her his source was from New Zealand, where they pretty much invented sheep. Of course, Patty was born on a sheep farm on Salt Spring

Island, but there was no telling the old man that. He said the sheep'd already been through enough recently, what with losing Edie and her home in the fire. Patty just shrugged and got to work. She flipped Bertie this way and that, and, with neat little strokes, took off half her coat.

I remember Patty shaking her head as Bertie trotted away, half bald.

Then the old man up and died, leaving poor Bertie looking like hell on a Harley, clumped and matted and fifty percent bald. I don't know if Prudence and Chubnuts had even noticed there was anything strange about her. Prudence spends all her time pacing around the property and yapping on her phone and cleaning and writing in that notebook of hers. Chubnuts just sits on the porch staring at his old house and watching me work.

But the little gaffer, Sara, it didn't take her long to start asking questions.

First she asked me what happened to the sheep. I wasn't going to tell her the whole goddamn story about the dead sheep and the barn and the old man and the New Zealander. I got better things to do. Not only that, but I don't like to speak ill of the dead. So I told her that Bertie only has half a haircut. Sara said she could see that. Then she asked where Bertie lived. I said she stayed in a shed near my cabin. It was more of a lean-to, really. A tarp over some pieces of plywood I put up for walls.

Little Miss Sara stood there, hands on her hips like a damn prison warden, and she didn't say nothing else, but the next day she came over and started reading to me from this book she got out of the library about sheep. She tells me that sheep are herd animals and that Bertie's probably unhappy because she's alone. I end up telling her about Edie and how Edie died and about the New Zealander and the old man. Kind of surprised me, the way the kid got it out of me.

She didn't say anything for a while or I couldn't hear her because I was pounding the last nails on the chicken shed. When I got done she told me things were looking good, goddamn bossy kid. Then she said she's going to have a talk with Prudence. That something needed to be done about Bertie. That it wasn't right to leave her like that.

I said, Fly at it. Like I said, the kid is bossy as hell.

Prudence

I dressed carefully for my appointment at the bank. My goal was to give the impression that I was a prosperous young farmer and entrepreneur, perhaps one of Whole Foods' organic garlic suppliers or an importer of rare, rainforest-friendly chocolate. I had no doubt that the facts would fit the image eventually, I just needed a little bit of time.

Unfortunately, the banker, Phyllis Snelling, seemed to require more from me in the way of assurances than a confident expression and neat clothes.

"So you inherited the old Woefield place," she said.

"Oh, yes. And it's an amazing piece of land. A truly wonderful property. I've got big plans," I said, holding my hands shoulder-width apart to show how big. "I'm certain I'll be able to help the farm achieve its potential."

Phyllis Snelling smiled. "Good. One of our mandates is to support small farmers."

I smiled. We were on the same page. I needed support. She and her bank wanted to give it. Excellent. This is going well, I thought. If Goldman Sachs qualifies for a bailout, so should I!

"So what's the plan?" she said.

"I think it's better described as plans," I told her. "I'm working on a multi-pronged approach intended to maximize productivity. We are going to be systematic and deliberate. I'm basing a lot of it on the theories of Joel Salatin. Grass farming, you know."

She seemed to want more details.

"Look, Phyllis," I said, using her name because businesspeople seem to like that. "Getting a farm going is not a quick process. It takes considerable time and thought."

Phyllis folded her hands onto her desk. Her small office was hot and smelled of vinyl furniture. Her hair was short and curly. "Is that so?" she said.

"So we may need a bit of extra time before we start repaying the loans. We're not asking for much here. Just give us, oh, say, until the end of August. I've got a great, hardworking team assembled. Things are coming together. By August we'll be ready to make our first payment. No question. We'll probably be fixtures at the farmers' market by then."

Phyllis leaned forward.

"What exactly are you growing?"

"Growing?"

"What crops are you planting?"

"Well, Phyllis, the question is really, what *aren't* we growing."

She cocked her head.

"We're putting in raised beds and I have plans to seed a hayfield. We're going to plant squash, tomatoes, peppers, eggplant. And potatoes, of course. A wide assortment of radishes. Everything organic!"

She didn't seem very impressed, so I added, "And chickens. We've got a selection of very nice chickens coming."

"Interesting," said Phyllis. Her short hair and sensible suit made me wonder if she used to have a career in law enforcement. "Because my family has farmed up near Woefield for two generations and I've never known that land to produce anything but a bit of hay and pasture for cows. Not a real productive parcel over there. And now you're telling me that you're going to make enough growing a few crops to support the place and pay back the loan."

I cleared my throat. Perhaps I shouldn't have been so forceful.

"That's the goal, yes."

"Unless I'm mistaken, your late uncle didn't make one red cent off that farm."

"He had other priorities. Farming wasn't his passion."

"But it's yours?" she said. She wasn't being rude. She was genuinely interested.

"It is. I believe farming is in my bones."

"Where are you from, Prudence?"

I cleared my throat.

"New York. Well, Brooklyn, actually." I thought about telling her about the cooperative rooftop garden I'd been involved in, but then I might have had to tell her about the partial roof collapse and the law-suit, so I decided to skip it.

"Prudence," said Phyllis, matching me first name for first name. "I was raised on a local farm. I live on a farm still. And I have to work full-time *off* the farm to help keep it going. Many of the smallhold farmers, at least those with less productive land, have jobs other than farming. That's how we pay our bills."

"I'm also a writer," I told her, concerned that the interview was going off the rails.

"How much do you earn doing that?"

"Earn?" I said, as though I were hearing impaired.

"Look, I appreciate your situation. The reason I handle the agricultural accounts is because I understand how difficult farming can be. But I can't delay your first payment unless I know you've got a solid, achievable plan to repay the loans."

"But I do!" I blurted. My conversation with Seth popped into my head. "We're turning the place into a . . . a treatment center. For people struggling with addictions. Farming will be part of the therapy. And so will writing. It's going to be a small, live-in center." I leaned closer, des-perate to convince her. "Treatment services are a lucrative and growing business!"

Phyllis Snelling stared deep into my eyes. I knew I didn't look guilty. I never do when I lie, probably because I only ever lie for good reasons.

"Have you got any clients?" she asked.

"Our first patient arrives this week," I said, getting into the spirit of the thing. "We're only catering to people who can pay a premium for care. Trust funders. People with extended health benefits."

She leaned back and tapped a pen against a folder.

"That could work," she said in a voice that suggested to me that she was sorry she hadn't thought of turning her farm into a treatment center. "Can you provide me with a copy of your business plan and income projections for the next six months?"

"Of course," I said. "I should have brought one with me. I forgot with all that's going on. I'll send you all our information, including our brochure. And our bookings."

"Good. If everything is in order, I am authorized to give you three months. By July 15 we will need you to make a mortgage payment, a payment on your line of credit and a payment on your outstanding property taxes, or we will have to put the farm into foreclosure."

I swallowed, which wasn't easy because my throat suddenly felt full of dirt.

"Of course," I said. "You won't be sorry."

SARA

I guess when you are trained to notice one kind of animal, it's only natural that you start noticing other kinds, too. We never specifically studied sheep in Poultry Club, but I saw some sheep at the 4-H fair and they sure didn't look anything like Bertie.

The ones the kids showed at 4-H were like sheep in a picture book or a dream or something. Fluffy and white with cute black noses and skinny black legs. Most of us bring only our best animals to shows, so those ones are probably extra special. But Bertie—that's Prudence's sheep's name—looks so bad you might not even know she was a sheep. It was hard to tell if she was gray or brown or white because she was so dirty. And she was missing half her coat. She was also very lonely. I could tell from the way she stared at people, which wasn't normal.

I went up to her and she didn't move. She was either very tame or really tired. She kind of reminded me of my mom. That's when I noticed her hooves were all messed up. It was terrible! I'm not an expert or very old and even I could tell she needed help. So I did what we learned to do in Poultry Club. I Took Action. I got a sheep book and figured out that Bertie needed her feet trimmed and medicated and she needed to be completely sheared. It's cruel to leave a sheep with all its hair in the summer, even only on one side, because they get very hot and matted. I took out a sheep-shearing video from the library and then I told Prudence what needed to be done. She told me that she was going to "delegate this one" and I should put someone in charge of sheep maintenance. Prudence has an excellent vocabulary, I have to say. That may be because she is from the United States where I think they have a different schooling system.

I did all this while getting my birds ready to move, which wasn't too hard, as well as going to school, which was hard because since I went to church with her, Bethany thinks we're best friends. I'm getting quite interested in Christianity because the minister had so many things to say about morals and he had definite leadership qualities that I don't get at home. I've also been reading that book Bethany's mom gave me, *Left Behind*. It's sort of scary and boring at the same time and probably more interesting if you're an adult. All I can say so far is that when the end time comes, there's a good chance I won't get left behind because I am doing everything possible to get ready for heaven. Although, now that I think about it, maybe getting left wouldn't be so bad. I kind of like it here, even though leadership is a lot of work.

SETH

I don't know how familiar you are with Def Leppard. Now there's a band that has seen some trouble. Sure, they sold more albums than just about anyone in the eighties. But they had tragedy, too. Steve Clark died of booze and drugs and Rick Allen, the drummer, lost his arm in a car crash.

After the scene at Home Depot I felt like Def Leppard in their darkest days, only without the album sales, the groupies or the fame. But the show must go on, you know. Look at Leppard. Those guys are still playing.

I was also trying to keep out of Sara's way. The kid was worse than Prudence for projects. She had Earl doctoring Bertie and I knew she wanted to get me in there, too.

Sure enough, she asked if I'd help and I had to tell her I wasn't feeling good. Which was true. I hadn't had a drink for two days and was feeling a little rough. I didn't have full-blown DTs. I've been there before and I highly recommend avoiding it. Sure, I had the shakes, and things that turned out not to be there kept flitting across the edges of my peripheral vision. But no full-blown delusions.

But even without DTs I wasn't at the top of my game, health-wise. My head felt like it'd been stuffed into an old boxing glove and then pounded on by every middleweight within a thousand miles.

I couldn't seem to update Celebutard, never mind Raging Metal. Some of my sources had been feeding me pictures and stories, and some of the material wasn't bad, either, like the cell-phone video of the supposedly sober Canadian celebrity falling down the stairs at a strip club in Vancouver, obviously out of his mind. I didn't end up posting it. You know why? I felt sorry for him. It's fucking hard being sober. It was starting to dawn on me that my days as a blogger might be numbered.

The kid came in when I was laying on the couch in the living room. It was maybe 1:00 in the afternoon or something. Prudence had gone out. Probably shopping for more supplies to turn this place into Green Acres. She wasn't picking up pizza, I'll tell you that much. She had us on a steady diet of beans and rice and this green leafy stuff that tasted like a vegetarian's ass. The only good thing about Prudence's healthy cooking was watching Earl's face as he ate it. Anyway, while she was out, I took a break from my job, which was using a wobbly old wheelbarrow to move dirt from the big pile out front over to the new raised beds me and Earl started building as soon as he finished with the chicken house. There are eight of the damn things and she's got plans for about a million more since she realized this place is basically dirt-free. There's only a one-inch layer over top of rocks and more rocks. I took Prudence's absence as an opportunity to lay on the couch to try and pull myself together. I heard the kid came in but I didn't move. I couldn't.

She walked just far enough into the room so she could see me on the couch.

"Can you help us with something?" she asked.

"Probably not."

"But you don't even know what it is."

"Is it outside?"

She nodded. She had this clipboard in her hands. Like a, I don't know, little wedding planner or a figure skating judge. Like she was taking notes on my performance. If I hadn't been feeling so near death, that clipboard might have cheered me up.

"If it's outside I can't do it," I told her. "I'm maxed on the great outdoors."

"Oh," she said.

From where I lay I could only see part of her. She was half hidden by the wall that divides the kitchen and the living room. She was really small.

"Me and Earl are trying to help Bertie," she said.

"Who's Bertie?"

"She's the sheep."

"Well, that's very Christian of you. But Bertie lives outside. Ergo, I am unable to help."

"You were outside a while ago. Pushing the dirt."

"Too sick now."

"Sometimes being outside makes people feel better."

"Not in my case. I'm fairly sure I could die if I was exposed to any more fresh air or sunlight."

During this conversation, she'd been inching her way into the living room so she was standing near my feet. She looked me up and down. She looked at the two cans of ginger ale beside me and the empty bag of Cheezies. I saw her eyes move to my laptop, which was sitting on the coffee table. I quickly minimized the screen shot of a woman who, according to the gossip site, may or may not have been Paul McCartney's ex-wife, doing something unmentionable with a vegetable.

Then the kid stared at me some more. Her expression was hard to figure and I found myself feeling sort of, oh, I don't know. Ashamed or something. But not in a way that made me mad at her. She looked at me like the guys in Leppard probably looked at Rick Allen when he wanted to give up because he didn't think he could be a one-armed drummer. I sat up.

"Earl's going to be in charge of the sheep," she said.

"That's good. That'll keep him out of trouble."

Not for the first time I felt glad to not be Earl. Sure, Bertie's just one sheep, but who knows where that kind of responsibility could end? Probably with a flock of hundreds. Also, that sheep looked deeply troubled to me.

"There's something wrong with her feet."

"I guess Earl will have to fix them."

"You ever read *Left Behind*?"

"What?"

"It's a book," she explained.

I thought maybe it was one of those kids' books that kids are always reading. Like *Harry Potter* or some shit. I'm not a book guy really. I'm more into music and the Internet. I prefer TV to movies.

"No. I haven't got to that one yet."

"It's about these people—" she started, but then she must have noticed me close my eyes. I felt like I was wearing a barrel filled with shattered glass over my head.

"I better go," she said. And *poof!* she disappeared.

When she was gone, I lay back and closed my eyes. I was nearly asleep when Prudence came zipping into the room, the way she does.

"Change of plans," she said.

What else is new, I thought. Far as I could tell, changing plans is all Prudence does. Actually, that's not strictly accurate. It's just that the second you finish one of her plans, she's got another one right behind it. She's a plan fiend, is what she is.

"The treatment center idea," she said. "I'd like to move forward on that."

"Treatment center?" I wasn't sure I was hearing her correctly.

She stood at the end of the couch, right where Sara had been a few minutes earlier. She was practically vibrating with, I don't know, energy or excitement or intention or something. For once she had on shoes instead of rubber boots. She was also wearing lipstick and her hair was in a neat little ponytail. I noted again that she was a seriously good-looking girl, kind of like Natalie Portman but broadcasting on a higher frequency.

"It was your suggestion and it was a brilliant one."

"It was?" I've been known to suggest bogus plans as a means of getting people off my back. No one had ever taken me seriously before.

"I may have misspoke," I said. The truth was that I'd been so hungover when we'd talked that I could barely remember the conversation.

"You're going to create all the marketing materials for our treatment center on your computer. That's what we'll show the bank. So they know we have a plan. It's the only way they'll delay our payment schedule."

"Whoa!" I said, heart suddenly accelerating. "Just hold up a minute." I groped around in my excuse bank for a decent objection. "But you aren't really starting a treatment center here?"

"Not exactly. This is more of an interim measure to buy us some time. I told the bank I was opening a treatment center and now they want to see my business plan and income projections."

"Holy shit," I said.

"Don't worry. Soon we'll be self-sustaining and this won't be an issue. We just need more time. This is where you come in. You're good on the computer. We're going to need a website and a brochure. It's got to be professional enough to convince the bank that we're for real."

"Dude," I said, "I'd love to help, but I think you can go to jail for doing shit like that. I've heard that banks are kind of humorless about fraud."

She smiled.

"Seth, if I can't get the bank to back off, they're going to put the place into foreclosure. That means we'll all be homeless. You, me, Earl and Sara's chickens. We need more time and this is the only way we can buy it."

"You're serious," I said, pulling at my hair and realizing that it needed a wash.

"The lady at the bank is expecting our plan tomorrow. If you need examples, you can look them up online."

"Well, then, I guess I better get going."

"So you'll do it?"

"What the hell," I said. I felt like Rick Allen the first time he picked up his stick after the accident and the band was so grateful. Essential. That's how I felt.

Prudence grinned at me.

"Thanks, Seth. We make a great team."

I pulled my hat down low because I didn't want her to see my face when she said that.

PRUDENCE

You might not think it due to his hair, but Seth has a flair for design.

His brochure for Ocean's Edge Treatment Center was extremely compelling. The text said it was a place of healing and change. First he wanted to call it Ocean's Edge Healing Path Treatment Center, but I said that sounded too much like a spa.

"Does it matter that we're not on the ocean?" he wondered.

"We're on an island. That should be enough," I said.

"You should promote it as an oceanside spa," he said. "Go for full-on false advertising. That way when the poor bastards get here, they'll be completely demoralized and ready for change. They'll take one look at this place and hit rock bottom right away."

"Seth," I reminded him. "There's nothing wrong with Woefield. And we aren't going to have any actual clients. Other than you."

"I don't know, man," he said, staring at the front page of his brochure on the screen. "Once people get a gander at this masterwork, you'll be turning them away by the wasted busload."

"No one is going to see the brochure except the bank lady," I told him. "Just to be on the safe side."

When I went to pick up the brochures from the copy shop where I'd had them printed, the tall, fleshy guy who'd taken my order heaved himself up from his desk. He wore a Pogues T-shirt. His hair was dyed black but light-brown roots showed at his greasy part. His skin had a gamer's pallor.

He wiped a pudgy, short-fingered hand covered in nacho chip dust on his T-shirt.

"Can I help you?"

"I'm here to pick up a brochure."

"Name?"

"Prudence Burns. I was in here yesterday to drop it off."

His eyes, which were red rimmed, darted over at me.

"You're the treatment center lady," he said.

I cleared my throat.

"Ah, yes. That's right."

"You gonna have sex offenders over there?"

I recoiled. "Pardon me?"

"Kiddy diddlers? Rapos? Dudes who beat on their old ladies?"

"What? No. Of course not."

"Your brochure doesn't specify. Treatment centers get some sick bastards."

"You *read* our brochure?" I said, thinking surely that must be an invasion of privacy.

"Had to read it to print it."

He reached under the desk and pulled out a short stack of neatly folded, glossy brochures.

"So who are you treating then? Ex-cons?" he continued.

"No," I said. I was starting to feel defensive about my fake treatment center. "It's just for people with addictions. Mild ones."

"For real?"

I nodded and took out my credit card.

"I looked you up on the Internet. You weren't listed on there."

"We're new. Our website is under construction, so at the moment we're just taking clients via word of mouth. And referral." I looked over my shoulder, as though checking to make sure that I wouldn't be overheard. "We're kind of exclusive," I whispered.

"No shit," said the guy. "So you might get some stars and stuff in there. That's cool, except good luck getting any privacy around here. Unless your patients are Howard Hughes and don't come out of their rooms, everyone around here's going to be all up your ass wanting to know your business."

"Great," I said.

My plan was to drop off the brochures at the bank and beat a rapid retreat before Phyllis could spot me and start asking questions. I put the brochures and business plan into a large manila envelope and handed the package to the short lady behind the semicircular reception desk that divided the banking offices from the tellers' counter. The receptionist was so short and the desk was so tall that she looked like a gnome.

"This is for Phyllis Snelling. She's expecting it." I turned to head quickly for the door.

"Wait!" said the small lady. "Are you the girl from the treatment center?"

All the people standing in the tellers' lineup turned to stare. So did the various bankers and tellers milling around.

"Girl *with* the treatment center," I said.

"Phyllis wanted me to let her know when you came in."

The small lady's head disappeared behind the desk when she got off her chair. As soon as she was out of view, I began to hurry toward the exit again.

"Prudence?"

Damn. Brady, the plumbing writer from the strawberry social, stood in the doorway, on his way in. He was dressed in work clothes and he beamed at me.

"You think any more about what I said?" he asked. "About teaching writing? We'd love to have a published novelist give us some pointers."

"Oh," I said. "I'm not really much of a . . ." From the corner of my eye I could see Phyllis Snelling coming out of her office.

"You are too modest," said Brady. "Don't worry. We won't take so much of your time that you can't write."

"How about you call me?" I said. "We can talk about it."

"Already tried," he said. "Your line wasn't working. You got her hooked up now? Maybe a cell-phone number?"

"I'll call you. I have your card. We'll set something up."

Phyllis Snelling was nearly on us.

"I got ideas," said Brady. "You'd think plumbing wouldn't give a guy a lot of inspiration for stories, but I'm here to tell you different."

"Great," I said. "Let's talk soon!"

As Brady stepped away, Phyllis reached out her hand to shake mine with a strong, dry grip.

"Prudence," she said.

"Oh hi!" The important thing was to maintain a positive and confident image.

Brady shouted from his place in the lineup. "Don't forget to call! We need you around here. Me especially!"

I nodded and smiled.

Phyllis stared at him. I could practically see her making a note to go and revoke his line of credit.

"I left our brochures and business plan with the receptionist."

"That's great," she said. Then she stepped in closer. People walked by in every direction. She eyed them as they walked past and lowered her voice.

"I was wondering," she said. "Whether you handle young people?"

"Young?"

"Under nineteen? My sister's daughter, Laureen, she's showing . . . I mean, she's got some . . . issues."

"Issues?"

"Drugs," said Phyllis quietly. "Not just pot either. Verna says she's been taking other stuff besides. Ecstasy, I think it's called."

"I see."

"She dresses strangely," said Phyllis. "Striped tights and she's got her hair cut into this weird shape. I think it's because of drugs."

"Hmmm."

"So do you treat kids?"

"No," I said firmly. "No kids. We aren't licensed for them."

She nodded her head sadly. "That's too bad. Verna's beside herself with worry."

"That's tough," I agreed. "Give her my sympathies."

Phyllis Snelling stepped in a little closer. "But you probably have addiction specialists on staff, right?"

I thought of our brochure. It mentioned certified counselors no less than three times.

"Yes, of course."

"Maybe Laureen could talk to one of them. Just for an hour or so. Something like an outpatient visit."

I exhaled. I could not afford to antagonize this woman.

"Well, our counselors are sort of busy. Getting ready for the big opening. You know."

"But you might be able to squeeze her in?"

"Well, I . . ."

"She'll pay. Of course. We're not trying to get anything for free."

I realized that it was one thing to tell the bank a lie to delay our payments but if we started taking money for counseling we could be in serious trouble.

"I'm sure we can work something out. Someone will be able see her for a little while. Have a talk. Off the books."

Phyllis smiled and her face became momentarily beautiful.

"That's great. Really great. Verna will be so happy. She'll call you. I'll give her one of your brochures."

"Excellent," I said.

Brady walked past.

"Don't let me interrupt!" he said. "See you soon! I can't tell you how grateful I am."

"He's right, you know," said Phyllis. "This town really needs you."

EARL

I didn't hardly have the chicken coop done and them boards packed full of dirt before the kid was on me about the goddamn sheep. She brung me a whole stack of books and one of them movie discs. I told her I didn't have no VHS or Betamax for watching movies and she said I'd need a DVD player, which I guess makes sense. I told her I didn't have one of them, either.

She said I could just read the books until she brought her DVD player from home and I told her I wasn't reading no goddamn books. I was wore out from making the raised beds and chicken coop. That kind of fine finishing takes it out of a man. She said that sheep care is more complicated than many people realize.

I told her if old Bertie needed shearing, she should call Patty from Salt Spring. Or maybe she should ask Chubnuts. The kid asked what a chubnuts was and I said it was just a word. And she said, You mean Seth, and I said I did. She said he was busy doing stuff on the computer all the time and that she already called and Patty had gone to Australia for a month for a sheep-shearing contest. And besides I was supposed to be in charge of the sheep now.

I said we should just leave her. She'd learn to stand to one side to catch the breeze. The kid thought I was making a joke but I wasn't.

Finally, the little bugger got me to agree to do Bertie's feet. I'd seen Patty wrassling with her. Didn't look too hard. So I said yes. Stupidest goddamn move I ever made. Besides not leaving here when I had the chance. That's the story of my life. Jesus Christ. I must have said that last part out loud, because the kid told me I should be careful or I'd get left behind.

I told her that, far as I knew, I already had.

SARA

Being a leader is very tiring but also rewarding. It's like we learned in Jr. Poultry: The secret for getting ahead is Getting Started. It seems like a lot of adults have trouble Getting Started. Or maybe they just get started on the wrong things.

Like my dad. He's always saying how he's had enough of his new boss on the construction crew and he's too well educated to do that kind of work. He always says he's going to tell his boss that he can shove the job up his you know what. But my dad never does. Instead he comes home and complains to my mom. The other thing my dad does is watch sports on TV. But he is always watching new sports that he has to learn about. He watches a whole bunch of soccer or maybe tennis and then he tells us all about it in a lot of detail. But when the people or teams he wants to win lose, he quits watching and says he hates the sport and that it's corrupt and everyone's on steroids. Once my mom told him he might like it better if he tried to play one of the sports and he threw the remote and broke it on the wall.

Being a leader gives me a lot of confidence, but it is also quite a lot of pressure. You have to think about everything. Like in the case of my chickens, what if I move them and they don't like it and get sick and die? That could happen. One of the kids at Poultry Club got twenty new pullets last year and the stress of being shipped killed all but four. Mr. Lymer said that the kid, whose name I won't mention, may have forgotten to plug in the heat lamp, but I like to think the best of people, even direct competitors, so I am going to assume it was stress that did it.

New things and places are often stressful. So are old ones. I was sure Bertie the sheep found it stressful to not be looked after properly. And because she's just a sheep, I can't even tell her that I'm going to make sure someone helps her.

I got Earl some books on sheep care and on sheep shearing but he isn't really a self-starter, I don't think. It shouldn't be too hard. All we have to do is fix her feet and finish shearing her. I hope that when Prudence sees what a good job we've done, she'll be so happy she'll want to get some more sheep.

Seth

First off, I never knew a sheep could kick like that. Especially not Bertie, who has always seemed more like a gob of phlegm hanging around the place than a farm animal. When I went outside I found Earl sitting down. He had Bertie by the back legs, or one back leg, anyway. And she was methodically kicking him in the arm and the chest with the other one. Just like *whump! whump! whump!* Steady like that.

"Holy shit," I said. As you may have noticed, Earl is old and played out as hell. I figured if that sheep hit him in the wrong place the old man could drop dead. It seemed like a real possibility.

Little Sara was standing beside them. She had hold of her book with one hand and with the other hand she kept trying to shove the sheep over onto its side. I have no idea why. I think it was just making matters worse.

Before I got in there to help, I took a picture. My blogging has probably given me a reporter's instincts.

Earl grunted *oof* every time a kick landed. Between Bertie's bleats and Earl's *oof*s, they sounded like an Oompa Loompa concert.

Anyway, once I got a little closer, I had no idea what to do. I didn't want to insert myself into the kicking, stinking, woolly tangle of old man and sheep.

"We've got to flip her over," said Sara. "I told Earl that, but he didn't listen."

So without even thinking about it too much, I took her, Bertie I mean, and flipped her over. The crazy thing is that she stopped struggling.

She reeked like some homeless dude's sweater. I held her on her back. To keep her there, I straddled her, crouching over her in this highly dangerous way for my family Js. I was glad we were behind the house so my mom and Bobby couldn't see me.

Sara handed Earl some clippers.

"Can't," he gasped.

No shit, I thought. Poor bastard's probably going to die in the next couple of minutes.

"Give them to me." I was as surprised as anyone to hear myself saying the words.

"We've got to trim her feet and then put Coppertox on them," said Sara.

"Got to keep the dirt out, too," said Earl, sucking air between each word.

"Okay, I'll hold the feet and you trim them," I said to Sara. So the kid took the massive bloody clippers, like garden shears, from me and started going after the sheep like she was Jack the Ripper and the sheep was a Victorian prostitute. The thing was, she wasn't getting anywhere near the sheep. No, those big fucking clackers were jabbing perilously close to my eye.

"Little dude," I said. "Watch it. You're going to maim somebody. I'll clip. You hold her feet."

This Sara could do. Once Bertie was on her back, she seemed to give up all hope and she had stopped kicking. The kid hung onto Bertie's hooves and I cut off a gnarly piece that looked like it was extra. How the fuck did I know, right? They smelled terrible, like the homeless guy's sweater had a gangrenous arm in it. After I'd cut as much as I could without amputating the poor sheep's foot entirely, Sara rubbed some of the toxic-smelling stuff from the tub on them. I could practically feel myself getting cancer from the smell alone.

"You should be wearing gloves," I told her.

By this time, Earl had caught his breath and was helping Sara. "How are we supposed to keep these bastards clean?" he asked. I think he was talking about Bertie's hooves. I'll say this about him: He's got a masterful and winning way with children and sheep.

"I can't hold her like this until June," I told them. I wasn't used to wrestling with sheep. Contrary to what some people from my high school might have said.

"I know!" said Sara. And she ran off into the house, leaving me and Earl to finish cutting Bertie's other three feet and putting the carcinogenic goop all over them. Earl had to do the back feet, because I couldn't hold her steady and turn myself around to face the other way.

We'd just trimmed the last foot when Sara came back. She was carrying a box of maxipads.

"Look, kid, you should talk to your mom about whatever's going on with you," I said, breathing hard myself now. I was also thinking that kids are insane and I was definitely going to wear a rubber if I ever got to have sex with another person and not just myself. Seriously. What a time for the kid to explore the wonders of menstruation. And to pick me and old Earl of all people.

Sara ignored me, pulled out a pad, ripped the adhesive strip off and folded it over one of Bertie's feet. She held the pad in place and told Earl to get the duct tape. Which he did. Together, they wrapped about twelve feet of duct tape around Bertie's little hoof. No dirt was getting in there anytime soon. The poor sheep looked like some dying raver in moon boots.

"Nice work," I said, impressed, even though I felt like Angus Young at the end of a show, totally wrung out from physical and emotional exhaustion.

Prudence got home just as Earl and Sara were putting a final sanitary napkin on Bertie's left back foot, while I held her front moon boots steady. Even in my weakened condition I could see that something wasn't right. I'd never seen Prudence walk slowly before.

"Hi," she said, in a flat voice. She walked right past us into the house while Bertie's maxipad-clad feet paddled in the wool-smelling wind.

PRUDENCE

I'd read numerous books in which New Yorkers make their escape from the big city and realize their dreams of becoming farmers. In every case they experience a small but entertaining setback or two, and eventually they become quite successful and never betray their values. One woman moved from New York to the Ozarks and became a renowned beekeeper and writer. Another woman moved to the east coast, bought a cow and started making world-famous yogurt. A third guy wrote a bestseller about living beside a saltwater marsh.

Not one of them talked about meetings with bankers or creating fake businesses in order to defer tax and mortgage payments. They certainly didn't mention getting roped into giving creative writing workshops. I admit to experiencing a moment of discouragement after my trip to the bank. I allowed the mood to continue for twenty minutes. Any longer than that would have been wallowing. Ultimately I knew all my problem solving would be good training for later, when I had to deal with things like harvesting and deciding how much seed to buy.

To cheer myself up I found the listing for the local farmers' market in the community paper and sent the organizer an email asking to reserve space for a table next month. I thought that would be an excellent incentive to get our garden growing, so to speak. The radish seeds I'd planted were already sprouting and I was sure the swiss chard, to which I'd devoted a whole bed, wouldn't be far behind.

I was hoping we'd become well known for one or two outstanding items. I had a friend in Brooklyn who used to go all the way to the little farmers' market outside the Botanical Gardens in the Bronx because she said one of the vendors there had the best honey crisp apples in the United States. I wanted our table to become a *destination* like that.

The arrival of Sara's chickens was a welcome change from the accumulating complications. When they came, a week late due to delays in the chicken coop construction, I felt as though we were really getting started, agriculturally speaking. As Michael Pollan points out in *The Omnivore's Dilemma,* what's missing from many farms in this era of conglomerate agriculture and monoculture crops is actual animals.

At Woefield, I wanted us to have a harmonious balance of animals and vegetable crops. Of course we already had Bertie the sheep, and the chickens were another step in the right direction, even if they were just boarders.

Earl finished painting the Chicken Hilton a few minutes before Sara's mother arrived with the birds. As I watched Earl work, I noticed that he seemed to have aged several years in only a couple of weeks. That got me thinking that perhaps in addition to standard crops, we should also grow some medicinal herbs. I mean, if that famous yogurt company could start from just one cow, perhaps we could put in a bed of Saint-John's-wort and some valerian and see where it leads.

Seth came outside to watch the action. He brought his laptop and a camera with him as though he was expecting a flock of celebrities rather than chickens.

He started snapping pictures as soon as Sara's mother came around the corner, lugging a large wire cage covered with a flowered sheet.

Sara rushed to meet her mother, calling out orders for how to proceed with the cage.

"Don't jostle them!" she instructed. "Be careful!"

"Sara," said her mother, who was pink and panting from exertion in the warm May morning, "just tell me where to put the damned things."

Sara ran to open the door of the chicken run, which was neatly enclosed on all sides with boards and wire fencing.

Mrs. Spratt stooped low to duck into the doorway of the run and set the big cage down inside.

"Careful!" said Sara.

"You're welcome," puffed Mrs. Spratt.

Earl, Seth and I stepped forward to get a look at the birds. Bright morning light dappled the cage and the grass was damp underfoot. The birds were still hidden by the sheet.

Mrs. Spratt joined us.

"Some debut, heh?" said Seth.

"You have no idea," said Mrs. Spratt.

Sara crouched over the cage inside the chicken run and, after peering under the sheet for several seconds, pulled it back and unclipped the cage door. Then she backed out of the coop.

After a minute or two, a chicken emerged. It walked with an odd back-and-forth motion that reminded me of a heartbeat. I gasped when it cleared the cage because it was no regular chicken. It had a glossy black body and a head topped with an elaborate arrangement of white feathers, like the sort of hat a British aristocrat might wear to a wedding.

"Check it," breathed Seth beside me.

"Don't that beat all," muttered Earl.

Mrs. Spratt said nothing.

As we watched, a second bird and then a third came out of the cage, each more striking than the last.

"They're incredible," I said.

"Holy shit," said Seth.

"Seth," I said, and nudged him with my elbow while casting a meaningful gaze Mrs. Spratt's way. But she didn't seem to notice his profanity.

"Just you wait," muttered Mrs. Spratt.

Sure enough, a fourth bird appeared out of the sheet-draped cage. This one was even bigger and glossier than the others and it had a huge plume on its head. It looked haughtily around its new surroundings. Then, with no real warning, it walked over to one of the smaller birds and leaped onto its back.

"Not again," said Mrs. Spratt.

"Are they fighting?" I asked.

"That bird is such a pig," said Mrs. Spratt.

"He's giving that other one the bone!" said Seth. "Look at him go!"

Earl took a few steps back.

"Sara, can you please do something about that animal?" asked Mrs. Spratt. She turned to us. "I thought he might calm down in a new situation."

But the bird showed no signs of calming down. He pumped busily away, while continuing to survey his new domain with a beady eye.

"He's multitasking," said Seth, his voice high and excited. "Taking care of his star player."

"Seth!" I said, although in light of the scene of chicken debauchery going on right in front of us, it seemed pointless to ask him to tone it down.

"Mom, can you get the frizzles?" said Sara.

Her mother sighed and clumped back toward the car.

Moments later Mrs. Spratt was back, this time struggling with a large cage draped with a couple of threadbare beach towels. She set the second cage down beside the first inside the run and Sara went through the routine of inspecting the birds inside, then opening the door to the cage and backing out of the enclosure.

I don't know quite what I was expecting. Even *more* impressive chickens, probably. Ones with tails like peacocks or elegant swan necks. But the birds that emerged were small, strange and bedraggled.

"What on earth—" I said, and then broke off.

"You can see why they call them frizzles," commented Earl. "Look pretty goddamn frizzled all right."

One by one the birds lurched out of the cage, each one messier and less prepossessing than the last.

Sara stood and beamed at them and then at us. Her small figure swelled with pride.

"These," she said, "are my frizzles."

I knew then that I had nearly everything to learn about farm livestock.

SETH

I nearly fell over when that second batch of birds came out. I should have known any birds belonging to the kid would be unusual. She is nothing if not radically strange. She's like the Ted Nugent of little kids or tweens or whatever you call people who are her age.

When she ordered her mom to "go get the frizzles" I thought she was asking for a snack. Then comes another cage, but instead of good-looking birds, out come these draggle-ass, used-Kleenex-looking chickens. It was awesome.

There was something perfect about her having the real fancy chickens and chickens who are about the saddest things that ever walked the earth. I mean, those frizzles were a mess. They looked like something J. Lo wore five years ago on her Latin American tour dates. They looked like they'd been bleached and then put in the dryer on high for about thirty-six hours. Their feathers were tattered and hanging off them and they had this very dim expression on their faces, even for chickens.

"What on earth are those?" said Prudence when the frizzles came poking out of their cage, looking like they'd been on a group meth bender for about a month and were about to go on the long ride to tweaker heaven.

"Those are the frizzles," said Sara. "My show birds."

Earl shook his head and grumbled something.

"And what are those called?" I pointed at the black chickens.

"Those are my white crested non-bearded black Polish. My backup birds."

"Get out of here," I said.

"My frizzles are top quality."

I wanted to understand. I may not know a chicken from a turkey, but I do know good-looking versus pathetic. I'm fairly solidly on one side of that dividing line and it's not the good-looking side.

"You got it all wrong," I told her. I pointed at the big black chicken, the one with the huge head of feathers that made him look like he was wearing a whole other fucking bird on his head. He'd finally gotten off the hen he'd been humping. The poor thing shook herself off and was eating a few bugs to try and regain her dignity. The black bastard was moving toward another unsuspecting hen with murderous lust in his little round eye. He reminded me of Gene Simmons, only attractive. Actually, he reminded me of Alec Baldwin.

"You need to understand something," I told Sara. "These here, the shiny black ones with the shit—sorry Mrs. Spratt—weird white feathers on their heads? These are your Baldwins. And that big one is the Alec Baldwin of the flock."

The others might let the kid continue telling herself lies about her chickens, but I wasn't about to.

I pointed at the scruffy little white birds. "These here are your Dog the Bounty Hunter and family chickens. They're low class. You can tell from their hair."

"Feathers," Sara corrected. "And for your information my frizzles are perfect. The B-list birds—"

"The Baldwins," I interrupted.

"The Polish non-bearded are my alternates because they have flaws."

"Bullshit," I said, and quickly added, "Sorry Mrs. Spratt. I've been watching old Alec Baldwin for a few minutes now. That bird has no flaws that I can see. At least not where it counts."

"He doesn't meet the Standard," said Sara, and something about the slightly wistful angle of her head made me think that deep in her heart she probably recognized Alec Baldwin's superiority.

"You're way too hung up on standards," I told her. "Is it because of the new kind of testing they do in schools now?"

"Sara means the Standard of Perfection," Mrs. Spratt finally spoke up. "It's the poultry fancier's bible."

"Don't that just curl your whiskers," said Earl, forgetting for once to take the Lord's name in vain.

"Then the Standard's wrong," I said. It was so obvious. Alec Baldwin was now going for broke on the second hen and she had the same long-suffering look as the first one. You know, I could relate to that hen. I've never been jumped by a rooster who didn't believe in even the most basic foreplay, but I have definitely been boned by life more than once.

All at once, I wanted to convince the kid I was right about these chickens. They aroused some sort of appreciator's passion in me. I had this vision of joining the poultry club and becoming a famous chicken fancier, which was kind of crazy since I never cared about even dogs or cats or any other kind of pet.

"I'm telling you, that one is a champion. Trust me. I've spent the last five years reading celebrity and music blogs. I know pretty much everything about A-lists and B-lists, all the way down to Z-lists. I have also learned to recognize quality. That bird there is A-list all the way," I said. "You know how I know? None of us can take our eyes off him."

It was true. Every single one of us was staring, mouths hanging open like we were frogs waiting for flies, while we watched Alec Baldwin.

Ten minutes before all I knew about chickens was that they came on Styrofoam trays at the supermarket, but it turns out that just like humans, some of them have a certain kind of star quality, like James Hetfield or Bruce Dickinson. It's like the golden proportion. They say that every species has one. The Polish chickens definitely did. Not a feather out of place. Their bodies were covered with a glossy black sheen that turned green when the light hit them a certain way. They reminded me of pictures I'd seen of Alec Baldwin's hair when he was younger. I don't know what it is about those Baldwin guys. They're fascinating. There's just something about them, even the fugly one and the fundamentalist Christian one, although now that I think of it, they may be the same person.

"I've obviously got to school you in recognizing beauty and natural charisma," I told Sara.

Prudence suggested that I should get back to painting the kitchen.

I came away from that chicken coop knowing that I wasn't going to have to look at porn online anymore because I would be able to get my sex and violence fix out at the chicken house.

Sara

Another thing we learned about leadership in Jr. Poultry Club is that winners stick with other winners. Or at least not with losers.

That's why I was kind of worried when I saw that girl and her mom go into the house the day after my chickens moved to the farm. I wasn't worried about the effect they might have on me or my birds, but I didn't think Seth or Earl should be near a bad influence like her.

The girl and her friends, who go to the high school, hang out near the Stop 'n' Save Corner Store. The store even posted a sign against them that says only two students are allowed in at a time. The lady who works there told me it's because some kids steal if too many of them are inside at once. She didn't say specifically that it was that girl, but I knew it was. The lady also said she hoped I didn't grow up to be like those kids. I found that kind of offensive, but I didn't say anything.

That girl and her three friends all wear dark clothes and keep their hoods pulled up over their heads. They sit against the wall at the side of the store, smoking, or sometimes they sit on the railing of the little overpass bridge like they might jump or push someone off. They sort of remind me of trolls.

My dad says they're rebates, at least I think that's the word, but he says that about nearly everyone, so I didn't think it meant too much. About a week before she showed up at the farm, I saw that girl and her friends when I went to the store with Bethany and her family after church.

Bethany's parents let me and Bethany go inside while her dad gassed

up their minivan and her mom stayed in the car. We were each supposed to choose a treat and her dad said he would pay for it. On our
way inside we had to pass by that girl and her friends, who were sitting
by the door.

There was a boy with them and he told us to give him our money.
He said it in a low voice so Bethany's dad wouldn't hear. The boy might
have been joking, but it scared Bethany. She stopped walking and just
stood there.

My leadership kicked in and I told the boy to leave us alone.

The boy told me to suck his dick, which is one of the worst things
anyone has said to me so far in my life. When he said that, that girl and
her friends laughed in this very mean way. I pushed Bethany to get her
going again.

Then the guy called Bethany a f%#$ retard. I feel bad even writing
those words.

What kind of person who is nearly an adult says something like that
to kids? I'll tell you who: a very bad person, one who better not get his
hopes up about being taken when the Rapture comes. The pastor at
Bethany's church had just been talking about the Rapture and it's an
extremely scary and exciting thing that most people who don't go to
Bethany's church don't know about.

When we got into the store I could tell Bethany was going to cry, so I
told her he was talking about me, which made her feel better. That was
lucky, because like a lot of leaders, I don't like it when people cry. My
mom cries all the time, especially when my dad starts complaining. It's
very hard on my stomach.

That day in the store I picked the biggest and most expensive treat. A
Häagen-Dazs chocolate-covered ice cream. I think I deserved it.

Anyway, I was very disappointed to see the girl at the farm with her
mother. I felt bad when they went inside and met with Prudence. I
hoped they weren't going to try and bring some animals here. I know
it's not good leadership to be jealous, but I kind of was. I have a bad
feeling about this. School is terrible mostly and so is home. I don't
want the farm to get ruined, too.

Prudence

When she was giving us the detailed instructions for building the chicken coop Sara neglected to mention that we were going to have to deal with a chicken apartheid situation. The frizzles aren't supposed to mate with the Polish non-bearded so her breeding line doesn't get screwed up. I pointed out that there wasn't going to be any breeding, because we are going to eat the eggs. Sara said that I had a point, but asked me to keep an eye on Alec Baldwin, which is what Seth had everyone calling the black rooster. If we see Alec "doing it" to a frizzle we're supposed to get in there and break it up. I decided to delegate that chore to Seth. Somehow, I couldn't see Earl going in the coop to pull that chicken off his romantic targets.

I would have liked to delegate the meeting with the banker's sister and her daughter to someone else as well. I'm not saying that I think we were doing anything particularly wrong with our little subterfuge about being a treatment center. It was a means to an end. But addictions services was outside my field of expertise. The key, I thought, was to do no harm and give no bad advice. Remain neutral. That was my goal.

Ten minutes before the girl and her mother were due for their consultation, I chased Seth out of the kitchen and looked around and tried to see the place through the eyes of a prospective patient. Would it pass as a treatment center? I'd covered much of the mismatched flooring with simple but attractive area rugs I'd found on a local used furnishings website. The bathroom, living room and kitchen had been painted white and I'd had Seth wash all the windows and I'd replaced the curtains.

Seth had also painted all the cupboard doors a soft dollar-bill green. The whole place smelled like cleanliness and fresh paint, and it looked cheery and bright.

For the sake of verisimilitude, I'd printed out some twelve-step slogans Seth found for me on the Internet and hung them on the fridge with magnets. "Keep it Simple, Stupid," read one. "First Things First," said another. Remedial stuff, but it was probably effective because it was so easy to remember.

My plan was to tell the girl and her mom that the treatment center wasn't set up to handle adolescents. I would give them the information that I'd had Seth gather, including a list of adolescent treatment centers, and send them on their way. Then I could get back outside to plant more of the raised beds and see if the radishes were any closer to being ready. I'd signed up for a table at the farmers' market in three weeks and radishes were the only things that looked like they'd be ready. To be safe, I'd planted two full beds of them: six varieties in all.

When the knock came at exactly 1:00 p.m., I answered the door to find an older, tireder version of Phyllis the banker standing on the porch. Verna was a few inches shorter than her sister and ten or twenty pounds heavier. Her no-nonsense curls had been tinted a red that was now faded and grown out, leaving a good inch of gray-brown at the roots. The red on her cheeks was more rosacea than rouge.

Her daughter wore tight, light wash jeans and a black hoodie advertising a band called Stench. The hood of the sweatshirt was pulled up and cinched tight around her face. She was thin but had round, baby cheeks. A few lank brown curls peeked out from under the hood and a ring pierced the septum of her nose. She glanced at me once with liner-ringed eyes and then stared at the floor.

"Stand up straight, Laureen," Verna instructed her daughter. She looked at me. "Hello, we're—" She stopped mid-introduction, apparently distracted by Laureen's slouch.

"She *used* to have perfect posture. I don't know what happened to it."

"Please, come in," I said.

Laureen took two steps into the hallway, still staring down at her feet, which were encased in black skate shoes.

"Phyllis said this is a *treatment center,*" Verna whispered.

"That's right. Or it will be. Once we get ready."

"So you know all about drugs."

At this, Laureen finally looked up, a little hungrily it seemed to me. Or maybe appraisingly.

"Oh yes. Quite a bit."

I wanted to get off the subject, so I invited them into the kitchen and asked them to sit down.

"So the . . . people, patients, I mean, live here?" asked Verna.

I nodded.

"Is it very messy?"

I frowned, not sure what she meant.

"When they go off the drugs. It's supposed to be very . . . noisy. A lot of vomiting. Some people have to wear diapers."

I'd seen people detox in movies, especially German ones, but wasn't sure how accurate that picture was. I didn't want to commit.

"Would you like some tea?" I asked.

Without waiting for an answer, I got up and put on the kettle and began pulling new cups from the cupboard.

"We, I mean, our clients will be more into the recovery phase of their . . . recovery, when they get here. The messy stuff happens somewhere else," I said.

"Detox," said Verna.

"That's right. Detox."

"I don't know if she'll need that."

Verna spoke about Laureen as though she wasn't in the room. Understandable, since the girl slouched at the table, inanimate as a squash.

I put the cups and teapot on the table. After I took my seat, Laureen finally spoke. "You got any sugar?"

I got up, went to the cupboard, pulled out the mason jar of brown sugar and set it in front of her.

She made a face. "You got any white sugar?"

"No," I said firmly. "That's not part of our program."

Then I turned to her mother. "As I'm sure Phyllis mentioned, we don't handle adolescents here. For legal reasons. We can't have young people here because some of our clients will be . . . old. You understand."

Verna nodded seriously.

"But I've printed off a list of centers that do handle adolescents." I slid the small stack of pages in front of Verna. The new bamboo tablecloth was yellow and printed with pictures of white daisies with green stems. Very pretty, really. Hugh the cab driver brought it over as a housewarming gift.

"Here you go. These should tell you everything you need to know. I've also included some excellent recovery slogans."

Verna ran a hand through her tired hair and frowned as she flipped through the sheets.

"Are any of these places local?"

"I think the closest one is in Vancouver."

"This Forest Grove Place," she said, stopping to read one of the pages. "Says here it's eight thousand dollars per month with a minimum stay of two months."

I nodded.

"We can't afford that," said Verna.

"Oh. I see. I'm sure there are publicly funded centers in there."

"I thought you being in the business, you'd have some idea which would be the best place for her."

I looked from mother to daughter and cleared my throat.

"Well, I guess it depends on your circumstances. And Laureen's particular needs."

"Our circumstances are she's turned herself into a damned drug addict."

Laureen managed to rouse herself. "Did not," she muttered.

"Oh no?" demanded her mother. "Then what are you?"

"If I did as much drugs as you drank, then maybe . . ." Laureen's voice trailed off.

Verna's face flushed scarlet. It made for an abrupt contrast with her washed-out hair.

"How dare you say that to me, young lady. After all I've done for you!"

I tried not to look yearningly at my stack of farming books on the counter. *The Self-Sustaining Life* seemed to radiate simplicity from the top of the pile.

"Often treatment programs will look at whole families," I said, sure I'd read that somewhere.

"I don't need looking at," said Verna. "Just because I have a few drinks now and then."

"That's what I used to say," said Seth, coming into the kitchen.

I saw with relief that he did not appear to be drunk. I also noticed that the combination of hard work and good food seemed to be having a positive effect on him. After only a few weeks on the farm his potbelly was gone and there was color in his face. Even his long hair appeared thicker and shinier, perhaps because it was tied into a neat ponytail.

"I said to myself, Seth, you just have a few drinks now and then. But when I got honest, the way you do in treatment, I had to admit the truth. I had a problem."

Verna's face had eased from purplish-red back to pink. I could still see a vein throbbing on her forehead.

"Seth," I said carefully. "We are here to talk to Laureen today. And *as you know,* we are not *qualified* to counsel minors."

"It's all the same. Young or"—here he paused and looked at Verna—"young enough. The key is to get honest. To communicate. To work together."

Now both Verna and Laureen were staring at him. The hostility was gone from Verna's face and the sullenness from Laureen's. There was something new in their eyes. Was that hope?

"You will get through this together," said Seth. "Here at Ocean Side Recovery House, our motto is 'Together we can.'" He clasped his hands together as though shaking his own hand. "There's no therapy like working together. That's what got Steven Tyler clean and sober. Rehab and the support of his band. He's got twenty years now. Same thing with Robert Downey. Only he's not in a band. *Ironman* is all the evidence you need, right?"

Outside a small voice yelled, "Alec Baldwin! Stop that!"

"Nature calls," said Seth. He swept out of the kitchen.

"Is he one of your counselors?" asked Verna in a throaty voice. "He seems really good."

"Alec Baldwin's here?" asked the girl, giving the first sign that she could be anything other than sullen and disagreeable.

"Uh, no, he's a client," I said.

"Alec Baldwin is?" said Laureen, actual excitement creeping into her voice.

"No. Seth is a client. Alec Baldwin is a chicken."

"He looks pretty young," said Verna. "I thought you said this was a place for old people."

"Older," I corrected. "He's over eighteen."

"What about that kid we saw out there when we were coming in?" asked Laureen.

"Who? Sara? Oh, she's a neighborhood child. She keeps her chickens for poultry club here. It's like a community service we provide. Just for her," I added quickly. "She's not allowed in the house."

"So the way that guy is, so positive, is that what you do for people here?" asked Verna.

"Was he that cool and nice before he came here?" asked Laureen.

"Seth? Positive?" I said, trying to get my bearings. "No. He wasn't *too* positive when he first got here."

"How long ago was that, approximately?" said Verna.

"I thought you weren't open yet," said Laureen.

I poured us all tea in an attempt to slow the flow of questions.

"He's what we in the business call a pilot client. They're like your first clients. The ones you experiment on."

"What kind of experiments?" asked Verna.

I took a long sip of my tea while I pulled the printouts toward me with one finger, hoping a useful phrase would leap out. A professional, expert-sounding recovery phrase. It was tough, since the pages were upside down.

"Supportive," I said.

Mother and daughter nodded at me. Laureen had even let her hood slide back so her entire face was showing.

"Facility," I said, catching a word near the bottom.

"A supportive facility," said Verna. "Right. And what else?"

The upside-down printouts weren't helping. My gaze drifted to my stack of books.

"Hard work. Farm work. Self-sufficiency. Working with animals. The land. Et cetera."

Verna was nodding, with me all the way.

"Now that makes sense to me. Good sense. Ever since we moved off the farm, this kid's been going to hell."

"Mooooom," mooed Laureen.

"You know I'm right. We never should have moved into a subdivision. Damn town kids are always hanging around and getting into trouble. Pissing their time away like they have nothing else to do. People who live on farms don't have time for drugs. There is too much work to be done."

"You never should have sold my horse," said Laureen, sensing that her mother seemed willing to shoulder at least some of the blame.

Verna spoke to me. "I thought, hell, she's not riding him anymore. I had no time to keep the place up since her dad and I split. I see now I made a mistake."

I frowned in a concerned and empathetic way. I thought about saying there are no mistakes, but I was fairly sure there are. In fact, I was beginning to wonder if trying to pass Woefield off as a treatment center was one of them.

"Look, this kid needs to get straightened out. I'll work on myself too. Maybe I do drink a few too many glasses of wine on the weekend. I would love for us to have a chance to pull ourselves together in a supportive facility like this. It would mean a lot to have experts around. The truth is, Miss Burns, I can't afford ten thousand dollars. I can't afford one thousand dollars. I just don't want to lose her."

"Aw, Mom," said Laureen, but with less conviction.

"Can we work for you? Volunteer? She doesn't have to come here as an inpatient and be around all the older clients. I can't imagine she'd be harmed by that pilot guy we just saw. In fact, someone like him would be nothing but good for her. And there is that other kid that you do community service on."

"I don't know," I hesitated. I could not afford to blow our cover with the banker's sister, and I felt some sympathy for Verna's situation. "Doesn't Phyllis live on a farm?" I asked. "Couldn't Laureen spend time there?"

"It's not the same. I think we've got to have the supportive atmosphere and the experts," said Verna. She looked right at me and I saw a woman getting old before her time. A woman on the verge of giving up. It was in the sag of her shoulders. I was sure I could do something for her.

"I'll think about it," I said. "I'll check the regulations and the, uh, insurance, and I'll let you know."

Verna stood up and grabbed my hand.

"Thank you, Miss Burns. We would be so grateful."

Laureen had retreated into her hoodie and laid her head on the table. She only raised it when her mother nudged her.

"Yeah, thanks," she said.

Earl

You know, I been watching TV by myself ever since the old man died. Can't say as I've missed the company. If the kid hadn't insisted, I'd have said no. But she wouldn't quit until I come in the house and set down. Said if we was going to care for Bertie proper, we needed to get educated. If you can beat that.

It was me and the kid and Chubnuts. I'll tell you one thing. There's cages of monkeys make less noise than that guy. When he first come here he didn't say boo to no one. Now you can't shut him up. The kid's a cool customer, but I'm starting to get the idea there's something wrong with her. She sure as hell don't act like no kid I ever heard of.

We got started at around 4:00 in the afternoon. The kid brought her DVD from home and Chubnuts got her all set up at the TV. He had soda pop and popcorn and them chips that's all orange and leave dust all over everything. He was in one of them moods he seems to get into now and then. It's not too bad if you can keep him working with his hands, but Jesus Christ you don't want him anywhere near a TV screen.

I come in and he made me sit down in what he called the chair of honor. There's no honor about it. Goddamn thing is the lumpiest chair in the place. Enough to give a guy problems down there if you know what I mean. But it's got decent arms so you can rest your drink and your elbows. And it was high enough I could get out of it without losing my pants or getting help.

Once I was settled, he says, What can we get you here at Palace Royale Theater of the Stars? Just like that. I told him I thought we were watching a damn sheep-shearing film, and he said of course but movies are better with snacks and he tried to get me to eat some of that black licorice. And I say to him hell no, I got dentures and plus no one should eat that shit, tastes like pitch out from between a dead woman's toes. And he says I don't have to be like that. Then he wrote something on that computer of his.

Miss Sara took some popcorn and some chips and some licorice, but she put down the black kind after I said that thing about the toes. She didn't smile or nothing, but she looked as happy as I'd seen her, so I laid off Chubnuts. I don't think it's right for a child to be so serious. I've known others was like that and they all had a good reason, if you know what I'm saying.

So the video starts up and Chubnuts asks us if we're ready. I asked him where Prudence was and he got a helluva sour look on his face and said she was busy.

I said she should be watching because it was her sheep. Before I could say anything else, Chubnuts turned up the volume and we started watching.

The kid took a lot of notes in her little book and Chubnuts made all kind of remarks and wrote on his computer.

I guess I must of drifted off. The damn video was nearly as long as a feature-length movie, which makes it too long by half in my opinion. But I was thinking about old times so I guess I didn't mind.

SETH

Remember Linda Hamilton in the first Terminator movie? How buff she was? Well, the girl in the sheep-shearing video was like that. There wasn't an ounce of fat on her, except, you know, where you'd want it.

I'm not a fitness guy myself, but I can appreciate a toned physique.

Also, the way she handled that sheep and the clipper, which was this lethal-looking thing with these big spikes coming out of it, took my breath away. Her fashion sense was pretty much farmer in the dell, but I don't mind that on a woman.

The shearer talked dirty, too, saying how you had to let the sheep empty out. At first I was so distracted by her pecs I didn't even pick up on what that might mean. I thought it was either draining the poor sheep of blood when you cut its neck with those clippers or . . . I don't know what.

Once she got shaving I was basically glued to my seat. The animal was almost as big as she was and she kept saying how she had to avoid its tits. I kid you not. Watching that video was like watching a slasher flick, only real and with sheep.

There was this huge blood spatter on the floor just to the left of the screen, probably left over from a previous shearing. Whoever was working the camera seemed to have a bit of the palsy or whatever because the camera swung around all over the place so you could see the blood sometimes. What must it be like to be a sheep and see what was practically a lake of blood off to the side when you're getting your annual haircut? It was enough to make me vegetarian, at least when it comes to sheep.

When the girl finished the first sheep, she moved right on to man-handling another huge brute. A ram, she called it. She went on about how you shouldn't cut off its pizzle and you have to be careful around its scrotum. I was thinking sweet Jesus, not only is this like a horror movie, it's also getting like a porno. And the whole time she was talk-ing, she was throwing that massive sheep around like he was a sack of feathers. When he started kicking, probably because she was getting too close to his pizzle, she put a headlock on him and that was the end of him acting up. You know those shows on Spike with the guys who jump motorbikes over flaming school buses? And the little warning at the end not to try this at home? Well, that about sums up sheep shear-ing for me. Seriously. I could barely watch but I couldn't tear my eyes away either. You can look at my archives if you want the full account. I live blogged the whole thing, the way some people do for the Academy Awards. I put it on this new blog I started called Farmer John. So far there haven't been any comments because it hasn't really caught on yet.

I couldn't believe Sara thought we should shave Bertie ourselves. I'd only stopped drinking like a week before and I could barely shave myself, for fuck's sake. The only consolation was that, since Bertie's female, we weren't going to be faced with a giant scrotum that we'd have to try not to cut off by accident. Personally, I'd be tempted to let that part stay hairy. I watched the video all the way until the credits so I could get the name of the sheep girl. I might try and look her up online.

Sara

Watching the video was really fun. It was nice to do something social with people who don't need their mom to remind them to close their mouth.

Seth made it especially fun because he had snacks and stuff. I knew he wasn't saved, like Bethany's pastor says people should be, but he does have some good qualities and was getting more attractive, although obviously he's quite old compared to me and I'm way too young to date anyone. I knew he'd get left behind when the Rapture came due to his swearing and probably also for having long hair and tight pants. Once we had Bertie fixed up, I thought I might talk to him about changing his ways.

We had popcorn and nachos and two kinds of pop and candy. It was great.

I took a lot of notes during the video, but it was sort of hard to know exactly what was going on because the sheep was moving and kicking and the girl who did the shaving talked too much. When it was over she held up a single piece of wool in the shape of a sheep and the sheep ran away all happy and bald.

Obviously, we can't do that with Bertie, since half her coat is already gone. I guess when Earl finishes he can hold up half a sheep. That will still be satisfying.

I think Prudence should have watched the video too, but she was too busy in the garden, which is a whole bunch of boxes full of dirt and really small greenhouses that she's made of plastic tubes and white plastic material and rocks. There is a lot growing in Prudence's garden, but it's all really small. Also, her potato patch isn't working out. Seth and Earl could only dig down an inch or so before they hit bedrock. Seth said this was no country for metalheads and old men and he was starting a union, and Prudence said fine, she'd need five more raised beds to grow potatoes.

Prudence works harder than anyone I ever saw. Once my mom dropped me off at the farm at six-thirty and Prudence was already working. She was picking rocks in the field and moving them to her rock pile using the wheelbarrow. The pile of rocks was almost up to her knees. I don't know what she's going to do with all those rocks. Maybe sell them. Anyway, Prudence is quite thin and I think that's why. Seth says she's like the Energizer Bunny, only hot. I don't agree because no matter how hard Prudence works, she never seems hot. Her face doesn't even get sweaty. She looks nice all the time.

Anyway, after the sheep video was over and we were finishing our pop and chips, even Earl, who drinks root beer, which kind of surprised me but I don't know why, Prudence came in and told us we had to go outside because she had some guests coming. She wasn't mean about it, though, so I didn't feel bad.

I decided that once I completely understood the Rapture and the risk of getting left behind, I would talk to Seth and Earl and Prudence about it. Prudence might seem like she would be saved because she works so hard and is nice and doesn't swear, but she doesn't go to church and that's important. At least, that's what the pastor says three or four times every service.

I hope that mean girl won't be coming around again.

Prudence

After I finished watering the raised beds and plotting out my rock garden, which would feature varieties of lavender, sage and thyme, I checked the radish crop. It wasn't growing fast enough, making me nervous about the farmers' market. I could only hope the radishes would have a sudden growth spurt over the next few days. With that in mind, I put five buckets of horse manure that I got from a farm nearby on them. I have no idea why people spend money buying compost when there's manure all over the place. Sure, it's a bit smelly, but you can't beat free!

Anyway, when I'd top-dressed the radishes (being careful not to bury their little shoots) I reluctantly prepared for the writing group. Earl, Seth and even Sara were watching television in the living room and I had to ask them to clear out. It was a shame to see them wasting a beautiful afternoon with such a pointless activity, but the key to being an effective employer/landlord is to pick one's battles. At least they were watching together and with luck they were building some team spirit. Also, I was distracted because I'd never taken a writing class in high school or in college and hadn't had time to research how to teach one.

When I wrote my book, my writer friends told me to write about something that mattered to me, hence the global warming/personal responsibility theme in *The Sun Doesn't Forgive*. The review I'd received made it clear that there was more to writing a successful YA novel than expressing passionate opinions. The reviewer said my book had an "inauthentic air" and "one-dimensional characters who talked like particularly preachy mini-adults." The book was set on a farm and my child characters were modeled on some of the kids I'd seen at the Brooklyn Flea in Fort Greene. I never got a chance to talk to any of those kids, but mine gave a lot of speeches on the need for government subsidies for sustainable agriculture practices and they talked knowledgably about the need for political change, similar to how I bet those Fort Greene Flea Market kids did. When drought sets in, my characters are forced to leave their farm to become nomad wanderers, similar to Cormac McCarthy's *The Road*, but with a greatly simplified vocabulary and a stronger emphasis on vegetarianism. Unfortunately, my characters are made into slave laborers by an evil corporation named Monpanto, which apparently was funny only to me. After my experience here at Woefield, I'd write a different book, obviously. All in all, I wasn't entirely confident about my ability to teach a writing class.

The kitchen table was too small, so I put all the furniture I could find in the living room. A long, lumpy gray couch, a small, stiff loveseat upholstered in something brown and scratchy, and assorted chairs, one of which had a rattan seat that looked like it could have been used as a weapon in *The Deer Hunter*. I decided to take that one out, for insurance reasons, and added "Look online for attractive, reasonably priced used furniture when funds permit" to my To Do list.

Presumably, people would want to write during the writing class, so I put hardcover books at each place. The writers could use those to balance their paper on. I felt bad about the seating arrangements but also hoped that the discomfort might cause people to leave early.

At 6:55 there was a knock on the door.

I opened it to find Brady and his entire writing group standing on the porch.

"We're early," said Brady. "I hope that's okay."

He wore a short-sleeved shirt with a palm tree pattern in sunset yellow and orange. I tore my gaze away to look at the rest of the group. There were four of them. A man in his shirtsleeves, a wide-shouldered woman wearing a pilled black sweater, and, to my surprise, Laureen and Verna.

"Oh," I said, when I saw them.

"This is the gang," said Brady. "We've recently picked up a couple of new members. When Verna heard we were coming here for writing class, she and Laureen wanted to join us."

I opened the door for the group and stood back to let them in. As Verna passed, she whispered, "When I saw Brady at the grocery store and he told me you were running this group, we were sure you wouldn't mind. You know, since it's open to the public."

"Of course I don't mind," I said, even though I did. The basic rules of civility require that one deal with the unexpected in a gracious way. I wondered whether she'd told Brady and the rest of the writing group that this was a treatment center. I pushed the thought to the back of my mind. There was nothing to be done about it now. Even if she had told them, what would it matter? Some prisons hold writing classes. Why wouldn't treatment centers?

The group stood awkwardly between the kitchen and the living room.

I gestured them over to the area I'd set up. "I thought we could work in here."

"Super!" enthused Brady.

The rest of the class nodded. Except Laureen. Was she on drugs? I hoped not but I couldn't tell. At least she wasn't trying to pick bugs out of her arm, which is something that serious addicts do according to my reading in the addiction memoir field.

After quickly checking my notes, I asked everyone to introduce themselves and to talk about what kind of writing they wanted to do. Brady interrupted.

"Novelists!" he said. "We're all aspiring novelists! That's why we're here. We've gone beyond the short story into the long form. The big business. The real thing. And we've come to learn from the master."

"I wouldn't go that far," I said. "Let's do introductions and you can tell me what kinds of novel you're working on. Perhaps we could start with you." I turned to the man in the dress shirt. He wore tasseled loafers. I hadn't seen a pair of loafers since I left New York.

"I'm Marvin," he said. "You can call me Marv. I'm working on a tale of intrigue and high finance involving the capital markets. Hedge funds. High rollers with big appetites. Dark markets."

"Wow," I said. "That sounds great."

"Just today, I was at a seminar. Heard a guy speaking about a new fund out of Calgary. High risk, high rewards. Damned exciting."

"Wow," I said again, then realized that as a master novelist, I should have a larger store of expletives to express myself. I thought of what one of my YA writer friends might say. "Holy cow," I added. Marv didn't notice.

"They've got all these new financial instruments coming out. Lot of 'em created after the meltdown of the subprime market. They're never going to regulate those boys. They're too smart. Betting on the losses. Now that takes some guts."

"For god's sake, Marv," said the big woman in the seen-better-days sweater. "Why don't you tell us what you had for lunch, too? It'd be as interesting."

Marv looked confused for a moment.

"Smoked salmon on those little croissants," he said finally. "At a mutual fund lunch."

She rolled her eyes.

"How about you?" I asked her.

"Me? I'm writing a tell-all about my fuckhead ex. It's gonna be a ball breaker. I just want to know how to get it published." She cast a quick look over at Laureen, who was studying her bitten fingernails. "Sorry."

"It's fine," said Verna with a tight smile.

The woman continued. "My name's Portia. Sounds like the car, spelled like the outhouse."

"Excellent," I said, working to maintain my smile. I turned to Brady.

"You know me!" he said. "I'm writing a book about . . . Well, it's hard to describe."

"Just a word or two will be fine," I said.

Brady's sunny face grew thoughtful for a moment. "Well, it's about a guy. He's got some issues."

"Pornhound," said Portia, spelled like the potty. "Guy's a perv. But it's not a half-bad story. I gotta hand it to Brady. The story's not half bad at all."

I nodded, like I could easily imagine how a story about a pornography addict would be quite captivating.

Then I turned reluctantly to Laureen and Verna.

"And you two?" I asked. "What are you working on?"

"A mother-daughter memoir," said Verna. "A healing story." Without being asked, she elaborated. "It's about how when trust is broken, only time and effort in a supportive environment will put things back together. Isn't that right, Laureen?"

Laureen made a face like someone about to undergo a cavity search.

Her mother continued. "It's about how when someone says she will be home at a certain hour, she better be home. And how if a parent finds rolling papers in a person's purse, that person better have a good explanation, because that person's parent doesn't want to have to put a second mortgage on their house to send that person to goddamn treatment in California or some damn place." Verna's voice had risen enough that she'd managed to grab the attention of the others in the group, no mean feat.

"That's got real dramatic potential!" said Brady.

"And sometimes that trust never comes back," added Portia. "Like if the fucker takes up with some slut he met at the Jinglepot Pub."

I waited for Marv to weigh in, but he was checking his BlackBerry.

"What do you think?" asked Verna. It took me a while to realize she was asking me. The supposed expert on the topic.

I thought for a moment. "Well . . ." I said carefully. "Working together on a project such as a book can certainly be, uh, useful. For establishing trust and a, uh, good working relationship. Which can be helpful."

Verna was nodding. "Good. Because I'm just about at my wit's end here. And we have nowhere to turn. I have got to get some cooperation from Miss Thing."

Brady nodded. "Cooperation. Support. The Mighty Pens are committed to that. I know I wouldn't have gotten to page ten without these guys cheering me along every step of the way."

"How many pages is your story?" I asked Brady, happy to move onto a safer topic.

A small frown appeared on his face.

"Eleven. Well, twelve if things go well today."

"Oh," I said. "How long have the Mighty Pens been meeting?"

"I'm the founder. And I was on my own for the first six months. But then Marv came along and then Portia. After her separation, you know. We've been meeting for, oh, I don't know, a year and a half or so," said Brady.

"Wow," I said, once again drawing upon my huge linguistic store. "That's great."

"Brady might only have eleven pages, but they're really good," said Portia.

"So what were you working on before the, uh, pornography project?"

"Been working on this the whole time," he said.

"Well," I said.

"I'm the prolific one," said Portia. "My book's nearly done. It's six hundred and twelve pages now."

I arranged my face into what I hoped was an admiring expression and turned to Marvin.

"I'm still in the planning stages. Making notes. Coming up with strategies," he said.

"Okay," I said. "Well, let's get writing, shall we?"

"Prudence?" asked Laureen, putting up her hand.

"Yes?"

"Can I use the bathroom?"

"No, you may not," said her mother. "You can wait until we get home. I'm not having you smoking out the bathroom window while I'm down here pretending to write a book!"

Laureen sighed so deeply she extinguished all the tea lights I'd put on the coffee table for atmosphere.

Brady looked confused.

"If anyone needs the bathroom it's upstairs. And the rest of us can get started."

There was a pause.

"Started on what?" asked Portia finally.

"A piece of writing," I said.

"About what?"

"Why don't you just start writing where you left off?"

"I didn't bring the printout of my book," said Portia. "It weighs a friggin' ton and I'm worried that I'll put my back out if I carry it too far."

"I didn't bring my laptop," said Marv. "Brady said we were going to do creativity exercises to help us improve our skills. The kind you used to help you get your writing career going."

I debated whether to tell them I had long since abandoned my writing career and moved into radishes and fraud, but decided the timing was wrong.

"Fine. No problem," I said. I looked around the room, waiting for an inspiration to hit. "Why don't we start with an exercise to help us to . . . write."

They all stared, expecting more.

" . . . interesting characters," I added.

They nodded in agreement.

"Let's start by describing someone interesting."

"Like someone we know?" asked Laureen.

"If you think you're going to write about that loser you've been seeing you can think again," said Verna.

"Fine. Whatever," said Laureen.

Brady nodded intently. The perfect student. "I'll write about my main character," he said. "He's got a lot of depth."

"Excellent."

"Can you hate the person you write about?" asked Portia.

"Sure," I said.

"I'm not really sure what I'm supposed to do," said Marv.

"That's cause you wouldn't know an interesting person if one crawled up your ass and started sending smoke signals," said Portia.

"Okay, let's get started," I said. "We'll take, oh, forty minutes."

The funny thing is that during that forty-minute exercise I wrote more than I had since I finished *The Sun Doesn't Forgive,* even though I was also keeping an eye on what could only loosely be called my class. Of course, what I wrote were additions to my To Do list, with more detail about each item. I also got some insight into why Brady had only written eleven pages in one and a half years. He spent the entire forty minutes staring off into the middle of the living room with his pen poised over his piece of paper. Thirty seconds before I called time, he scribbled something.

Portia wrote so hard she pushed her pen right through her paper. She had covered at least ten pages.

Marv would write a few words, then check his BlackBerry. Write a few words, and surreptitiously check to make sure his fly was closed. Or scratch himself. Then he'd write a few more words before using the tip of his pinky finger to feel around in his nose.

Laureen started slowly and then began to write furiously. Verna kept sneaking glances at Laureen's paper, until I suggested that everyone keep their eyes on their own work. Then she began writing almost as fast and as hard as Portia.

I heard a few muffled shouts and bangs from outside, but I figured it was just Seth helping Sara coach Alec Baldwin on how to pose for the judges. I was pleased to see him coming out of his shell and taking an interest in the animal husbandry side of things and leaving the house without being coaxed.

Right before it was time to call a break, the doorbell rang.

I smiled at the writers.

"I guess we can stop there."

The doorbell sounded again, followed quickly by a knock.

I got up and opened the door. Earl stood on the porch. There was a cut over his eyebrow and there was blood and something brown and foul-smelling all over his green checked work shirt.

I chose not to ask about it.

"Yes?" I said.

"You need to come outside."

"We have a few minutes to go here. Perhaps you could take care of whatever it is? I'm teaching a class."

"What the hell are you teaching 'em?" he asked, craning his head around to get a look at the Mighty Pens.

"Writing."

"They don't know how to write? At their age?"

"We're working on creative writing."

"Jesus," said Earl. "That's no way for grownups to spend their time."

"Earl, I'll be outside in a few minutes. We just need to finish up here."

I closed the door gently but firmly in his face, and went back and joined the group.

"Okay. Let's read our work, shall we? Who would like to go first?"

Brady put up his hand.

"Brady. Go ahead."

He rubbed his forehead with his index finger a couple of times and studied his page.

"Any time you're ready."

He cleared his throat like a singer getting ready for a performance.

"It was rock hard," he read.

"Oh my goodness," I said and looked over at Laureen. She was pretending to be oblivious, but I could see the corners of her lips curving up.

"I don't know though," said Brady. "Do you think it might be better to say, 'It was hard as a rock'?"

Verna flashed him a look of loathing.

"Either's good," I said. "Well done." I offered up a little prayer of thanks that Brady was such a slow writer. "Anyone else?"

That's when the shouting outside turned into screams.

I made one of those split-second decisions one must make sometimes.

"I'm afraid that unforeseen circumstances are going to require that we call it a night early. I'd like to suggest that you all take these character studies, work on them some more at home, and those who wish can bring them back for our next class."

They all nodded.

"I just have to pop outside and deal with some, um, farming. Do you mind letting yourselves out?" I was already up and in the doorway. The writers stood and milled around uncertainly and I turned and headed for the door. I trotted down the porch steps and around the side of the house.

I stopped dead in my tracks.

Seth lay on the ground. He had Bertie clutched to his chest like a favorite stuffed toy. Both of them were covered in blood. There were blood-matted bits of wool everywhere. Seth's white Iron Maiden T-shirt was soaked. The entire area looked like an abattoir run by a blind man.

"Oh my goodness," I said.

Little Sara stood on the side, her eyes huge. She had a death grip on her binder, unconsciously mimicking Seth and Bertie.

At first I couldn't see any movement from the two combatants, partly because the light was fading, but then Bertie weakly kicked one hind leg. Seth made a low groaning noise.

"What's happening here?" I asked, even though I was not at all sure I wanted to know.

"We got fired up from watching the video," Earl said. "We were all set to shear her but she put up a hell of a fight. Kicked out with her front hoof when he was bending over and clipped him in the head. He bled like nothing I've ever seen before."

"So that's Seth's blood?" I said, feeling relieved.

"Some of the blood got in his eyes. That's probably how he ended up nicking her so good. I'd say ten percent of it is her blood. Also, she crapped all over him."

That explained the smell.

We needed a triage approach to the chaos. While I was deciding whether to call a vet, a doctor or a cop, Brady and Portia and the rest of the Mighty Pens appeared around the corner. When they saw Seth and Bertie they took a step back in unison like a group of well-practiced line dancers.

I felt I had to explain.

"Seth was shearing our sheep. There was a small accident."

"Killing that poor sheep, more like," said Laureen. She turned to her mother. "*This* is where you want me to hang out? I'm going to end up on hard drugs if I spend too much time here."

The look on Verna's face said she didn't entirely disagree with her daughter's analysis.

"Gory, isn't it?" said Brady, whose powers of description nearly rivaled mine.

"Reminds me of the last tiff I had with my ex," said Portia. "Only in our case the blood was all his."

"Right," I said. "So as you can see, life is full of fodder for writers. I'm sure some of you will get a good story out of this."

Brady nodded seriously.

"Now please excuse me. I need to call an ambulance."

"He don't need a goddamn ambulance," said Earl. "Scalp wounds always bleed like hell. Look after the sheep."

"Maybe if he let the poor sheep out of the Vulcan death grip," suggested Laureen.

"Can't let her go," said Earl. "We'll never catch her again. I don't goddamn blame her."

"Isn't that bloody guy your pilot patient?" asked Verna, pointing at Seth.

"Are those maxipads on that sheep's feet?" asked Portia.

One of Bertie's silver duct-tape hoof protectors had come loose and the sanitary napkin beneath it flapped in the wind.

"That's right. Seth is a recent alumnus of our program," I said, trying to maintain a professional tone.

"What kind of program?" asked Brady.

Through all this, Marvin had been quiet. Too quiet. When he fainted he hit the ground with a thud like a side of beef falling from a hook. We all turned to look. His slack face was the color of suet.

"Maybe it was the smoked salmon croissants he ate at his mutual fund meeting," said Portia, a noticeable lack of compassion in her voice.

I wasn't sure which emergency I should attend to first. I turned in circles a couple of times, like the chickens that were wandering all over the place. Alec Baldwin had made his way to the edge of the scene and kept darting in to peck at bits of bloody wool.

"How did the chickens get out?" I asked.

"Seth and Bertie broke the fence," said Sara.

"Bertie ran right into it but he hung on. He's got more grit to him than I would of thought," said Earl.

Fortunately, the loose chickens helped to focus my attention.

"Sara, you and Earl get the birds while I deal with Bertie." Portia was reluctantly helping Marvin to his feet.

Seth moaned.

"I'll be right with you," I said, attempting to sound comfortingly brisk and efficient, which is important in crisis situations.

Earl and Sara began to walk after the birds with their arms out-stretched—an elderly poultry Messiah and his young disciple. The chickens ignored them.

"Get Alec Baldwin first. He's the ringleader," I suggested.

Laureen's head shot up at the name.

"Not that Alec Baldwin," I said and her interest evaporated.

Brady was leaning over staring at Seth and Bertie's prone, bloodied bodies.

"Forgot to hold the skin, huh?"

"My hands. Kept slipping," gasped Seth. "So. Much. Blood. Like an Ozzy show."

Brady kept staring. "I'd say it's just a few nicks. You, I'm not so sure."

"You know about shearing?" I asked the plumber who was also a pornographic writer.

"I've shorn a few sheep in my time," said Brady modestly.

"What should we do?"

"Well, you should keep a spray bottle of disinfectant handy before you start. In case you make a mistake."

"We don't have any disinfectant," I said.

"You can make some up easy enough. Your sheep's still got quite a bit of her coat on. I might as well finish shearing her. Then you'll want to bandage her up to keep the dirt out."

A few minutes later, Bertie was shaved and the Mighty Pens were on their way home. Each left me ten dollars for the writing lesson. I told Brady to keep his in exchange for services rendered. We wrapped Bertie's nicks and scratches with a combination of feminine protection and masking tape, which was better for her skin than duct tape. I had no idea those things were such an important part of farm life.

EARL

I've never been one to get the government involved, but some things is just plain wrong. That poor old sheep. I knew Chubnuts wasn't the man to handle those shears, but I been sorer than hell ever since Bertie kicked the shit out of me the other day. People don't realize how tough a sheep can be, even a depressed one.

That feller in the funny shirt did a helluva job, considering he don't even know how to write. But I still wasn't feeling good about it. So I called up the vet's office and told the girl on the phone that I had an anonymous tip about a sheep getting abused.

I wasn't trying to get no one in trouble. But I seen what can happen when good men do nothing. Saw it in my own family. I'm not sure this outfit should have animals. The kid's chickens is one thing. At least she's got her head screwed on tight. But the best thing for old Bertie'd be for the government to pick her up.

Didn't matter, since the girl at the vet office said they don't handle that kind of thing. That I should call the CSPCA or something like that. I don't trust any of them groups that's all letters and no names. CIA, CSIS, FBI. I guess that's my American side showing.

So I give up then. I knew we were supposed to keep Bertie's cuts clean and make sure she didn't pull off her bandages. Least, that's what the feller in the Hawaii shirt said.

Well, hell, how's a person supposed to keep a sheep clean? It's a sheep for Christ's sake. She's got maxipads on her feet and she's trussed up in about three hundred yards of tape. No wonder the poor goddamn thing is depressed.

I decided to keep her on my porch for the night, since she'd had a bad time and shouldn't be out wandering around. Prudence took Chubnuts, who ain't even all that chubby no more, inside to try and stop the bleeding on his head, at least the part of the blood that didn't get mopped up by that hair of his. I used a couple of ropes to make a halter and lead, and I somehow got Bertie to my cabin and pulled her up them stairs. I closed her in with some busted-up chairs. No one sits on my goddamn porch anyway.

This is some kind of half-assed operation, I'll tell you. I figure that one of these days I might just have to call someone else about what goes on here.

Seth

No one cared about me. There I was, covered in blood, kicked half to death, lying there trying to hold onto that miserable fucking shitsack of a sheep and all anyone could say was "Is the sheep okay?" "What happened to the sheep?" "Oh, poor sheep."

Not one of those dudes Prudence was teaching showed the slightest concern about me and the potential extent of my injuries. Even the falling giant. When he woke up, all he could say was how much he hated to see animals suffer.

I was relieved when the Hawaiian shirt guy from the funeral took over the shearing. Dude's got some skills.

The thing that gets me most is that Prudence barely even complimented me on my *effort*. I did most of the job, I mean after Bertie kicked me in the head and before I nicked her so bad. I also held onto her when she took off and I didn't let go even when she slammed me head-first into the chicken run. There are Hollywood stuntmen who wouldn't have hung on like that. It was like being a mixed martial artist grappling with a . . . I don't know, a fucking panic-stricken farm animal.

Not only that, but later, after Brady took over, I helped catch the rest of the chickens and got them settled and helped Sara fix the sides of the chicken coop, by like, reapplying the chicken wire, even though my eyes were nearly glued shut with dried blood and I probably had a concussion that would later cause me to develop the kind of dementia football players get. I'm probably going to end up killing a bunch of people before I'm forty as a result. Earl told me I shouldn't have been listening to my headphones while trying to shear a sheep, but I was nervous and listening to Nazareth relaxes me. Now my MP3 player's busted. Basically, I gave that task everything I had, which makes me heroic. A little public recognition would have been nice. Also, I worried about the poor sheep living on Earl's porch. God only knows how much danger she'll be in if he gets lonely some night.

I really wasn't too sure I was cut out for life on a farm even if it was located right across the street from where I grew up. Plus it felt like it had been about six years since I'd had a drink and I wasn't sure I was cut out for sobriety, either. Tell you the truth, after the shearing, I didn't know what I wanted, probably because of the undiagnosed head injury.

SARA

I thought that I liked to go to the farm because of the chickens and because my parents—well, my dad—fight a lot and it's not very relaxing at our house. But then we had the thing with the sheep at the farm and it was kind of stressful but still very interesting. It didn't make my stomach hurt, not even when Bertie and Seth knocked down the chicken run and some of the frizzles and Alec Baldwin got out. I guess I like adventure more than I thought. This is probably what it would be like if I had a lot of brothers and sisters instead of just me.

Part of me didn't want to get too attached to any of it. That's because I was still reading *Left Behind*. It doesn't have a very good plot, but it's easier to read than the Bible, which Mrs. Blaine also lent to me. I've been to church with them five times now and they always ask how I like the books. Mrs. Blaine told me that *Left Behind* was based on real events that will take place in the future. What is going to happen is that good people who have been saved and are religious are going to get taken away by God. But they won't get any warning. He'll just take them, even if they are driving or flying planes with other people in them. So that will cause a lot of accidents for the people who are left behind. It's kind of an irresponsible way for God to handle it, if you think about it. You would think that if God was going to do a Rapture, which is what it's called when God takes all the people, he would do it when they weren't busy. But I think the point is that the people who are left behind get what they deserve.

The funny thing is that in the book, none of the people who get taken away sound very fun or nice. The whole book is about the ones who get left because they are more interesting.

Still, just in case there's a Rapture and I got taken, I tried not to do anything that would put other people in danger. Like at school I refused to hold the climbing rope steady because what if I got Raptured and someone fell? If it was Tilda Best who fell I wouldn't mind, because she's not very nice and sometimes teases me because of Poultry Club, but still. When my mom asked me to help with dinner, I would wash salad and open cans but I wouldn't boil water. I'm not saying my mother is going to get left behind, because I'm not God and such things are not for me to know, as the pastor at Bethany's church says even though I can tell he thinks he does know, but I have my suspicions. I'm also about ninety percent sure my dad will be here forever.

Same with everyone at the farm. They are all probably getting left. Earl swears and is in a bad mood a lot, Seth swears even more and he drinks sometimes, and Prudence is an unmarried girl who lives with people who swear and drink.

Even though I didn't like to take on positions of responsibility in case of Rapture, I told Prudence I'd help her find fencing for Bertie. I figured as long as I wasn't driving, which I wouldn't be because I'm too young, it should be okay.

PRUDENCE

The morning after the shearing incident, Sara and I were outside the Grow Right before it opened. She seemed to know a lot about fencing options. It's probably one of the many topics they cover at Junior Poultry Fancier's Club. I'm not sure why I felt so strongly about getting some fencing in place right after the shearing incident. A fence wouldn't have prevented Bertie's unfortunate haircut, but at least afterward we'd have had some place to put her other than Earl's porch. Earl was convinced she'd run away if we didn't contain her and I had to agree that if ever a sheep had cause to bolt, she did. Perhaps I was also feeling like some measure of control and containment was in order.

Sara, who has a tendency to appear undersized even in the confines of the chicken coop, looked positively minuscule sitting on the wide bench seat of the old Dodge. Her feet dangled far above the floor. She reminded me a bit of that children's book character Flat Stanley, trapped there under her seatbelt. If she hadn't held it down, the strap would have extended right across her face.

Once I'd exhausted her on the subject of portable fencing, I tried some other conversational gambits.

"Must be hard to get up so early on weekends," I said. As soon as she moved her chickens over, Sara started to arrive first thing in the morning. Saturdays and Sundays I would get up at 6:30 a.m. and find her already feeding her chickens or sitting on the porch reading one of her poultry-keeping books. She told me her mom dropped her off on her way to work at the grocery store.

"I don't mind," said Sara. "I'm a morning person."

"You don't miss sleeping in? Staying up late with your friends? Going to sleepovers and all that?"

"Mornings are the best time to handle chickens."

"I wasn't aware of that. I'm really impressed with how much you know about them."

"Our leader says a person shouldn't have an animal if that person doesn't know how to take care of it," she said.

Her leader had a point. After the debacle with Bertie, I'd decided it was time to get serious about sheep care. We couldn't have her living on Earl's porch forever.

I wondered if I should send Seth and Earl to go to Sara's poultry club. Maybe there was a sheep version they could attend.

"Well, I like the sound of that club of yours. Maybe you'd like to be a vet when you grow up."

"I'm getting a C in science," she said.

"Oh."

I pulled into the Grow Right parking lot. It wasn't yet eight-thirty in the morning but on either side of us farmers were already parked, waiting for the store to open. It was a marvelous feeling. There we were, a row of early risers waiting in our trucks for the feed store to open. One old guy to my left nodded at me and I was filled with a sense of camaraderie.

At exactly 8:30 a.m. a Grow Right clerk in a green smock shirt unlocked the front door. As one, the farmers around us opened their truck doors. The morning sky was bright and cloudless and the air was crisp in my nostrils. I thought I could smell a hint of the ocean.

"Come on, Sara," I said, as we joined the lineup of farmers filtering into the store.

I sent Sara to pick out a halter and a lead rope, a large water bucket and a black rubber feed bucket. It was high time Bertie had something to drink out of other than the old pasta pot, especially considering all she'd been through. We could do better than that for her. I asked the clerk about the best kind of fencing for a portable corral.

"You want the one-inch Flex-Fencing," she said. "And the Stomp 'Er polyethylene posts."

"Easy to put up?"

"You betcha," she said. "The posts are dead easy. Some people bring them on trail rides and set them up overnight for their horses so they don't have to hobble 'em. Easier and cheaper than driving wood posts and putting up board fences."

"Perfect!"

The Omnivore's Dilemma, in addition to changing the way I think about corn, also introduced me to the work of Joel Salatin, who runs Polyface Farm in Virginia. His father bought a worn-out farm in 1961 and now it's one of the most productive acreages in America and it supports three generations of the family. They specialize in "beyond organic" meat and produce. I could see Woefield being that kind of success story. I really could. According to Salatin, it's all about understanding perennial prairie polycultures, respecting animal individuality and soil health. At Polyface they move the animals around all the time to achieve maximal grass growth. It's a revolutionary concept in this era of big agribusiness and monocultures! And it all depends on local knowledge.

Of course, the Salatins are a big family and so they have an abundance of workers. I'm not planning to have children, because of my concerns about overpopulation, but I believe that many people are eager to find useful and meaningful work.

The other thing I thought about as we shopped for fencing was the quote on Joel Salatin's website about respecting the "pigness of the pig." I love that. It was time we started respecting the sheepness of our sheep. I was just having trouble getting a handle on what Bertie's sheepness was, if you catch my meaning. She was so inexpressive. I think it might have been easier to start with a pig.

After some discussion with the clerk, during which I revealed my ignorance of metric and standard farm measurements, I bought enough tape fencing and posts to make a quarter-acre enclosure.

"The good thing about this kind of fast fencing is you can move it around," she told me. She was a woman in her thirties with sun-damaged skin and an opt-out approach to fashion. "Once your animals have eaten down an area, you can move the fence somewhere else. If you have the room to do that."

"That's exactly what I intend to do," I said. "We definitely have the room."

When she finished writing the receipt, she said, "Are you the girl who moved into the old Woefield place? Harold's daughter?"

"Harold's niece," I said.

"Hell," she said. "I knew Harold. He was a good guy."

"Thanks," I said.

"You're the one putting in the halfway house,."

"Pardon me? I mean, no, that's not correct."

"House for wayward girls? Ex-cons?"

"None of the above," I said. "I better get going. Our sheep is unwell. We need to get the fence up as soon as possible."

She handed over the receipt. Her fingernails were dirty. "Someone at the counter will ring you through. Then you can drive around back to the warehouse and we'll load up your truck."

Sara joined me at the counter, carrying buckets and a welter of rope and colorful nylon webbing.

"Is that everything?" I asked.

She nodded, solemn under her fishing hat.

"I think Bertie'll look nice in this."

She'd picked out a bright purple halter decorated with rhinestone trim. I wasn't sure it was in keeping with Bertie's sheepness, but staff must be allowed to express their ideas.

"I'm sure she will."

As we joined the lineup I overheard a snippet of conversation between the clerk and her customer.

"Should castrate 'em," said the clerk. The customer, an older man wearing patched work pants, nodded in agreement. "Just cut 'em right off."

I thought about saying something about how I didn't know April was when the animals got neutered or fixed or whatever it's properly called, but decided to hold my tongue.

"Now I know how them nimrods feel," said another clerk, who was loitering around in the cash area not even attempting to look busy.

"I think you mean NIMBYs," said the one operating the till.

"Yeah, that's right. The 'don't put your garbage in my yard' people. Sex offenders and drug fiends staying right in our backyard."

They all seemed to notice me at once and fell abruptly silent. Had they been talking about me? About my fictional treatment center? How did they all know?

"Makes me sick," muttered the clerk.

"Should be a law," said the one at the till.

This was ridiculous. I was offended on behalf of my imaginary clients.

So you want people suffering from addictions to just die? I imagined saying. *Doesn't the Bible say something about being kind and understanding?* I had no evidence these were religious people, but since they were making incorrect assumptions about me and my treatment center I felt justified in making a few about them.

After the farmer left, the clerk rang me through with a noticeable absence of small talk. I got no opportunity to defend Woefield or the need for residential treatment facilities.

"Thank you very much," I said in a stiffly formal tone as Sara and I walked out. The thing that kept me from being too upset was the idea that they'd all be coming to me for advice once they realized that Woefield was a marvel of sustainability and productivity, probably as a result of our performance at the farmers' market.

Seth

I was already on edge after the thing with Bertie. Like I said, my back was royally screwed and my headphones were busted and not drinking was grating on my nerves, but I was outside anyway like some damaged old indentured farmhand. I was thinking there must be some way to chase Bobby and his helicopter parts out of my room. Maybe I could set up the old tent in the backyard. Anything was better than getting worked to death.

Prudence brought home all this fencing and asked Earl and me to put it up. She didn't ask about my back or my headphones or anything. She was acting like I was her kid or something, which was bullshit since I'm only three years younger than her. I didn't take it personally, though, since she acts like that with Earl too and he's as old as most of the mineral deposits around here.

"Shouldn't you stick around to supervise?" I asked. I was starting to get nervous about doing stuff by ourselves.

"Sara can do it," she said.

"Sara is going to supervise?"

I turned to look at Sara, who was standing slightly behind Prudence and staring at me like I was some kind of creature in a zoo. Not a warthog or a masturbating chimp or anything, but more like something she'd never seen before.

"Sara, how old are you?" I asked her.

"Eleven."

"How much fencing have you put up?"

"I watched my dad fix our fence once. After he ran into it with the lawnmower and broke a board."

"So none."

Prudence just smiled affectionately at me and said the coffee was made.

When I got to the house, Earl was sitting on the porch with a cup in his hand. Every time he took a sip he made a face.

"Something wrong with the coffee?" I asked, even though I knew the answer. Earl's one of those guys who likes hot water with a bit of old dishwater thrown in. Prudence makes coffee that could burn the nuts off a lumberjack. She said she'd been a barista in New York at one of those places that considers coffee making this high art form.

Earl muttered something about drinking engine grease.

"It'll give you energy for putting up fences," said Prudence. "The three of you should have no problem. This type of fencing is extremely easy to install."

Earl muttered something about not for goddamn monkeys, probably unconsciously picking up on my earlier zoo thoughts.

"What are you going to do?" I asked her.

"I've got some things to take care of."

Before I could tell her that I was worried my back injury might turn into a chronic pain–type condition if I were to mess it up further while putting up fences, which I was certain was backbreaking work, as well as the worst and hardest job on any farm besides shoveling shit, she was gone.

Fine, I thought. I'll put up fences but if I end up crippled, I'll sue. Get an addition put on my mom's piece-of-shit house, climb in there with a lifetime supply of beer, vodka and Pringles, and an Internet connection, and never come out. Of course I knew Prudence and the farm had shit-all in the way of assets and probably no insurance, so I'd be screwed, but a guy likes to dream.

EARL

I told her before we even started that tape fencing was no good for sheep. A sheep'll just put her head under it and push on through. Sheep are slipperier than people think. When they want to get someplace only a few things'll stop them. Electric fences won't do it. You got to have that special sheep fencing.

But Prudence didn't listen. Said how Bertie didn't have a fence at all before and she didn't go nowhere. I knew that the only reason was because she was too goddamn depressed.

I didn't tell Prudence that, though. If there's one thing I've learned over the years, it's that people don't change their minds. Not when they get them made up.

The whole thing put me in a hell of a mood. Last time I did any fencing was the last time I saw Pride. The band was home from tour for two weeks. That was rare, because Merle wasn't one to take time off. People think life on the road is all fine hotels and fancy women. Hell, that's what I thought when I first set off with Merle and the boys. What did I know? I was only sixteen. Life on the road is all bad food and arguing over small stuff and gig after gig.

But Pride never minded the road. He said he liked to get out of Kentucky and he was one of them guys that liked to meet new people. People liked him back, maybe more than they liked Merle, which might a been part of the trouble.

Anyway, we were gone for a good three months. Pride stayed behind with Penny, our older sister, who kept the place up when we were on the road.

Almost as soon as we pulled in Merle told me to get to mending fences. He was tyrantical like that. But I didn't argue. I was so glad to get out of that car and away from them boys.

I looked around for Pride and asked Penny and she said he was on a run. I don't think I knew what she meant until I saw him. I was out in the back pasture nailing up new boards when up comes Pride. He was walking like he had a helluva wind at his back, all sideways and tilted. When he got closer I could tell he'd been drunk a long time. His face was yellow and his whiskers was patchy. You had to look hard to see the charm.

He said, So you're home. His eyes were so wet from the drink it was like he was crying.

I said yessir, because I was used to talking to Merle.

He asked how the tour was and I said it was okay. Long.

He asked if they liked me and I said I guessed they did. Enough, anyway.

Of course they liked you, he said. Kid like you up there with the band.

He was right. The audiences liked me and for just the reason he said. I could play. I could sing. And I was a kid.

I asked how everything was with him, just to change the subject.

He sat down in the grass. I guess fell might be the better description. He pulled a bottle out of his pocket.

He said he didn't think he was cut out for life on the farm.

I told him I'd switch with him. I said I'd do it in a minute. That I'd rather fix fences than stay on the road with Merle and all his orders.

Pride threw his head back and laughed. He was a handsome man, even when he hadn't drawn a sober breath in a month. Maybe I'd have liked the stage better if I looked like my brother Pride.

I told him I'd talk to Merle. See about getting him back with the band. He could take my place. I said Merle was probably done being mad at him by now.

I thought Pride would just laugh. Or that he'd say he didn't care. But instead this little gleam came in his eye. I think it was hope. Give me a funny feeling, that look did.

He said for me to finish up here and get the fences mended. That he'd go and talk to Merle himself. He said maybe the three of us could play.

He pushed himself off the ground and brushed off his trousers and rubbed his face, like he could wipe off all the signs of hard living. Then he headed to the house and I could see he was making an effort to walk straight.

I hammered up the rest of the new boards and reattached the ones'd fallen down. And when I got back to the house it was all over and Pride was gone.

Sara

I'm not sure if you can get left behind for who you spend time with. Like for instance, when I helped Earl and Seth put up the fences, they swore A LOT. It was f#$& this and f^%@ that. At first they said sorry to me because I'm young, but later they got so mad at each other that they even forgot to say sorry anymore.

Earl hated it when Seth kept dropping the fence posts so he could hold his back and talk about how much it hurt. I thought Earl might pass out a couple of times because his face went all red and his eyes bulged. He said how the fence posts only weighed a few pounds. Then Seth called him dude and told him to keep it in his pants because he, Seth, was injured. I'm not sure why he mentioned Earl's pants. Anyway, then he dropped all the stuff he was holding and walked off a ways and lay down. I don't know if he stared up at the sky or not because he had his mirrored sunglasses on. Me and Earl were just left standing there.

Earl said some more swear words and kicked the dirt.

I didn't know what to say, so I didn't say anything and just thought about God, which the pastor at Bethany's church said you should do when the road gets rough.

I wondered if God would let me win at the fair this year. Mr. Lymer says my frizzles are top-notch, but there's a lot of competition. Seth still thinks Alec Baldwin could win, but I told him there's no way. Alec has started to get some white feathers on his rear end and that's an automatic disqualification.

"We'll pluck them out. Dye them," he said. "No white feathers. No problem."

I never thought of that because it's cheating.

When Seth got up again after a few minutes, he grabbed the post again. But now Earl started swinging the big hammer sort of close to Seth's hand and even sometimes near his head.

"Jesus Christ, dude!" yelled Seth, swearing *and* taking the Lord's name in vain, after the hammer just barely missed both his head and his hand. "Watch what you're doing!"

Earl said Seth should shut the hell up.

And Seth said there was a fucking kid present and don't tell him to shut the fuck up.

You know what's weird? They were yelling and everything and my stomach didn't hurt. Not at all. I think it's because they like each other. I mean, they don't like each other very much. But it was like they were playing a game to see who could be more mean and cranky. It wasn't real.

I said I could hold a stake because Seth was complaining so much, and he said, "That's okay, Squid. You might get your finger caught."

Which was really nice. Like all at once he went from mad and yelling to being worried about my finger and he called me a funny nickname, which no one had ever really done before. My dad could never do that. Once he's yelling, he's yelling at everyone. The night before my mom had served tuna surprise casserole and he threw his plate on the floor because he said he hated casseroles. It broke and made a big mess. If I went to pick it up, which I didn't in case he threw something else, there's no way he would have been worried that I'd cut my hand.

After my dad threw the casserole, my mom went and sat in the car by herself and I went to my room and read *Left Behind*. When we came out again he'd cleaned up the mess. I sort of hoped he'd cut his finger. Which wasn't nice and was the kind of thinking that could get me left behind.

I like Seth. I even think I might have feelings for him, just like some of the girls at school do about Shia LaBeouf. I think Seth may be a musician. He dresses like one and is kind of misunderstood and is pretty skinny now that his tummy isn't fat anymore. It's too bad that I like him because he has no hope of getting Raptured when end times come. I wouldn't miss my dad, but I'll definitely miss Seth and maybe even Earl, who also nodded when Seth said that thing about not wanting me to hit my finger.

Then the man in the truck showed up.

Prudence

I was just planning a drip irrigation system for the raised beds so Seth wouldn't have to stand out there with a hose for a couple of hours every evening, when the knock came. I was feeling very pleased because my research told me that I'd be able to put in a drip system for a fraction of what some other options, such as automatic sprinklers, would cost. I could get used hoses and prepare them myself. People think you need a lot of money to farm. I think what you really need is a lot of help.

Back to the knock. When I heard it, I thought it might be Seth. He'd come to the door four times that afternoon muttering that Earl was trying to maim him. Seth lacks the stoicism I associate with the agricultural world.

"What is it?" I called out.

I couldn't hear the reply, so I got up and opened the door. I had to jerk it because the doorjamb is a bit sticky, and the old but now clean flowered curtain fluttered into my face.

A man stood on the porch. He wore jeans, a plaid shirt and a modified cowboy hat. His belt buckle featured a large cow head with horns on it. His boots were brown and scuffed. His lips were heavy and nicely curved. I found myself blinking at him because he was so good-looking.

"Yes?" I said, trying to smooth my composure and my hair at the same time. "Hello?"

He didn't say anything. I wondered if he was also under the impression that we were a treatment center. I would have been more than happy to sign him up.

"My name is Eustace Smith. I'm a vet. I have a clinic down the way." His voice was low and serious. "Do you have an animal in need of medical attention here? A sheep?"

I felt myself stiffen, despite my conviction that we were completely innocent of any wrongdoing. One of the Mighty Pens must have called the vet about Bertie. I wondered if that was the same as calling the SPCA. Maybe it was worse. I thought of Bertie: bald, scratched, feet encased in maxipads and duct-tape booties. Her belly cinched up with masking tape and lined with still more feminine hygiene products. She looked like one of those unfortunate creatures you see on the animal abuse websites. This handsome man wouldn't understand and it wouldn't do for us to get arrested. We'd end up in the papers, exposed as false treatment center operators and animal cruelty practitioners.

Subterfuge was called for.

"Sheep?" I said.

His perfect lips formed a funny little half smile.

"That's right," he said.

Bertie was still on Earl's porch, eating the expensive Washington meadow grass hay I got for her at the feed store and drinking the healing spring water I bought for her at the health food store. I didn't want her roaming around until she'd recovered from her shearing and had a fenced pasture to go into.

I shook my head.

He stared into my face. "No sheep?" he asked, as though trying to lip-read.

"We have some very nice chickens, though. Would you like to have a look at them?"

"I saw them as I came in."

"Oh. Right. Of course you did. They're right there."

"But you don't have any sheep," he repeated.

"No. No sheep."

"What's going in the little corral out there?"

Time for more quick thinking in aid of sustainability and viability.

"We were thinking of getting a mule." I'd been reading about mules in one of my self-sufficiency books.

"Is that right?"

I nodded. "They are supposed to be good for plowing," I said, nodding again. "They're stronger than horses."

"No tractor?"

"We are interested in sustainable farming practices."

Another smile. He looked right in my eyes.

"Right," he said. "I can see that."

"Did someone lose one?" I asked.

"A tractor?"

"No, a sheep."

"We got a call. Something about a sheep in distress. I thought I'd check it out. My receptionist must have misunderstood."

"That happens a lot with receptionists." I spoke as though I'd had many receptionists over the years. In fact, I'd been a receptionist for a music producer in Williamsburg once. After two days the producer told me it wasn't working out because my clothes weren't tight enough. Just as well. He had terrible energy and was messy.

Dr. Eustace Smith took his hat off, revealing a full head of short-cropped curly hair, similar to that found on a young Greek god. His forearms were very brown and muscular. He continued staring at me.

"You know," he said, "you look familiar."

"Well. Farm women probably all look alike after a while."

He grinned, and dimples creased his lean cheeks.

"I wouldn't say that exactly."

We stood like that for a long moment.

"Well, I'd better be going. I hate to interrupt a farm woman during her busy day."

Something about the way he said "farm woman" made me look down at myself. I had on a T-shirt from The Moth and a skirt printed with antique airplanes I'd purchased in SoHo and my tall French rubber boots.

"I'm new to farming," I said.

"You and your husband?"

"Married? No. I'm on my own," I told him.

His grin widened.

"Huh," he said. "Okay then." He replaced the hat, which was made of some kind of leather or oiled canvas. He turned and stepped down the stairs. He was on the third step when he turned back to me.

"This is probably inappropriate," he said. "And I hope you won't call the cops or the veterinary board. But would you like to go out sometime?"

I felt the blush rush through my cheeks and down the rest of my body.

"Yes, I would."

Straight white teeth gleamed against his tanned face.

"How about tonight? Seven o'clock? I'll take you to dinner."

"That would be nice," I said.

"See you then," he said and touched the brim of his hat. Then he disappeared around the side of the house. I was left staring after Eustace Smith, the world's handsomest vet. A minute or so later I heard a vehicle start up out back.

When I focused again I saw Earl, Seth and Sara all staring at me from where they stood a few yards away in the midst of a jumble of fencing.

Seth

When I realized she was going on a date, I felt maimed. Like somebody chopped my leg off or something. It's not like I thought we had anything going. I'm not delusional. It was just, I don't know, a trigger.

I was in the living room resting my feet after a demanding day, and I noticed she was bustling around even more than normal, which is some serious bustling, I can tell you.

She probably saw me noticing, because on about her fortieth pass by the living room she stopped and told me she wouldn't be home for dinner.

I asked her if she could order a pizza. Normally she cooks brown rice and beans and vegetables and stuff like that, but there was no way I was going to put that in my mouth if I didn't have to.

Look at the situation from my perspective. I'd been sober for quite a few days. I wasn't shaky at all. I was as detoxed as I was going to get. I was beginning to feel like a clean-living, hardworking man. A little pizza wasn't out of the question. I deserved something.

Right away she said she would call for pizza, and that was so unexpected that I looked at her closer. That's when I noticed she was all sparkling and clean and dressed up nice. All of a sudden I didn't feel so wholesome anymore. You know how some people can have that effect on you? Maybe you don't.

I asked her where she was going. I tried to put a don't-give-a-fuck spin on the question, but I'm not sure it came across.

She just smiled and I knew. Knew who it was, too.

"Got a date?" I asked.

"Sort of."

"With that big dude who came by here this afternoon?"

She nodded and smiled some more.

I wanted to say something then. I wanted to say lots of things. Every one of them was totally wrong. Instead I just asked if she could remember to order the pizza before she went.

She said she was running late and would I mind ordering it myself. She'd leave out some money.

The way she said it really got me. Like I was a kid and a useless deadbeat one, at that. I was essentially doing everything around the place. Holding fence posts and nearly getting knocked out by uncoordinated hammer-wielding ancients. Consulting with local youth on their competition chickens. Having the shit kicked out of me by sick sheep. Painting. Cleaning. Not drinking so people would think this hellhole was some kind of treatment center. And I was being given no credit for any of it. At least that's how it felt.

I've never been good at disappointment. Seriously. I don't know what my parents did to make me this way. They sure as hell didn't spoil me. The last time I felt that ripped off was with the drama teacher. Anyway, the next time Prudence went upstairs, I just got up and left. My time as a farmhand was over.

Sara

It started when my dad asked where I was all day. I didn't answer because I didn't think he wanted to know. Usually, he just likes asking questions but never listens to the answers. Then he asked my mom where she was all day. She said she was running errands. And he said, well, she sure as sh#*^ wasn't grocery shopping.

He said that because she made the tuna casserole surprise again. Even after what happened last night.

My mom said she was going outside to get some air. Which is what she always says when she's going outside to sit in the car.

But this time my dad wouldn't let her. He said she could stay inside and cook him something he could actually eat and how he'd had a hard day at the construction site. She whispered something about "And whose fault is that?" and "Maybe you should've thought of that before you bezzled from the bank," and then she walked to the door and this time he threw his plate at her and hit her in the back. She screamed. Before I knew what was happening she picked it off the floor and threw it back in his face, only he put up his arm and blocked it.

That's when I threw up my tuna surprise all over the table. I didn't even get the sore stomach first.

My dad and mom kind of stood there and then he said some swears and told my mom it was her fault and she asked me if I was okay. I said I was and I just needed to go to my room. She said that was okay. I don't know what they did after that.

I was too sick to even read *Left Behind,* never mind the Bible, which has very small type and pages that are easy to tear. Instead I read *The Standard of Perfection* because looking at chickens, especially the fancy ones, makes me feel better most times.

That's when I got the idea to run away to the farm.

I packed my knapsack with some clothes and my homework and a toothbrush, and went out to where my mom was sitting in the car with her head leaning back and her eyes shut. I didn't see my dad because I went out the back door.

I told my mom I wanted to go to Woefield and she looked at me. Her face was sort of puffy and red. She told me she thought that was maybe a good idea.

I got in and she drove me over there.

When we pulled in, I asked her if she wanted to come. I said it was a big house and there was probably room for both of us. But she said no.

When I knocked on the door there was no one home, so I waited.

Earl

Who the hell knows what could have happened to the kid if I didn't come along when I did. It was black as pitch outside and I just come up to the house to get the *TV Guide*. They got that program guide on channel two but the goddamn words move so fast and are so scrunched together I don't know who the hell could read it.

Anyway, I come up the porch and seen the house was dark. Figured Chubnuts and Prudence was out. That was okay with me. I'd already seen enough of them two that day to last a month. But when I reached the door I heard this little cough and I damned near jumped out a my pants. My suspenders was the only thing keeping them on.

Jesus Christ! I says. Once I caught hold of myself, I looked a little harder and I see the kid sitting way away in the corner of the porch. In the goddamn dark. And she's got a hold of a chicken. It was that black bastard, Allan, or whatever Chubnuts calls him.

I told her she give me a shock, sitting in the dark like that.

The kid didn't say nothing. There was something funny going on, I knew. She was too young to be sitting in the dark by herself.

So I asked her how she got here and she said her mom dropped her off.

I back up a few steps and look around the edge of the porch. I was damn sure I didn't see no car in the driveway when I come up. I asked if the kid's mom was coming back for her. The kid just shrugged her shoulders. I didn't know what the hell that meant, but I was pretty sure it didn't mean her mom was coming back any time soon.

That's when I realized I was stuck there with her. Hell if I knew what to do with a kid. Jesus Christ, I thought. This place.

I asked if she'd knocked on the door and she said she did, but no one was home. So I asked how long she was waiting outside and she just give me another one of them shrugs.

Poor little gaffer. Sitting out there with her chicken.

I was torn up about what to do. I could let her in the house but then she'd be alone in there. Or I could bring her down to the cabin. But then she'd be alone with me. And to tell you the goddamn truth, I didn't know which was worse for the kid. I really didn't. An old man's house is no place for a little girl. What the hell would I say to her?

I thought about Chubnuts and Prudence. There was no telling what time people like that might come home. People like them could be out all night.

I'll tell you what, I says to the kid. How about you put the bird back in his chicken shed and you and me can go inside the house? You eat dinner?

She shook her head.

I tell her we better call up the pizza parlor then. Get them to deliver. We can eat while we watch the idiot box.

And she said, The idiot box?

I explain that's the other name for the TV. There's a hell of a lot kids don't know.

Prudence

I decided it was best to meet him on the road. Earl had let Bertie off the porch for some fresh grass and I didn't want Dr. Eustace to see her. She still looked as though we'd put Hannibal Lecter in charge of her shearing and had hired the special effects team from *Night of the Living Dead* to bandage her. All for her own good, of course, but someone unfamiliar with the situation could misunderstand.

I admit that I was excited to be going out with a vet. Especially one with as much animal magnetism at Dr. Smith. Those lips of his . . . well, you know. Also, from a farmer's perspective, it's hard to imagine a more valuable friend. Only someone with a combine or a biofueled tractor might be more useful.

Naturally, I was looking forward to spending time with someone who was not only extremely attractive but also likely a fountain of knowledge about local agriculture. I could bounce my crop ideas off him and get hints about organic fertilizers and best practices in the region.

The date was even taking my mind off my nerves about the farmers' market in the morning. I really only had radishes to sell and the ones I'd pulled to see how they were doing had been a bit small. That's why I didn't pull any more. I thought I'd let them keep growing overnight. I'd probably accidentally pulled a couple of runts. We had Burpee Whites, April Cross, Cherry Belles, Champions and White Icicles as well as Easter Eggs and several other varieties growing. I'd wanted to plant Early Scarlet Globes, too, but the seeds hadn't arrived with the others. All the varieties were supposed to be fast growers. I had prepared radish recipe cards to give away and a poster listing the history and nutritional properties of radishes for the front of the table. Not a lot of people know that radishes can help you clear your sinuses and that they are anti-inflammatories and were eaten by the Romans. This would all be added value for our customers and I hoped it would distract from the fact that radishes were all we had.

But back to the date. I wore a pretty summer dress with my yellow soy and silk cardigan over top, and I found myself shivering a bit in the breeze. There was no trace of the rendering plant, just the scent of new grass and fresh dirt. I took a moment to thank the powers that be for my great fortune in finding myself in such a place.

As I stood at the end of the driveway, trying to appear casual, a sign hanging on a fence post caught my eye. It was mostly hidden behind some weeds and a scrubby shrub. The letters had been haphazardly chip-carved and burned into a rough-sawn piece of board.

WoeFiEld, it announced with a marked lack of confidence or familiarity with the basic rules of capitalization.

A large, rusted nail had been used to affix the board to the post. I can't stand to see things off center, so I scrambled across the dry ditch that lined the right side of the driveway and straightened the board. I told myself that when I had the time and money I'd replace the sign with something a bit more professional looking. Still rustic, of course, but more in keeping with the rest of the rapidly improving property.

For now, straightening would have to do.

I jumped back across the little culvert and lost a flip-flop. My bare foot slipped down into the ditch, which wasn't quite as dry as it looked. Under the dry crust was a thin layer of swamp mud with the consistency of a particularly sludgy petrochemical by-product.

"Shoot," I muttered as I picked up the recycled rubber-tired sandal with hemp straps I'd bought at the Fort Greene Flea Market, and then crouched down to try and clean my foot. I was just removing some of the mud from between my toes with a hand that was now as dirty as my foot when I heard the vehicle approach. As I stood up quickly, I noticed movement in Seth's mother's home, which was directly across the street. A curtain fell back across the window as though someone had been looking out. The place had a steady stream of traffic coming and going during business hours. I wondered whether Seth's mother ran some sort of hair salon. I made a note to ask him, because my hair was starting to need a cut and I'd feel less self-indulgent if I didn't have to drive to have it done.

I was just slipping my shoe back on when an enormous white truck stopped in front of me. It had a reinforced, extra-wide box with four tires instead of the usual two on the back and an extended cab. I smelled diesel. The truck's engine must have been vast to require the half acre of hood that covered it.

I could practically see the carbon belching out into the atmosphere and I wondered why a country vet needed so much extra horsepower to get around. Maybe he had to tow dead animals out of ponds or something.

The driver's-side window rolled silently down. Actually, it might not have been silent, but I couldn't hear it over the noise of the engine, which eclipsed the sounds of the birds in the trees.

Dr. Eustace's perfect lips curled into a smile and his eyes crinkled. "Are you sneaking out?" he asked. "Keeping me a secret from your parents?"

"I thought I'd save you the drive up to the house. Global warming and all."

His grin expanded.

I realized with surprise that I felt slightly giddy. It was an odd sensation since I almost never feel off balance. It's just not part of my nature.

We stared at each other for another long moment. A motorcycle roared by and I had to step back as it drove down the road between us. It took several seconds for the noise from the bike to subside and then we were left with the low grumble of the truck. I wondered why Dr. Eustace Smith didn't turn off the engine. Didn't he know how damaging it was to let a vehicle's engine idle?

"So you getting in?" he asked, still grinning. "Or should I come out there and get you?"

An odd, unfamiliar little quiver ran through my knees as I walked across the narrow, paved road.

SETH

When I walked into my house, my mom and Bobby were playing cards at the kitchen table. Well, cribbage. I don't know if that counts as cards, due to the board game aspect of it. My mom acted as though she'd been expecting me.

"Hi, honey," she said. Like we were just one happy family.

They were drinking rye and Cokes from pint glasses. I looked at them—my mom and Bobby and the rye and Cokes—and I realized that if I stayed for more than ten minutes I was going to get loaded. I'm not saying my mom made me drink, because she didn't. I'm just saying that I knew I couldn't be around the booze. Of course, part of the reason I went over there was because I was tired of the teetotaling approach and the working lifestyle in general. Still, the insight was a big revelation for some reason. My dad, Prince of Pubs, my mom, Aunt Elsie. We are the natives of a tiny island nation sinking into an ocean of alcohol.

I looked at my mom and Bobby, and the thought flashed through my mind that I wasn't genetically cut out for being sober. That's probably true for a lot of people attracted to the heavy metal lifestyle, with the obvious exception of straightedges such as Ted Nugent, who is a freak in other ways.

I didn't want to start off with the news that I quit my job or at least planned to, so I just asked for a drink.

"Sure, honey. There are glasses in the sink."

The kitchen was pretty messy, like always. I guess Bobby wasn't any more of a housekeeper than me or my mom. The funny thing about our house is that it looks more like a trailer than an actual trailer. It's so rectangular and prefab and plastic it's like the builder was trying to create an optical illusion of trailerness. I filled up a coffee mug with a mix of three parts rye and one part Coke. I downed it standing over the sink and then poured another one.

My mom asked if I'd eaten and I said no. She asked if I wanted to join them, and I said sure. She said there was some Hamburger Helper in the cupboard and I could put a can of tuna in it.

And I said, at least I think I said, "You won't even cook for me? I've been gone for weeks."

"We're playing crib, Seth. Just make the food. You're not helpless."

"I don't know if you noticed, but I kind of fucking am."

Her and Bobby looked at me then.

"I'm quitting my job," I said. "And moving back in here."

That's when Bobby decided to pipe up. I couldn't even look at him, partly because the rye was having this very instant and extremely negative impact on my eyesight and partly because I was afraid of what I was going to see in his mustache.

"Seth, your mom wants to see you become more independent."

"Whatever, man. She's also interested in winning the lottery and getting on Home and Garden TV for her crafts and we both know that shit's not happening."

"We know you had a tough break there. With your teacher. But your mom and I have been talking and she feels like she let you overreact."

"Overreact?" I said. I could feel myself shaking all over. This fucking mustache-wearing, helicopter-parts-selling dickweed having the balls to talk like he knew anything about what happened to me.

"So you were embarrassed," he said. He could see that I was on the edge and he didn't sound so sure of himself.

"Bobby," said my mother. I don't know whether she meant for him to stop or she was just trying to get a word in edgewise.

"Embarrassed? You think I was *embarrassed*? You fuck," I said. "You total fuck. Don't you talk to me about being embarrassed."

"Seth," said my mother. "Go to your room. Calm down."

"Go to my room? I can't even get in there because there are fucking rotors all over the place."

"Go to the living room, then," she said. "Cool down. I'll make us some Hamburger Helper. Then we can talk."

Bobby was trying to look stern, but he wasn't looking me in the eye. I thought about putting a fist through one of the walls, but last time I did that, not long after all the shit with the drama teacher happened, I hit a stud and broke my wrist. Hurt like a bitch and I could barely use my computer for a month.

Instead I downed a second mug of rye and Coke, poured another one and walked into the living room. I could see my mom and Bobby sitting in the kitchen, but at least it was dark in the living room with the curtains closed and I was sort of alone. I thought about what Bobby said. Embarrassed. Was that all I was? It sure felt worse than that.

The drama teacher came to our school when I was in eleventh grade. It's a terrible, shitty story and I fucking hate telling it.

Anyway, I took her class as an elective. I guess I was sort of interested in doing music or set design or something a little different. Maybe get a job doing concert production or something. Plus, my marks were for shit and I thought drama might be an easy credit. Those fruitcakes in the drama department all seemed to have A-plus-plus averages. At least to hear them talk they did.

So I walked into drama class and my connection with this teacher was instant. Sparks like flamethrowers. It was crazy. Like nothing I ever experienced before. Right away, she took a special interest. Now you have to understand, man. No one was taking a special interest in me at home or anywhere else right then. I had a few buddies and I had my music and I spent a lot of time online, but I wasn't too connected to other people. People thought I was a burner, but I wasn't really because smoking pot fucked up my drinking and made me paranoid. Basically, I just went to school and drank at home sometimes with my mom and the Prince of Pubs or once in a blue moon I went out with some guys. Mostly I drank in front of the computer.

Pretty soon me and the drama teacher crossed the line. Like Vili and Mary Kay, only I was seventeen, not like twelve or whatever, and she wasn't a full-fledged crazy. Also, we weren't officially having sex, but it was close. She let me do stuff to her and she did stuff to me. I don't want to get into all the Bill Clinton details. Anyway, she said I had potential in all these different areas. If I learned to play the guitar better she said she could see me fronting a band or if I got better at writing, maybe being a reporter for like *Revolver* or *Metal Maniacs* or even a more mainstream magazine, like *Spin* or *Rolling Stone* or something. She believed I could be somebody, as crushingly lame as that sounds.

In addition to our personal time in the drama room, which really got her going, we also hung out in her car. I started writing songs and singing them to her. They were mostly pretty terrible, I admit, but she dug them. She said I had more passion than even *I* knew. Which I know makes no sense but felt really *true* somehow and deep. During that period, I wasn't drinking too much because, I don't know. I just wasn't.

She was working on the big school production of *Jesus Christ Superstar,* which I thought was cool. Sebastian Bach starred in that show on like Broadway at one point. Anyway, I was helping with the sound system, and I was learning a lot. The whole year was like this blur of feeling. I loved her. She didn't look like anything much, to be honest. I mean, she wasn't all *Real Housewives* or anything. She was maybe forty, short hair, black clothes, not too skinny or anything. But she had this animal quality to her and she made me feel like I had potential.

A week or so before the play was due to start she broke up with me because she said she couldn't afford to lose her career or her marriage. Yeah, she was married. To some stiff who worked for the credit union. Poor bastard. Anyway, when she dumped me I guess I lost it. It was like I'd been floating down a stream and all of a sudden I went over a waterfall and into some class five rapids. My shit spun out of control pretty much immediately.

I said some things to her and she fired me off the production, "for both our sakes," as she put it. But I wouldn't leave it alone. I called her house and hung up when her husband answered. I wrote her letters and dropped them on her desk. I left single flowers under her windshield wiper. It was almost unbelievably lame and sad. The night of the premiere, or whatever, I got loaded and went down to the school. My memory of the night's a little sketchy, but I'm pretty sure every person in Cedar was there. I was too shittered to notice that little detail, unfortunately.

I waited in my seat off to the side until everyone was seated and the curtains were going to be opened in a few minutes. Then I made my move. I got up there on the stage with my boom box, hit play and started singing one of the songs that I wrote for the drama teacher. It was a direct rip-off of "Love Hurts" by Nazareth. I mean it was very, very similar. The teacher's name was Beverly, so I put that in there: "Bev hurts, Bev wounds." You get the picture.

And as I sang, I started kind of taking off my clothes. I guess I was trying to express my emotional nakedness or something.

Because the audience was there to see *Jesus Christ Superstar,* and I have long hair, at the beginning no one clued in that I shouldn't be up there. Not until I had my pants half off and fell over because I forgot to take my goddamned shoes off first and my feet got trapped. That's when I started crying. I was lying there with my pants around my ankles and I was too drunk to get up. But I was also still sort of trying to sing. "Bev hurts. Bev kills." Like that.

By this time everyone had realized that I wasn't part of the program. The principal told a couple of guys from the hockey team, who had girlfriends in the play, to do something, and they climbed up and tried to drag me off the stage. I started screaming at them not to touch me, but my fucking pants had me trapped so I was crawling around up there with my shirt off and my underpants in the air. I tried to evade capture and ended up basically plummeting off the stage, a drop of at least four feet.

Where's the blackout when you need one?

I landed just in time for the drama teacher's credit union husband to take a run at me. Then it was him and the hockey team and the principal and the vice principal, who was also the head of the phys-ed program, and everyone was pulling on everyone else and everyone was pulling on me.

They got me out of the gym and called my old man to come and get me. The next day there were questions from the cops and from the school. They wanted to know if the drama teacher did bad touching on me and whether we had an inappropriate relationship and I didn't want to ruin her career, because what we shared had been intense, so I said I had a crush on her and she had no idea about any of it.

I have no idea how the play went. No idea what happened with the drama teacher. All I know is I never went back to school, especially not after the cell-phone video someone took of the whole fucking thing went viral and killed my chances of a career as a musician or metal music reporter. Basically, I went into seclusion. At least until the farm. Which is its own form of seclusion.

Anyway, I replayed the whole horror show of my life in my mind while I sat in our dark living room. And when it was over, for some reason, I got up and pulled the curtain open to look over at the farm. Prudence was standing at the end of the driveway. Not really standing. She was dicking around with the old sign, then she fell in a ditch and after she got out, she hopped around trying to clean up her foot. She was such a nice-looking girl. Fast moving, but decent. My heart kind of hurt when I looked at her. Not because I was in love, but because I could tell from looking at her that she didn't hate herself. Not only didn't she seem to hate herself, she barely seemed to think about herself. How fucking glorious must that be?

While I was watching, a big white truck pulled up. It was the same one from the afternoon. I let the curtains fall closed. I really didn't want to see her get in that truck.

When I was sure they were gone, I got an idea. I walked out of the living room, like I was going to go use the john, but ducked into my mom's bedroom and found Bobby's wallet on the dresser my mom had decoupaged with flowers and leaves from old wrapping paper. It actually looks okay, that dresser. I took fifty bucks and then called a cab.

Prudence

Up close the truck was even larger than I'd thought. I had to step onto a running board to get in. But it was quiet. A country song played on the stereo. The seats were leather. When I pulled my seat belt around me, I was reminded of Sara in Earl's old truck. How she'd looked so small. In this truck, my feet, like hers, dangled above the floor.

As Eustace turned the steering wheel, I found myself staring at the sleeve of his blue-jean shirt, pulled back revealing a few inches of his forearm and his wrist. I don't particularly approve of leather, but the smell of it was oddly intoxicating.

After driving along the narrow, two-lane road for several minutes, he turned onto a gravel road with a painted sign that announced the Duck and Bob. The place was done up like a British country pub. A lot of attention had been paid to landscaping. Fancy ducks and geese and black and white swans swam around on the large pond off to the side of the parking lot. A flagstone path led through a vine-covered trellis to the heavy wooden front door. Tidy, shaded beds filled with impatiens and hostas and young ferns flanked the walkway.

Inside the pub, the walls were whitewashed. The roof was supported with dark beams, and mirrors advertising British ales were hung throughout. The tables were wood and so were the upholstered chairs. Dr. Eustace had to duck his head when he went through the doorway. As far as I could see in the dim light, the customers were mostly grey-haired. I liked the place very much for its orderly and well-established atmosphere.

"Is this okay? I thought we'd go out into the garden to eat," said Eustace.

I smiled and he put an arm around my shoulders. We walked straight ahead to the counter, where a barman was taking orders. To the left were seating areas and a fireplace. To the right and through a doorway was another room. Most of the tables were full.

I wondered if Earl ever came here and then decided probably not. He didn't seem like the British pub type.

"Hey, Doctor E.," said the young barman. His ears were pierced with those lobe-stretching earrings and his head was shaved to reveal a nicely shaped skull.

"Hey," said Eustace. "How you doing?"

"Good, good. We missed you on Tuesday."

"Had to work."

"Don't stay away too long. That would set a bad example."

Eustace laughed and said he wouldn't.

We peered at a blackboard menu on the far wall behind the bartender.

"I'll take the plowman's special," said Eustace. "And an iced tea."

"The crab cakes are excellent," said the barman to me, when he could see I was still deciding. "So are the oysters."

"Okay, I'll take the pan-fried oysters. And a soda water." In another circumstance I might have had a glass of wine, but I was running a fake treatment center.

Eustace maneuvered me through the dining area to the right and out another doorway that led to a fenced lawn. Cedar picnic tables with large umbrellas stuck in the middle were arranged on the grass, and a few cedar camp chairs faced out toward the large garden just beyond the fence. I could see rhododendrons lush with papery pink and red blooms and ferns rising like sculptures out of the beds of mounded bark mulch. It was very beautiful even though not all the plants looked native.

Eustace took our drinks over to two of the camp chairs and set them down on the small table between them. He shifted the chairs so they faced each other slightly. When he sat down, his knee brushed mine.

"So what did you miss on Tuesday?" I asked.

"Oh, I get together with some guys," he said.

"You had to work?"

"I got a little behind. I was giving some cattle implants."

"Vaccinating them?"

"No. I had to put implants in their ears. It's a hell of a job. It was just me and the farmer. We could have used two more guys. Big guys."

"Implants? Do you mean ID tags?"

He laughed and took a sip of his iced tea. He licked foam from his upper lip, which momentarily made it hard for me to focus on what he was saying.

"No. Implants that administer a low dose of hormones."

"Hormones!" I said. "You mean that stuff that gives boys man-boobs and women breast cancer?"

His eyes went squinty. "Ah, I see you're up on your nonsense science."

"Excuse me?"

"Look, the implants administer natural hormones. It's perfectly safe. You want to feed everybody? You've got to use every advantage. Farmers can't compete otherwise."

I knew he was wrong. I'd read all about it.

"You don't inject them with antibiotics, do you?"

"Sure," he said. "They get sick, I inject them. It's what vets do."

I vaguely remembered James Herriot writing about the wonders of sulfa drugs, but obviously that wasn't the same as the wholesale over-use of antibiotics in the agricultural industry. I took a deep breath.

"Not all of them administer unnecessary drugs. Some vets confine themselves to helping injured animals."

"And they use medications to do that. Just like me. When an animal gets sick I treat it."

"Probably most of the animals you treat have illnesses due to an unnatural life caused by industrial agricultural practices. Animals raised on small farms don't get sick as often." To be honest, I didn't know whether that last part was true, but I'd read it somewhere and it made sense. Sometimes in an argument you have to extrapolate from the available data.

"You realize that domesticated animals were essentially created by humans?" he said, leaning in toward me.

"But that doesn't mean they should be . . . abused. This is why Canada is a hotbed of mad cow disease."

He frowned.

"Canada is not a hotbed of . . . never mind. Look, bovine spongiform encephalopathy is caused not by medication but by feeding cows animal by-products, including contaminated beef."

"Yeah, but vets invented it."

"Vets invented mad cow disease?"

"No. The idea of feeding cows to other cows. You never saw James Herriot telling his clients to feed dead animals to their herbivores."

"Actually, it was British vets in the eighties who started this ball rolling. Wanted to keep their beef production competitive and didn't treat the protein supplements properly. Which reminds me, why are we having this conversation?"

I really wanted to let him know that I disapproved of industrial farming techniques and the vets who made it possible for farmers to raise animals in unnatural conditions. But I didn't want to get too strident because that would ruin our date and he was very good-looking.

"I disapprove of industrial farming," I said. "Just so you know."

"I'm not crazy about the Canucks lineup this year. And you are very pretty," he said. His knee was back on mine.

I decided to change his values later.

A young waitress, dressed as though she'd just gotten off the couch where she'd been watching Saturday morning cartoons on TV, arrived with our meals.

She placed a plate with four large oysters and a tossed green salad in front of me. The oysters had been lightly breaded and fried to a golden, crispy perfection. A small ramekin filled with homemade tartar sauce flecked with bits of onion and pickle, and four slices of lemon surrounded the oysters.

On Eustace's plate was a small loaf of bread, a large wedge of white cheese, red grapes, a green salad with cherry tomatoes and bright radishes, and a scoop of potato salad.

"Enjoy," said our server. "Let me know if you need anything else."

I lightly salted the oyster, cut a small piece and tasted it.

"Oh my goodness," I said as the flavors and textures settled on my tongue.

Eustace nodded.

"You have to try it." I cut another small section and added a swipe of tartar and a squeeze of lemon. I picked the morsel up on my fork and moved it to his mouth, my free hand under the fork to catch any juice.

He ate it and we grinned at each other.

"I think peak oil is a load of crap," he said, offering me a morsel of aged cheddar on a torn piece of crusty bread.

"I think people who drive unsustainable vehicles are killing the rest of us," I said, feeding him another slice of oyster.

"David Suzuki is the greatest conspiracy theorist of our time," he whispered, giving me a grape.

"I don't even know who that is," I said, feeding him a cherry tomato from my salad.

When we'd finished everything on our plates, I sighed with satisfaction. "That was amazing."

There was something in his eyes when he looked at me and I had an inkling of what he looked like right after sex.

"I don't get what all the hippies are bitching about," he said.

"Rednecks are a drag," I replied.

He leaned over the table. I could feel the warmth of his lips before they even touched mine. Just as my nose filled with the smell of garden and soap and man, a loud, slurred voice pierced the evening.

"Dude, I know two things: heavy metal and celebrities. And if you want integrity, pick a metal musician every time. That actress's publicists want you to think she's all that, you know, with the adopting starving kids and buying up villages. But it's a sales job. Tits and ass. Same as all the rest."

Startled, I jerked my head and the kiss became teeth knocking against my ear.

"Umf," Eustace said, pulling away and rubbing his mouth.

"I'm sorry. I just heard something."

The voice continued.

"She's a total whore. Just like a certain someone who works at the high school. Well, actually, she might not work there anymore. I haven't kept in touch. Fact is, I been home ever since I left school. 'Cept for this one trip I took to like Home Depot. This shit here is like my coming-out party."

There was a pause and then the voice sounded again. It was decibels louder than any other in earshot and it was coming from inside the bar.

"Don't get upset, dude. You'll fuck up your oxygen tank."

What was Seth doing here? Wasn't he supposed to be eating pizza back at the farm? When did he get drunk? He'd been doing so well.

Eustace was listening, too, with a smile on his face that looked like a combination of pity and annoyance.

"Always has to be one," he said.

I took a small sip of my drink and tried to think. Seth was supposed to be a patient in my treatment center. People gossip in small towns. I couldn't let anyone know that my one patient was out drinking at the local establishments. Seth's behavior was endangering my whole plan.

"Good thing there are places like yours for people like that," said Eustace.

Soda water threatened to burst from my nose and possibly out of my eyes.

"Pardon me?"

"It's okay. Everyone knows that you're turning that old place of yours into a treatment center. A few people have complained, but almost everybody knows somebody who should be in a treatment center. Your neighbors will get over it. I think it's a great thing."

Before he could continue he was interrupted by a shriek. "That bitch!" Seth's disembodied voice cried. "He couldn't rock a decent hairdo never mind a fucking band. That is some lame-ass bullshit right there. And after what I experienced in our educational system, I think I know about lame."

"Yeah, that's definitely a potential customer for you, right there," said Eustace.

I gave him a weak smile.

Sara

Me and Earl watched some really good shows on TV. We watched one where a guy trained his mule to pull a plow. He said a mule's like a horse, only smarter and stronger and better-looking. And Earl said, "Ain't that the truth." Then we watched a show where this big man with really blond hair was upset about people's houses because they weren't built right, and Earl said, "That's God's own truth." Earl likes TV a lot, even though he calls it an idiot box.

We had pizza with pineapple on it. He pronounced pizza funny, like "pee-ssssah," and said kids need to eat fruit so they can grow. It was nice of him to think about ways to keep me healthy. I enjoyed eating something that was not casserole. When I get older, I will probably not ever eat casseroles.

It was getting late and everything, like probably 9:00 or so, when Earl got up and went to the john, which is what he calls the bathroom. And I used the remote, which he calls the clicker, to look at some other channels to see what we'd watch next. I stopped on this music channel. There was an old man on there. He had a big gray cowboy hat and a fancy gray suit. He looked really famous because he didn't show his face or anything. At first he just stood there on the stage with his head down holding his guitar and then after everyone was waiting for him, he started playing and singing. He had a high voice, sort of like a girl or church people. I liked it a lot. It was sort of sad music but also happy. It went pretty fast and my toe started tapping, almost by itself.

I was nearly dancing when Earl came back in the living room. I didn't see him at first because he stopped at the doorway and stared at the TV. I only noticed him when the song was over and everyone clapped a lot and screamed, even me, and the announcer said that was bluegrass legend Merle Clemente making a rare appearance at the country music awards.

"Turn it off," said Earl and I was really surprised, because I didn't know he was standing back there and I thought we were going to watch some more shows about country life.

"But it's good. Don't you like music?"

"Not my brother's," he said. Then he walked outside. I went and sat on the porch with him and told him how my dad hit my mom with the tuna casserole. He told me some things about when he was a kid and said that families was damned complicated. It was the first time he swore the whole night, which was a sign that he's trying. I think Earl is one of my best friends that I know.

EARL

Goddamn Merle, I thought. How many times does he got to go on TV
in one year? Seeing him again so soon made it hard to catch my breath.
I had to set down outside to get myself right. The kid came out and
set beside me and didn't say a word for a long time. She's a funny little
thing. Real good company. She never complained about what was on
the idiot box. Watched everything like she was studying for a test on it
later. A hell of a good personality, you have to admit.

I guess that's why I told her that Merle was my brother. That and the
business with them parents of hers. She just nodded and said it must
be strange to know someone on TV and I said she had that right.

After a spell she said she wondered how Bertie was doing over there
on my porch.

I told her fine, but it was probably time to change her dressings. I
been doing that every day and it's a bitch of a job for one man. I didn't
say that to the kid, though.

She asked me if I thought Bertie liked living on my porch and I said
probably it's better than nothing, but not much. She said how a sheep
should have a proper shelter and other sheep. I said that was probably
true.

My breath was coming easier by then. Nights is pretty around the
old place. The air is clean and except for when the Riggins boys get
to partying and drive their trucks too fast down the road, it's quiet. A
person could close his eyes and imagine he was somewhere else.

The kid said just about what I was thinking, that it was real nice sitting outside in the dark. The old moon was hanging low over the trees at the far edge of the property and every so often a bat'd fly through the little patch of light from the lamp mounted on a post at the side of the house. I never understood who the hell put that lamp up there. It don't light up anything anyone'd need to see. Typical of this place. But at least it lets a person see the bats flying.

Kid said, Earl, those are bats, aren't they?

It was funny the way she was noticing what I was noticing. Maybe all kids can do that. I don't know.

I told her they were and they were hunting bugs.

She said that was good because bats are natural something or others. The kid wasn't a bit scared of them bats. That impressed me, I'll tell you.

I was just getting ready to say it was time to go inside. I was going to tell her to bunk down on the couch. I figured I'd set out on the porch or maybe in the kitchen until Prudence and Chubnuts came home, but then we heard a car pull up. There was some kind of ruckus and afore I knew what was happening, I seen somebody running down toward my cabin.

Goddamn if it wasn't Chubnuts, drunker than a skunk, no shirt on, skin white as half a moon, running for all he was worth, which wasn't much, because he fell on his face soon as he made it past where we was sitting.

I told the kid to go inside. She didn't need to see that.

She asked me if that was Seth and I said it was and she should go inside because he wasn't feeling good.

Do you mean he's drunk? she says.

Before I could answer, he was up again and running hell bent for election, yelling his head off about a teacher.

Jesus Christ, I said and took off after him. I'm not going to tell you I went fast, because I don't move fast no more even in the best part of the day never mind the middle of the goddamn night. I could see the little bastard because he practically glowed. He had a good head start on me when he hit my cabin and damned if he didn't bust open that barrier keeping Bertie on the deck. Next thing I know she goes skittering down the stairs like she's on fire. Poor goddamn sheep never gets a moment's peace. She ran past me and I made a grab for her, but she was pretty slick since she got sheared and I fell flat on my face.

Then Chubnuts was breathing his beer breath on me and asking if I was okay.

I told him, No thanks to you goddamn it, and Are you trying to kill the goddamn sheep? And he said he wanted her to try out the new corral and that no matter what had happened to Bertie, she needed to be out in the world. And I said, In the middle of the goddamn night? and We haven't even put a gate on it yet.

But he wasn't listening no more. He was heading back to the house and yelling for Sara to get the halter. I had no idea where poor old Bertie had got to. I figured if she had half a brain she'd a run away. By the time I picked myself out of the dirt and got back to the house, there was no one there. I walked around back to the parking lot and found the kid standing over Chubnuts. He'd gone down again, face first, and he wasn't moving.

I asked the kid where the sheep was and she pointed. Bertie was standing in the middle of the driveway. The tape on her belly had come loose and was dangling out behind. There was twigs and grass and all kinds of crap stuck to it. One of her booties was half off. She looked a sight I can tell you. That's when the truck pulled in.

PRUDENCE

We nearly got out of the Duck and Bob without incident. After Eustace returned from a trip to the washroom, I told him that I had to get home to deal with an unexpected situation.

"What's going on?" he asked.

I hated to lie to him, but nor did I want to get into a long explanation that might be misunderstood.

So I told him we had a problem with our septic system. I'd heard they were very tricky and could cause situations. There probably *were* problems with the septic at Woefield. The smell in the neighborhood couldn't all come from the rendering plant.

"Someone call you?" he asked.

I made a movement with my head that he could interpret in any way he wanted. I wouldn't say I lied, exactly. It was more of a deflection.

Eustace looked disappointed. Around us people were having a wonderful time. The garden was lit with little electric torches. Under other circumstances it would have been heaven to sit there with a handsome, if unsustainable, man.

Seth's voice floated out over the noise of the crowd again and I did my best to ignore it, although I was becoming increasingly concerned about him. What had upset him so badly?

"That guy is wasted," said Eustace.

"Hmmm," I said.

"He's crashed a table full of older people who look terrified. He's wearing an Anthrax T-shirt and mirrored shades. I give it ten minutes before he gets kicked out."

"We should go," I said, standing abruptly.

Eustace turned, ready to walk back through the pub the way we'd come in.

"Let's leave through the garden. I'd like to see the flower beds," I said, deciding it was best to make our exit around the side of the building and back to the parking lot.

"I thought you were in a hurry?"

"We'll look at the flowers quickly. It's busy in the bar. I don't like crowds."

"I wouldn't expect that from a New York girl."

"I lived in Brooklyn. It's quieter."

Like a competitor in a race walk, I led us through the back garden gate and pulled Eustace around the perimeter of the central garden bed, which twinkled with the tiny lights set amongst the flowers, shrubs and ferns. Very pretty. I elbowed past couples who lingered hand-in-hand and then, letting go of Eustace's elbow (he'd begun to resist my pushing and pulling), I race-walked toward the side of the pub. Soon I was in the packed parking lot. I found the huge white truck almost immediately and sidled up to the passenger door so I was hidden in the shadows. I waited for Eustace to catch up.

"Hello?" I heard him call out. His voice sounded like it was coming from the middle of the parking lot. "Prudence?"

"Yes?"

"The truck's over here."

"Oh."

I hurried out from my hiding spot and walked down a few more rows until I spotted another enormous white truck. Eustace stood near the bumper and when I reached him, he took my shoulders in his hands. In spite of my rush, I felt myself go limp.

"Is everything okay with you?" he asked, leaning down and staring into my eyes.

I shook my head slightly. He bent to kiss me and his hands slid from my shoulders onto my back.

When we drew apart to take a breath, he said, "You taste good."

"So do you. In spite of your terrible politics."

We nearly jumped out of our skins when someone behind us screamed, "POLITICS!"

Seth stood swaying in the road.

"NEVER DISCUSS POLITICS!"

He was being supported by a pair of silver-haired gentlemen who appeared to be in their early seventies. They seemed unconcerned by his severe intoxication. Maybe it's a generational thing.

"With apologies," said one of them, suavely.

I waited for Seth to blow my cover by speaking to me directly.

"WOMEN!" bellowed Seth. "YOU CAN'T TRUST THE BITCHES. NO MATTER HOW MUCH YOU LOVE THEM."

Eustace reached over and opened the passenger door. "Get in," he said, quietly.

"I loved a bitch once," Seth slurred, quieter now. He leaned forward so the men had to struggle to keep him up.

"Then she fucked me. Well, not physically. I wanted her to. But she never did. Nobody's ever really fucked me. I've fucked myself plenty, though."

He sagged to the side, putting an extra burden on the men holding him up.

Headlights appeared and a yellow taxicab pulled up. I was sorry to see that it wasn't Hugh's cab.

Seth craned his head. "I'm sorry," he said, speaking in the general direction of the taxi.

He took two unsteady steps toward the car and propped himself against the hood. He turned back and faced us. I couldn't tell who he was staring at because it was dark and he still had on his mirrored glasses, which he'd fixed with a lump of duct tape after the episode with Bertie. I moved to put one foot up on the running board of Eustace's truck.

"You wanna hear a song I wrote? I think you'd get it. You being a woman and all."

"That's okay," said Eustace, stepping to block Seth's view of me. Firm but polite.

Seth lurched violently and somehow ended up in the backseat of the cab. It moved off and so did Seth's escorts, after they'd said good night. Eustace and I were left in silence. A duck waddled through the spotlight of an overhead lamp.

Eustace leaned his head back and smoothed his curly hair from his temples. He took a deep breath.

"You ready?"

"I'm sorry?"

"To go."

"Oh, yes. Of course," I said. There is really nothing I hate more than a messy situation and I was very pleased that one was over.

Eustace and I semi-made out all the way back to Woefield. His hand traveled as he drove. So did mine. The truck had bucket seats or I'd have sat right beside him, like in old movies about small towns.

As the truck drove up our driveway and my hand moved up his leg he made a noise in his throat. Then he gasped, "What the—!" The truck skidded to a stop on the hard-packed dirt road.

I peered out the windshield. In the powerful headlights stood a small, white creature tangled up in some kind of tape. Bertie.

Eustace was out the door in an instant. He nearly dragged me with him because my hand was still in his pocket. Something to the left of Bertie caught my eye. When I realized what it was, I was tempted not to get out of the truck.

Sara

The guy who drove Prudence home got out of his truck and walked up to Bertie like he was scared she would run away, but I think she was too tired. He wrapped a piece of dirty duct tape around her head and neck to make a lead rope and halter. I was impressed because he was making do with what was at hand, which Mr. Lymer says is part of having leadership qualities.

"Do you want me to get her halter?" I asked. "She's got a new one."

He looked at me funny and said, "Are you okay?" Like he thought I might be sick or something.

"I'm okay. But Seth isn't. Are you a doctor?"

"I'm a vet," he said. "Whose sheep is this?"

"Well, I guess she's Prudence's. We all sort of take care of her though."

Prudence walked up and the vet said, "So you do have a sheep."

"It's quite an interesting story," she said, but he put his hand out the way my dad does when he wants to say stuff and no one's allowed to say anything back.

After that, he only talked to me.

"Let's bring her into the light. And if you have a proper halter you should go get it."

But I didn't go because I didn't want to miss anything.

The vet stopped leading Bertie when he saw Seth and said a swear. I'm practically inoculated against swearing now, since I've heard so much of it.

"That's Seth," I told the vet. "He lives here. With Earl and Prudence.
I'm staying here too right now."

"In the treatment center?" he said.

"I don't know. I guess so."

Still holding onto Bertie's lead rope, the vet knelt and put his fingers
on Seth's throat. Seth made a noise like he was going to throw up and
the vet took his hand away really fast.

Earl, who was standing in the shadows, said a couple of swears and
the vet jumped because I don't think he knew Earl was there.

"He going to be all right?" Earl asked.

And the vet said that he was a vet, not a detox expert, and that we
should take better care of our patients and his main concern was the
sheep.

Earl just shook his head like he was sad and said hell if he knew. I
can say hell because it's in the Bible and also in *Left Behind*.

Prudence bent over Seth and was saying something. I think she was
trying to get him up.

"You probably have the wrong impression," she said. At first it
seemed like she was talking to Seth, even though he was sleeping. But I
think she was really talking to the vet, even though he wasn't listening.
He'd pulled Bertie over into the light on the side of the house and was
looking at all the parts we had covered up so they wouldn't get dirty.

I told him how she got some cuts when we sheared her.

"I see that," said the vet.

"Earl and Seth got cut too. She kicked them, especially when we put
the medicine on her feet. Earl couldn't breathe."

The vet, who was tall and smelled nice, like a perfumed cowboy,
called her a poor old girl. But he didn't sound as mad.

When he finished looking her over, he told me to hold her while he
went to get something from his truck. When he got back we were all
standing around. Well, except for Seth, who was still sleeping in the
driveway.

The vet put some stuff on Bertie's cuts and gave it to me and said I
should dress her wounds twice a day and they weren't that bad and it

was probably best to let them heal in the air instead of covering them with feminine protection pads and I should clean them before I put the medicine on.

"What about her feet?" Prudence asked.

He ignored Prudence and told me we should keep the booties on for another few days.

Prudence asked how much we owed him for the medicine and the vet told me he'd think about it. Then Prudence said she was surprised to hear that he carried anything other than bovine growth hormone in his truck.

He just kind of snorted and told me that some people should focus on running their businesses and they could start by getting the clients off the ground in the parking lot.

Then Earl said it was time to put Bertie to bed and me, too.

It was an extremely full and interesting night.

SETH

She was leaning over me when I opened my eyes. It was like a dream, or a nightmare, one in which my usual hangover, Phil the Fucker, was joined by his psychotic older brother, Bruiser, who'd just completed three tours of duty in Iraq and come back nursing a grudge and a raging case of PTSD.

"Seth?" she said, quietly.

I couldn't figure out how she got so tall and my bed got so low.

Bits and pieces of the night before started coming back to me, unwelcome as a case of the clap. I remembered yelling at a bunch of old people. Prudence was there with some guy. He had a big truck.

"Seth?" she said again.

I tried to focus on her face. She smelled nice and looked pretty. Her brown eyes were soft, so maybe she wasn't too mad, but it was hard to tell through the fog of pain.

"Yes?"

"We have to talk," she said.

"About last night," I croaked, reaching for some plausible excuses. Bad seafood, negative interactions between small amounts of alcohol and completely legitimate allergy medicines. Artistic temperament. Low blood sugar.

That's when I noticed that I was on the floor. Not on the linoleum floor in my bedroom, but on a wood plank floor. I looked to the side and saw a piece of sky beyond the roofline. Patches of light pierced the gray. It was either dawn or dusk.

"Am I on the porch?"

"Yes. Look, I have something I need to say to you."

"Why am I on the porch?"

"Because you wet your pants. But that's not what I want to talk to you about."

I squeezed my eyes shut. "Okay," I whispered. If it was possible to drown from fucking shame there'd have been nothing left but the last few bubbles right about then.

Wetting one's pants is no kind of self-esteem builder.

"Seth, I've made some mistakes. All with the best intentions, of course. But I want to apologize to you most of all."

"Why? I'm the one who got loaded after you said no more drinking."

She patted my leg and I felt like I was a palliative case who'd been hanging on a little too long.

"Am I fired?" I asked.

"I haven't decided yet. Your jeans are in the washing machine and when I get home from the farmers' market we're having a house meeting. We have a lot to discuss."

"Is it morning?"

"It's five o'clock. So, yes, it's morning."

"I'm not sure I can—"

"You can go to sleep until I get home. But then I want you at that meeting. You need to be part of this discussion."

She stood and I was left staring at her ankles, which were nice, and then at nothing when she walked away.

I closed my eyes and prayed for death to take me.

Sara

Sometimes when you wake up in a new place you don't know where you are right away and it's a creepy feeling. But when I woke up at Woefield, even though it was really early, I knew exactly where I was.

Sometimes at my house I get confused because I dream I am somewhere else and when I wake up I'm disappointed that I'm not. So in some ways, waking up at Woefield was like a dream come true.

I didn't get why Prudence was asleep on the little couch across from me. She had her own room.

She looked funny because her mouth was open and her legs were hanging over top of the arm of the couch and her bare feet were poking out from under the blanket and there were papers with numbers written on them and lists all around her. She'd started writing after I told her the interesting news that Earl has a famous brother and she asked his name and I remembered because it rhymes with Earl's name, which means they probably got teased when they were at school. Prudence went on the Internet and looked Earl's brother up. As she was reading she kept saying, "no way" and "oh my god." When she was done she printed off her radish recipes and fact sheets for the farmers' market.

I tried to be really quiet. I thought about putting my blanket on her feet, so they wouldn't be so cold, but I was worried that might wake her up. She went to bed really late. I went outside because I was excited to see my birds right away. When I kept them at home, I used to go outside to see them as soon as I got up. I missed doing that after they went to Woefield, even though I came over really early lots of times.

I went into the coop and opened the door of the henhouse. When I walked back past the porch, I heard a whistling noise and it turned out to be Seth. He was sleeping on some garbage bags on the floor of the porch and there were some old blankets over him. He looked extremely terrible. I don't think I ever saw anyone look that terrible.

At first I thought he was sleeping, but when I went a little bit closer, he opened his eyes. I nearly jumped back from how they looked. Plus, he smelled bad.

"Sara," he said in a low, devil voice that didn't even sound like him.

I stayed quiet. I was back to wondering if he might be a child abuser because of how sick he looked. And how he smelled.

"It's okay," he said.

That was nice, so I tried talking to him.

"Are you sick?"

When I asked that question his skin changed from yellow to white and he told me wait by putting up his finger. So I did. Wait, I mean.

A minute or two later, he said, "Sara, don't ever drink."

I already knew that, so I just nodded.

"How are the champions?" he asked. I knew he meant my birds. Also, I could kind of tell that he didn't want to be alone, probably because he was scared from being so sick.

I sat on the first step of the porch. I didn't want to sit any closer because of the smell.

"They're good," I said.

He said he was glad.

I didn't say anything and neither did he for a while. I just watched my birds start coming out of their little house into the chicken run. They looked especially nice in the morning.

"Sara," he said, after a while. "Dude, I think I'm okay. I'm going to get up and go in the house to pull myself together. You should go see your birds now."

I didn't turn to look at him, because it seemed like he might need privacy.

"Okay," I said. And I went back to my chicken coop.

Mornings at Woefield are definitely nicer than they are at my house. Especially when Prudence got up and asked me to help her sell radishes at the farmers' market.

PRUDENCE

I admit that I wasn't as fresh as I'd have liked the day of the farmers' market. And I also admit that my wares weren't as comprehensive as some of the other vendors.' But I hoped that the sheer variety of my radishes, plus the added value of the radish recipes and informational flyers, would help make up for it.

Sara and I arrived at six-thirty to get set up. We'd have been there earlier, but I discovered that my Round Black Spanish and my Chinese Whites were barely developed. They had big tops and almost no roots. It was a bit of a blow as, according to the information on the seed packets, they should have been ready. Worse, even my Easter Eggs, Snow Belles and Champions were a bit . . . scrawny. They looked like little red worms clinging to the end of a plant. The only radishes that even looked like radishes were the Cherry Belles and the French Breakfast. I considered not pulling the other varieties, but the table would have been absolutely barren if I'd only had the two. I guess I didn't thin them enough or maybe the radish beds are too shady.

I scoured the raised beds for other crops I could bring, but all I could safely cut was a sprig or two of Italian flat-leaf parsley and a few stalks of baby swiss chard. I asked Sara whether we had enough eggs to sell and she said they'd only laid three the day before because of all the excitement and that we ate the rest at breakfast. She suggested I could sell some crafts. I told her I appreciated her suggestion but we only had an hour before the market and I was pretty sure most crafts, such as knitting and crocheting and making jam and so on, would take more time than that.

With no other options, I washed the twenty or so radishes and the small pile of extra radish greens and bundled them into a corner of the cooler. Sara looked inside and asked where the rest of the stuff was.

"This is it," I told her.

"But that's not very much," she said.

"Sara, we are just getting started. By the end of the season our table will be overflowing with fresh organic produce."

"Oh," she said. Then she found an egg carton and put the three fresh eggs in it and put that in the cooler.

I put two more empty coolers in the truck to give the impression of abundance. As we drove out of the yard I cast a somewhat longing look in Bertie's direction. I'm not saying I wanted to quickly butcher her, after all, old mutton is no one's idea of delicious, but maybe I could milk her or something. Then I looked toward Seth's window. Would it be weird to sell his old heavy metal records at the farmers' market?

In the end I took a deep breath and went with what we had.

When we got the market, which was held in a dirt parking lot beside the baseball diamond, I backed the truck in. That process took longer than it did for Sara and me to arrange the radishes and the three eggs. I left the two empty coolers in the back of the truck to suggest that I had a lot of other produce I would be bringing out when the time was right. Maybe people would think, when they saw our paltry display, that we were sold out?

We put the swiss chard and the parsley in water glasses flanking the small mound of radish greens and the five complete bundles of actual radishes. Sara ripped away most of the egg carton so it didn't look so empty. I fanned out the radish information at the front of the table. Sara wrote out the names of the varieties on stickers and put them on sticks that lay on the table. We couldn't attach them to actual bundles because then people might wonder where the China Rose and Icicles were. It would have been embarrassing to admit that all we had were French Breakfast and Cherry Belles.

All around us were trucks and table straining under the weight of mountains of baby potatoes, herbs, freezers full of meat, breads, baked goods, baby carrots. Worse, every table seemed to be heaped with beautiful radishes of all different types. The other vendors' radishes differed from ours in that there were large roots attached to the greens.

I pretended not to notice. Sara, however, was afflicted with the honesty of youth.

Sara

I felt sort of bad for Prudence. She tries really hard but that's not always enough. For example, I once spent two whole days on a poster for our Poultry Club bake sale and it didn't get chosen. Mary-Ellen Scottolini's did and I know for a fact that she barely spent half an hour on hers. She didn't even spell "poultry" right! Mr. Lymer chose hers as the winner because Mrs. Scottolini always wears low-cut shirts. Even Bethany knew it wasn't fair.

The other people selling stuff at the farmers' market were nice, except the lady with the fresh baked bread with stuff on it. She acted very competitive even though we had nothing to compete with. The other sellers waved and said hello and didn't say anything about our radishes, which didn't have hardly any radishes on them. The customers were meaner, though.

One lady who had a lot of hair on her face asked if we were joking and Prudence got this funny look that I think was supposed to be a smile. She tried to give the lady a recipe for pasta with radish greens. The lady asked Prudence what she was playing at and Prudence asked me to look after things while she went to "inspect the coolers." Then she stared into an empty cooler while the lady told her friend that the farmers' market was really going downhill.

That lady wasn't even the meanest one. This one man with a German accent brought over his whole family and picked up our whole display of radish greens and our three eggs and laughed and laughed and said things in German or maybe it was English that just sounded

German and was very rude. Prudence did her fake smile again.

The only good points were when a couple of ladies at the local food security booth came over and bought all of Prudence's radish recipes and radish fact pamphlets for five dollars and invited her to join their collective. Prudence's smile got real then. They were very nice ladies and I think they felt sorry for her like I did. The bad part was that then all we had were our radish greens and the miniature radishes, which Prudence called the "fetal radishes," and our eggs and people kept walking by and looking at us kind of quickly and then turning away. Prudence excused herself, saying she needed to take a walk and clear her head. She probably had a headache from staring into the empty coolers for so long. She'd been gone about five minutes when the nice vet came by and bought everything! Even the little leaves we had in glasses for decoration! He left us forty dollars! He told me not to tell Prudence he bought our stuff and I promised. He asked how Bertie was and I said she wasn't up when we left but I thought she was fine, since Earl takes very good care of her on the porch. And he sort of frowned and then laughed and told me to have a good day and to remember our deal.

When Prudence came back, I gave her the money and her face went a bit funny, like she was going to cry and she asked who bought the radishes and I said a customer. And she said, "Well, that's that then. I guess we can go."

We were putting away our table when the man who runs the market came by and asked if we'd be back next week and Prudence said she'd get in touch! Then she gave him some of her money. I'm excited because I really like the farmers' market.

Prudence

We were home from the market by nine-thirty. I wasted no time. It was clear to me that serious measures were required. We weren't going to be able to count on our produce to carry us for a while yet. As soon as I got the coolers washed and put away and prepared a snack for Sara, I headed for Earl's cabin. By the time I was halfway across the field I'd forgotten the embarrassment of the market. The morning was glorious—wisps of cloud made their way west across the lid of the sky. The grass was sparse, yes, but damp and deeply rooted beneath my feet. No little radish setback was going to take me down or dislodge me from this place. The field, the house, the fences. The air. The rocks that popped relentlessly from the bedrock below. It was all mine to keep or lose. I stopped for a moment and took a deep, calming breath.

I felt slightly giddy from lack of sleep and from the intensity of the market.

When I got to the porch, I peered over the barrier at the top of the steps. Bertie, still wearing the duct-tape booties, was lying on Earl's porch on a bed of hay and newspaper, munching contentedly. The menstrual absorbent pads were gone and the cuts were healing nicely. She looked more comfortable and she was certainly less embarrassing than she had been. I thought about Eustace and last night, and I gave my head a shake. I had to focus on the farm. On the future.

It would soon be time to move Bertie into the new enclosure, which Seth said was shaped like either a pile of fast-food vomit or a paramecium.

I'd promised everyone that we would put up proper fences and build a barn before winter, but I didn't have enough money and I knew when I made the promises I was not being entirely truthful. Lying had become habitual since I became a farmer. When I lifted my leg over the barrier that kept Bertie confined on the porch, she stared at me with those peculiar yellow eyes of hers with rectangular black irises.

That's when I noticed it. A guitar or maybe a banjo making lonely, country-sounding music. It sent a quiver running from the base of my spine into my scalp.

I hadn't had the best handle on Earl, at least until Sara told me about his brother and I looked up their history on Wikipedia. After all, Earl looked like a farmer and talked like a trucker and, at the risk of sounding rude, he had a tendency to wander around looking lost and irritated any time there was something to do. I had been beginning to doubt whether he actually knew much about farming. My uncle Harold wouldn't have known if Earl wasn't a good farmer because, as had become apparent, Uncle Harold never did any farming. I suspect that for Harold, the fact that Earl looked the part would have been enough.

The music grew louder, which is probably why Earl didn't hear me when I tripped climbing over the final piece of the barrier, which consisted of an old couch, two broken chairs that he'd taken from the porch on the big house and two lengths of frayed rope. The assemblage of furniture made it appear as though Bertie had barricaded herself up there.

Curiosity made me look in the window before I knocked on the door. The music was coming from Earl. He sat at the kitchen table, playing his banjo and singing. Keening, almost. A song so high and sweet that it made the breath catch in my throat. He was singing about sitting alone, too lonesome to cry, and then about water that rose high and a woman who left. A woman! Who left him!

Earl's fingers moved over the banjo in this way that made me think that maybe he wasn't the lifelong bachelor virgin I'd assumed.

A minute later the song was over and he'd moved into another song, this one faster. His fingers flew over the fret board. His head wobbled as he played, and he was singing sweet and clear.

It was like watching a great painter at work or reading a masterpiece. It was moving and startling and I knew that what I'd read online was true: Earl was an amazing musician from a famous musical family. And he lived on my farm!

When the song finished, I stepped to the side of the window so he wouldn't see me if he looked out. Then I waited five minutes before I knocked on the door to tell him about the house meeting.

EARL

First she told us she told the bank that she turned the place into a treatment center. I don't even know what in the high holy hell that is, but I sure as goddamn don't want no part of it. Then she says she's changed her mind and something about integrity and right livelihood and voodooists. I told her I didn't want nothing to do with voodooists and Prudence said not voodooists, Buddhists. To tell the truth, I couldn't figure out what the hell she was saying.

And Chubnuts was laying on the couch in the living room in his bathrobe, stinking like the worst rubbie you ever walked past in the city. He kept making these noises, like a sick heifer going into labor. Every time Prudence talked, he made one of them mooing noises. Them noises of his was enough to get on a deaf man's nerves.

Then there was the kid. I didn't even know if she should be listening. In a lot of ways, it was immoral, all Prudence's talk about rehabs. The kid was already more worried about morals than a TV preacher man. But the kid wasn't paying much attention. Prudence asked her to put the hen she was fooling with away after it crapped on the kitchen table. I'm having second thoughts about eating meals in that kitchen, I'll tell you. Between Chubnuts and them birds, you're as likely to catch bird flu as a full belly. Even the old man kept a better house than his niece.

I was thinking on that and wondering whether I might want to move up my plan to get the new camper and get the hell out when I realized they were all staring at me.

I asked what the hell they were all staring at.

Prudence said what did I think about her plan.

So I said, What plan? Because I was thinking on my camper and heading south and wasn't really paying attention.

A concert, she said. Now she'd really lost me.

What concert are you talking about? I wanted to know.

The kid was all excited and said because I'm famous. And my brother was on TV.

And I thought to myself, No goddamn way I'm going down that road. Prudence could stick that plan in her ear and give it a jerk.

That's when the kid's mother showed up and took a bad situation and made it worse.

Seth

Even in my extremely weakened condition, I was able to work up some sympathy for Mrs. Spratt. I saw her husband at the strawberry party when I first moved over here and a bigger douche bag would be hard to find.

Prudence was talking all sorts of nonsense about a concert. Some kind of hillbilly hoedown–type concept. She'd also said some highly offensive shit about me sobering up and how no one on the farm was going to "enable me" anymore because it was bad for all of us, but that everyone, even someone like me, deserved at least one more chance. Like we were on an episode of celebrity rehab without any celebrities.

She seemed to think Earl was going to be the big attraction at her concert. At that point I was pretty sure she'd lost her mind. She was never completely, you know, sane, what with the wanting to live on the scabby-ass farm and all, but the shit she was talking during this house meeting was like Britney at her baldest. I half expected her to step out for a second to shave her head or go to a gas station bathroom in her bare feet.

I tried to get things back on track by asking a few clarifying questions, but I was too sick. All I could do was groan to give her some sense of audience reaction. When I tried to speak, vomit surged up in my throat, so I kept it general.

Then the kid's mother showed up.

"Excuse me," I heard her say. "Am I interrupting?"

It was pretty clear she was. There were three people sitting around the kitchen table and I was listening hard from the living room. You could tell from the way my head was angled.

Mrs. Spratt stepped into the kitchen. She looked thrashed. Deeply, internally thrashed. Worse than me after the premiere of Harewood Technical's production of *Jesus Christ Superstar*. Sara's mom had on a blue cardigan and a blue flowered dress made out of some clingy nylon or rayon or something. Not clingy sexy, but clingy from static. She had on these terrible light brown not-quite-leather shoes. It was a horrible outfit, and I'm a person with virtually no standards. It was the outfit of a woman who has given up some time ago. Her face was pale and puffy *and* wrinkly, which is the worst combination and one of my biggest fears. Before I came here and started being force-fed health food, I used to eat a lot of carbs but I made of point of not worrying about MSG because I'd rather go with straight puff than wrinkly puff.

"Hi honey," she said to Sara.

The kid looked up and I couldn't tell you what was going on in her blank little face. Something complicated and too old by half.

"Hi Mom," she said.

Mrs. Spratt seemed to be trying to act normal, but you could see she was a short step from a total crack-up.

"Thanks so much for letting her here stay last night," she said.

I was like, oh shit. I hoped the kid hadn't seen me when I got home. I wasn't in very good shape. Not that I remember any of it. On the other hand, with an asshole father like hers, she's probably seen worse than a guy passed out in his own piss. Still, it wasn't the image of myself that I wanted to promote.

"It was our pleasure, Mrs. Spratt," said Prudence. And she meant it. She's pretty open-hearted. Plus, we all like the kid. She's very cool, for a kid, and she's the only one of us who has it half together. Of course, she'll lose that when she gets older.

Mrs. Spratt coughed into her hand in a weird-ass gesture. Her hand was all red, like she did a lot of housework without using gloves or Palmolive or anything.

"I need to go away for a couple of days. I know it's short notice, but could you keep Sara?"

Earl looked at Prudence and I looked at the kid and Prudence looked at Mrs. Spratt.

"Oh, of course. I mean, as long as . . ."

"Is that okay with you, honey?" asked Mrs. Spratt.

The kid nodded, solemn as a little judge at family court.

"Your dad might come by. If he does, just tell him I've gone to your aunt Steph's for a few days. Tell him I've made arrangements for you to stay here. So you can be closer to your birds."

"He won't come," said Sara.

Mrs. Spratt kept going like Sara hadn't spoken.

"I packed some things for you." She set down a small suitcase on the floor.

"I already have everything I need," said Sara.

"Thank you so much," said Mrs. Spratt, looking from Prudence to Earl to me, anywhere but at Sara, as she backed out of the kitchen.

And a minute later she was gone and the kid was stone and I felt so bad for her that it even overwhelmed my hangover. Somewhat.

Sara

When my mom came to the farm, it was embarrassing but also good because I think Prudence and Earl were about to have an argument because Prudence said Earl was a banjo player and he got insulted. I can understand that. If I played an instrument, I'd probably want it to be the drums. Plus, it's probably embarrassing to be so old and play music.

Anyway, after my mom came and asked if I could stay for longer, everyone was really quiet and talked in that low way that people do when something bad has happened and they don't want things to get worse. And that was okay too, because living with my parents has made me kind of sensitive to sudden noises. I didn't hug my mom good-bye because we were in public and that probably would have made it worse. But I did try to show her with my eyes that I was really glad that I got to stay at Woefield instead of with Bethany.

After she left, Prudence asked if anyone wanted breakfast, just like at a real farm. We all did. When she put the pancakes and eggs on the table, Seth made a noise in his throat and got up **and** ran to the bath-room. But pretty soon he came back.

It was a good breakfast.

Later, Seth said he'd help me practice with my chickens. The Junior Poultry Show was coming up. I was pretty excited. I guess it's true when they say that kids are resilient. I think I might be. Also, it sort of seemed like I might have got left behind. But I was okay with it.

EARL

I'll say one thing for that girl. She can fry an egg and make a decent hotcake. No meat, of course. She's not like one of them chefs on the shows with all the lights and counters. Lunch and dinner's almost always brown mush with greens I never saw before, but even that's not bad once you get used to it. I felt better than I did when the old man and me lived on takeout and tinned beans.

The breakfast was almost good enough that I could forget that damned fool idea of hers. Concert. Jesus Christ. I ain't played in front of nobody since I left the band when I was seventeen years old. Sure, I still play some, but only when there's nothing on TV. The old man used to spend hours listening. I figured I might as well play for him since we weren't doing nothing anyway.

Anyhow, at least now we had some idea why the kid was here. That mother of hers was a sad sight, I'll tell you. She must be in some kind of tough shape if she thinks this is the right place to leave a kid. Might as well dump her off outside the goddamn casino for all the moral guidance she'll get around here. With Chubnuts running around and passing out all over the place and Prudence, well, she barely has as much sense as those chickens out there. And me, I got no kid experience at all.

Still, I figured if we were going to be looking after her for the time being, we better get this place straightened around. I had my camper-buying plan, but I guessed that could wait. That breakfast was a hell of a good start. I wasn't going to need to eat again until lunch.

Also, I knew I'd be a damned fool to walk away from the place. Not when I was due ten percent of the proceeds of the sale if Prudence ever sold it. To be real honest, I figured she'd forget about the concert idea. She's always going in twenty different directions. Who the hell was going to go to a concert to hear me play?

Prudence

I wouldn't say Earl was into it, precisely, but he didn't refuse. Well, he said, "No goddamn way" and "Jesus Christ Almighty, what the hell are you talking about now?" as well as "That's the stupidest idea I ever heard." But he didn't say he'd leave and take his banjo with him. So I took that as a yes. I was sure he'd become more enthusiastic when he got used to the idea and once he realized that I was going to reunite him with his brother.

My idea was that one reasonably successful concert could get us through the winter and maybe pay for some sort of a barn and more livestock, which somewhat ironically is what you need to get the grass to grow. The more animals eat your grass, the better it grows and the more productive your farm.

After the mix-up with Eustace, I realized that I was going to have to be more honest. No more lying, even in aid of a worthy goal, such as keeping the farm going. I know I should have fired Seth, but I couldn't help feel that my lack of clarity about his problem hadn't helped. I decided to give him one more chance.

Here's what I was thinking. It was okay for our farm to be small. It only had to support us, at least at first. Small is beautiful is one of the main principles of the back to the land movement. But the thing that couldn't be too small was our bluegrass concert. I knew that large concerts were lucrative because I once read an article that said that most successful musicians make most of their money on touring rather than from music sales. Some of the big musicians, like Madonna and the Rolling Stones, make millions.

Of course, I was aware that Earl is no Madonna, but I figured if I could get his brother to come, we'd have a shot at a real event with several hundred people. That was my theory, at least.

During the first few minutes of the house meeting, Seth kept his eyes squeezed shut and pretended to be asleep in the living room. I carried a small ice cream pail over and put it beside him in case he needed to be sick. I didn't want him throwing up on the coffee table because that would have gotten the meeting off on the wrong foot.

Back in the kitchen I laid the situation out in a way I thought everyone could understand.

"I called us all here this morning because there are things we need to discuss," I said, forcefully but reasonably. "We need to clear the air. Make some changes. As you know, I am new to farming. Living off the land. Whatever you want to call it. I have always had the purest of intentions, but it's possible that my methods haven't been the best."

"Prudence, sorry man, but I'm dying here," said Seth, from the living room. "Can you move it along? If you're going to fire me can you do it quick?"

My spine straightened.

"Seth, your condition goes exactly to the heart of what I'm talking about. It was a mistake to tell the bank this was a treatment center. It wasn't honest, and more importantly, it wasn't fair to you."

He peered out from eyes that looked like two fertilized raw eggs. I was glad when he shut them again.

"I want to clear things up. Right livelihood, as the Buddhists call it, is all-encompassing," I said. "If we're going to make a go of this, we're going to have to do it honestly."

"Ah, Jesus," grumbled Earl.

But Sara was nodding. I doubt she had any idea what I was talking about. But that was okay. She was on my side. I would take any support I could get.

"I want this farm to survive. In order to do that, the people on it need to be nurtured and so does the land. Things are coming along. The raised beds are going gangbusters now. Soon we'll have enough chard and other produce to go back to the farmers' market with our heads held high. I'm going to clear the situation up with the bank as soon as possible. But in the meantime, Seth, you have a problem and you need to deal with it. You need to get some help, real help, or you will have to move out."

His raw egg eyes flew open at this news.

"We won't continue enabling you. From now on, this is a clean and sober farm as far as you are concerned. Our focus is going to be on farming. And music."

I turned to Earl.

"This brings me to my next point. Earl "

He turned to me, his head cocked on his wattled old neck, and for a moment I lost my nerve and found myself patting my mug of coffee.

"You are a musician," I said. Not a question. A statement of fact.

He stared at me.

"A terrific musician. I know because I've looked you up online."

Sara looked from me to Earl. Seth's hideous eyes were open and he was staring at us.

"But you are not a very good farm foreman."

Before Earl could swear or protest, I continued.

"We need to make some money to make the first payments on this farm and to get the place going. And with all of us, except perhaps Sara, being inexperienced at actual farming, we are going to have do it through non-conventional but legal and ethical means."

I had their attention.

"We're going to put on a bluegrass festival in July. Featuring you and your banjo, Earl. We're going to invite people from all over the island. All over Canada and the US. Maybe even Japan. We'll invite great musicians to back you up. The concert will make enough money for us to get our grass farm off the ground. That and my writing lessons."

"Grass farm? You think a grow-op is right livelihood?" said Seth, struggling to keep up.

"I mean actual grass," I told him.

Earl told me I was full of shit and no goddamn way. But he didn't get up and leave. Seth said this would be just like Woodstock only with no good bands, no offense, and he hoped there wouldn't be as many naked hippies because he had a weak stomach. Then Sara's mom showed up. And after that I made breakfast and told them all to leave it to me.

So really, it went well.

Seth

I was barely well enough to sit upright, so I was proud of myself for being of service to the kid at all. She needed help. I mean, there was the thing with her parents, which was extremely social services and all. Then there were all her crazy ideas about end times and the Bible and so on. Someone really did a number on that kid's head. At least I had rock and roll when I was growing up. All she's got is chickens.

Here's the deal. Her best bird, Alec Baldwin, has some flaws, which she thinks are going to disqualify him from the upcoming poultry competition. I didn't spend most of three years writing about celebrities and rock musicians without figuring out that it's the flaws make the star. The more damaged a person is, the more likely they are to succeed. I've even worked out a mathematical equation for it. The whole celebrity worship dynamic is composed of one part envy, one part desire and one part sheer contempt. A star has to have charisma and total self-involvement, both of which that black bastard rooster with the white floppy feathers on his head had to burn.

"But Seth," Sara said, when I tried to tell her for the eighth time that Alec Baldwin should be the one to front the band, so to speak, "he's got white feathers coming in."

"So we dye them," I said, which was a little assy of me, seeing as how I didn't know whether feathers would take dye. "Or maybe we could just color them with a felt pen. There's nothing wrong with assisting nature when it comes to beauty. Just ask anyone working in the porn industry."

"It's cheating," said Sara. "Even if you're selling used stuff."

"Sara, honey. You're referring to *pawn*. Porn is selling used people. Anyway, you're looking at this all wrong," I told her. Although in truth she was looking at it just about right. Much as I'm a competitive person, I was also a hungover one and my judgment was possibly impaired. There was a chance that I was permanently brain damaged.

"It's not fair," said Sara.

For a kid she can be pretty relentless.

"You tell him, Sara."

I turned around and saw a tall guy standing on the first step of the porch. He looked sort of familiar. Then again, after I've been on a tear, even my own mother seems only sort of familiar.

"Can I help you?" I asked. It seemed like he was a friend of Sara's. Probably a cousin or something, stopping by.

"Hi, Dr. Eustace," she said.

I took another look at him. Then it came to me. Outdoorsy, checked shirt with the sleeves rolled at the forearms. Biceps straining the fabric. Probably a guy who could give a real gun show if he was in the mood. He was Prudence's date from the night before. Why did he have to look like *that*?

All at once Phil was prowling around my belly again, looking to floss his teeth on a shred of my stomach lining.

"How are you doing today?" the guy asked me, all sincere and concerned.

I was acutely conscious of how red my eyes were and of the puffy, yellowish look of my skin, which is caused by the sugars in booze and by the fattening effect of shame. I told myself to push through it, even though it would have been easier if I had a drink or two or some decent narcotics. Then I remembered that the guy was a veterinarian. He probably had narcotics up the ass in his truck. Was there any way to get in there without him noticing?

"That good, eh?" he said. I realized I'd forgotten to answer him and was just staring at him, basically slack-jawed with envy and self-loathing.

"Prudence is inside."

"I'm here to see you," he said.

I'd been using a piece of doweling to push Alec Baldwin's reluctant little rooster butt down the "runway," which was actually an old door we'd laid over two chairs. The resistant little bastard kept stopping halfway. Sara didn't have the fortitude to keep him moving. I'd been telling her to tell him to "bring it" the way Tyra does her Top Models. Then I showed her, maneuvering him down the door using an advanced dowel technique that many a hockey player would have envied. When the big vet said he was there to see me, the stick clattered to the ground and I had to fight not to scream with pain at the noise.

Sara grabbed Alec off the table and I bent to get the stick, and whacked my battered, brain-damaged head on the door.

"Fuck," I said, grabbing my forehead, which I could see was bleeding a little when I pulled my hand away.

Sara looked from me to the vet. She may be young, but I'm fairly sure she noticed the contrast between us.

"Your birds are looking good, Sara. You bringing them to the fair on the weekend?" he asked. I hated that he knew about Sara's fair. And that he was better looking than me and probably never got his guts chewed out by a hangover more powerful than a thousand dragons and had never fallen down with his pants around his ankles while trying to serenade a drama teacher.

Sara nodded.

"You going to show your birds?'

Another nod.

"Good for you. Look, I want to talk to Seth here about something. You mind giving us a few minutes?"

He didn't talk to her like she was a little kid. He didn't disrespect her or condescend. To tell you the truth, I even felt sort of flattered that he knew my name. Good-looking people get away with murder.

Sara picked up Alec and said she was going to practice over near the coop. And I said, "Sure, sounds good," trying to sound like I was some high-level chicken show coach or something.

The guy, who was pretty buff as well as tall, came over and sat down across the door from me. There was this intensity to him, a clarity. He was seriously handsome. In metal terms, he made me feel like Lemmy standing next to Bret Michaels circa 1989, only the big guy was less skeezy than Michaels and I was several orders of magnitude less cool than Lemmy. When you spend all day, every day, on the Internet you develop an image of yourself in relation to the world. You know what I mean? It's like your looks or lack of them are manageable. Because you focus on other people and no one can see you and if you make the odd crack about yourself, well, that's just you being human and relatable. But when you get confronted by a demigod with an advanced degree in old jeans, well that kind of fuckery plays hell with the whole construction.

I went to run my hand through my hair, but realized I was doing it in an "I wish my hair was like yours" way, so I stopped. Plus I had on a hat and I hadn't washed my hair for a while. Instead I put my hands between my legs so he wouldn't see them shake.

"You feeling better?" he asked.

"Sure," I said. I wasn't about to get into it. I had just started to feel almost like I was going to make it through the aftermath. No way was I about to start dissecting my feelings. That was a whole swamp full of alligators and pythons right there.

"I couldn't help but notice that you were a bit shitfaced last night."

"Sherlock fucking Holmes, at your service," I muttered, and then felt bad.

The guy soldiered on and it occurred to me that Prudence might have hired him. Or he was from some religious group. Either way, I decided to stonewall him to get the visit over as soon as possible.

"It doesn't have to be like this," he said.

I was on the verge of making a crack about being on the porch, pushing a chicken around with a piece of doweling, but I didn't. I didn't say anything.

"You've heard of AA, right?" he said.

Fuck me. I should have known. Although, to be completely honest, most of what I know about the whole self-help thing I learned from

TV, like when Dexter landed himself a crazy bitch sponsor at an NA meeting and that guy on one of those FBI shows had to go to AA after he got shot and turned into a total lush and a pill head. My parents talked about AA sometimes like it was exactly the thing you wanted to avoid, because if you went there you had to quit drinking and that would be the worst possible thing that could happen to a successful drinking career.

I was weirded out that AA had sent their best-looking ambassador to get me. It was like getting recruited to Scientology by Tom Cruise or to the Jehovah's Witnesses by Prince or something.

I cleared my throat.

"If you want to keep drinking it's your business," he said. "If you want to stop, there's help." Just like on the late-night TV spot. Only he seemed sort of embarrassed as he said it.

"Prudence ask you to talk to me?"

He frowned. "No. I saw you, drew my own conclusions. This has nothing to do with Prudence. I just thought I'd put it out there for you. Someone did the same for me."

This bastard was in a self-help program? For what? Square-jawed, cleft-chin sufferers? Handsome Bastards Anonymous?

"So what, you want me to go to some meeting? Join a club? Make a vow?"

"If you feel like things are getting out of hand, I'll take you to a meeting. You don't have to be a fuckup your whole life. Trust me. If I can pull it together . . ."

The crazy thing is I believed him. Partly because I could see he wasn't enjoying saying all this to me.

I got this sudden, clear as a police siren on Sunday morning image of Prudence pulling off my piss-soaked jeans as I lay on the porch. I thought of the kid this morning, looking at me the way you'd look at someone who was dying. Like I was Ivan Ilyich from that Russian story and Sara was the farm boy. Oh, I was lost, all right. And right there the shaky little foundations I'd tried to rebuild around myself in the past couple of hours fell apart in a heap of busted nails and splintered lumber.

"So if I wanted to go to a meeting, what time would we have to go?" I asked him, like I was very busy. I might have been willing to try something new, but I didn't want the guy thinking I was free all the time.

Sara

Things sure changed after I started staying here. For one thing, everyone was very busy. Seth started going out with Dr. Eustace every night. I wished I could go with them because it seemed like they had really good talks. If I wasn't into leadership, which Mr. Lymer says means minding your own business except when you are asked for your opinion, I'd have definitely wanted to listen in.

Earl was building a platform out in the field, with a back wall and a roof that Prudence said was going to be the bandstand. Seth was helping and Prudence hired a few other people, too, like the nice man who drives a cab and one of the writers that she teaches. Personally, I thought Prudence should get people to work on a barn, but Prudence said that's going to come after the festival. Earl was hardly talking, even to swear.

I think Prudence is one of the busiest people who ever lived. Probably only God and Jesus and the devil are more busy than Prudence. When she wasn't telling Earl what to do, she was on the phone or she was walking all over the property saying how this area is going to be camping and this area over here is going to be parking during the festival and I couldn't tell how she was deciding because the two areas looked exactly the same. Seth kept warning her about mud pits full of hippies.

I think everyone enjoyed it when the reporter came and started asking questions, even though he was mostly just interested in Earl. I could tell he was disappointed that I didn't have more stories about him, but he tried to hide it and that was nice. In addition, I could tell that the reporter was getting interested in my chickens. Everyone does, eventually. He said he wished he could come to the fair with us so he could take photos for his magazine. He said his editor would like the "local color." I told him we'd tell him all about it when we got back.

To get ready, I had to give the frizzles two baths. White chickens are a lot of work to prepare. I didn't know that when I bought them or I might have chosen to get red ones instead. You have to dip the white ones in this bluing stuff and let them dry. Then you have to do it again. It's good that Prudence is letting me keep them on the porch because they'd just get dirty again if they went in the coop.

Almost all of the animals here live on porches. I think that makes us unique. I hope the reporter mentions that in his article.

Earl

I was damned happy to get off the farm to go with the kid to her poultry show, although I might not have said that at the time. I'd been working my tail off ever since Prudence started up with all that shit about having a concert and needing a bandstand and ticket booth and whatnot. I figured nothing would come of it. Even when that reporter feller showed up and started hanging around the place, asking questions about me and Merle and the High Lonesome Boys, I didn't think much of it. I figured he was making it up about that magazine of his. *Bluegrass Revival* sounds like it'd have about four goddamn readers. I was surprised as hell when he showed me a copy. We had so many people hanging around the place doing Christ only knows what one more didn't make a frog's hair worth of difference.

Anyway, it's too bad he had to go do a conference call with his editor or he'd have seen that they put on a good fair down there. Not many places do anymore. A lot of fairs have developed a—what do you call it—dependence on rides run by all them tattooed carnie buggers, look like goddamn criminals. I would have made sure to go with the kid no matter what, knowing them bastards was around. But this fair had some good stuff too.

Course, everything was a cock-up from the start. First, Chubnuts was having one of his days. Ever since he give up the bottle, he's been kind of funny. Not down, like you'd expect. Sorta chatty-like. Talking all kinds of personal business that a person doesn't want to hear unless it's on TV. It was like Chubnuts, who was looking a hell of a lot better, specially since he trimmed that hair of his and started washing it regular, was taking *his* prize chickens to the fair. He couldn't shut up or calm down and he must have changed his goddamn clothes three times. First he put on them tight jeans, don't know how he gets his feet into them, then the white track pants with the racing stripes at the sides that are too long and drag on the ground. Like those were his Sunday-go-to-meeting pants. Then back into jeans, only these ones were black and tighter than a banker's fist.

The kid though, she was calm, packing up her birds into their cages, putting the bedsheet over them so the birds wouldn't get too worked up. I helped her put them in the back of the truck and then she went and sat on the porch steps. Considering what she's got for parents, that girl is something else. Her old lady called every day at 4:00 p.m. She talked to the kid for five or ten minutes. Kid hardly said a word. Just yes, no. Nods. Even I could hear her mother crying on the other end.

Then her mother would ask the kid to put Prudence on the phone and Prudence would be stuck there for a good thirty minutes.

It was no situation for a little kid.

I figure the more people who aren't crying around her the better. Especially in a stressful situation like a poultry show.

We had to wait around for a good hour or more, until Chubnuts picked his clothes and put his perfume on and got the red snot rag tied around his head just right. He came out dragging this big bag of I don't know what all. Like a traveling hairdresser, with fancy brushes and rags and a blow dryer. He said it was in case one of the birds stepped in a water dish and needed to be dried.

I told him that if he put a dryer on one of them hens she was likely to die of a conniption fit, and he told me that I don't understand the cutthroat world of competitive poultry. And he might have had a point there.

Then he said we had to stop and pick up his sponsor. And Prudence said to Sara, I didn't know you got a sponsor for the show. And Chubnuts says, no he means *his* sponsor.

So I said to him, What the hell you need a sponsor for? You don't even have birds entered. Where were they going to advertise? And he told us he didn't mean a commercial sponsor, he meant a spiritual sponsor.

This seemed to mean something to Prudence because she shut right up.

So I said, We're going and I can't fit no one else in the truck and whoever wants to come better get in the truck now.

The kid and Prudence climbed in and Chubnuts said he was going to wait for his spiritual sponsor to pick him up because he needed to talk to him.

We were driving away and Chubnuts was still talking, saying, Do you think Robert Downey or Steven Tyler go to events without their sponsors? Then he started telling Sara that he'd be right behind her and Don't worry and Don't let Earl anywhere near Alec Baldwin!

We're on the road about five minutes and the kid said, I like Seth. He always makes me feel more confident.

See what I mean? Kids is a goddamn mystery.

PRUDENCE

My favorite part of the Cedar Agricultural Fair was the animals, in particular the sheep. They took my breath away. Bertie had almost entirely recovered from her hoof trim and shearing. The cuts had healed nicely and she seemed in better spirits because I think she liked living on Earl's porch. We'd made that her semi-permanent home because she pushed her way under the strands of the portable corral as soon as we put her into it and she went straight back up Earl's stairs. But as I looked around that fair, I had to admit that she was no show sheep, even on her best day.

The sheep at the fair were spotlessly white and soft and fluffy—like summer clouds. And so docile! They allowed their owners to lead them around without any argument at all. No kicking, no bleating, no trying to pull on the rope and run away. They were half a step away from being pillows.

I helped Earl carry the cages to the chicken building but left quickly. It was smelly and noisy, even first thing in the morning and only a quarter full. I told Sara that Earl would look after her and that I had to go and see some people. This was somewhat true. It was also true that I was avoiding Eustace, which was an odd experience because I'd never avoided anyone before. I'd never had to. My feelings were all mixed up. Sure, I'd lied to him, but it certainly wasn't out of malice or anything like that. A small misdirection aimed at a bank is hardly a capital crime! Minor white lies barely count. To be honest, considering the greed of the banking industry, I think we should be applauded.

I considered apologizing, but decided not to. Apologizing muddies the waters, in my experience.

Anyway, my focus at the fair was on promoting the concert. I'd never put on a concert before, so I was glad to have Travis, the music journalist, as a resource. My research told me that bluegrass fans travel extensively to attend jamborees and festivals, often in their RVs and campers, but until I talked to Travis I don't think I quite understood how popular bluegrass is. Dozens, if not hundreds, of musicians and bands play at festivals year round, and a lot of events have bluegrass workshops where aspiring players can learn to yodel and play banjo and what have you. It's a huge and growing movement and we were going to be a part of it!

I couldn't find a how-to guide for putting on a concert but was relieved to learn from Travis that all we really needed was a place for camping, a place for the bands to play, another for workshops, a beer garden, as well as microphones, amplifiers and speakers, contracts and insurance. It was just fabulous of Travis to offer to help with everything, especially given the fact that he was supposed to be working on his article about Earl.

With the bandstand nearly complete, and the posters and flyers that Seth designed already printed and the website up, I was really quite excited about our progress. I was sure there was no better place to advertise a bluegrass concert than an agricultural fair.

As I'd mentioned to Travis when he first arrived, I'd written to Earl's brother, Merle, or at least his management company, right away, but hadn't heard back yet. I was convinced he'd come. That's why it was fine that I advertised him as our special guest on the flyers and posters. It's important to be confident and optimistic when putting together any sort of party or gathering.

Seth

Although a person might not be able to tell from my personal history, I have a competitive streak. I just kept it hidden until the chicken show. I didn't do that well at school and my blogs weren't the most popular or whatever, but sometimes I think that's because I didn't want my hard-driving aspect to get out of hand. Enough shit in my life was out of control, which was something I learned from hanging out with Eustace. I also learned that I have a superabundance of character defects. That's the technical term for the unpleasant parts of yourself that cause your life to suck.

I don't want to go into a lot of detail, but I found out that I'm basically crippled by character defects. Seriously. When people talk about their defects in meetings, even the hardcore ex-cons and people like that, I turn into a bobblehead. That's how much I relate. No one has mentioned a defect that I do not have. You'd think there'd be at least one. But not so far.

What I'm trying to say is that extreme competitiveness is something I have to watch. I probably used to try and drink it away, like I did everything else, but I'm not going that way anymore. I'm like the Nuge now. Mr. Clean.

That said, I had to remind myself not to bug out when I got to the fairgrounds and saw all those birds Sara and Alec would be competing against.

Fuck me, I thought. We've got some serious competition here.

I was already kind of disappointed that Eustace bailed on me. He had an emergency to attend to. Some cow went through a fence and cut herself open from shoulder to hip and Eustace had to go and sew her up. I don't want to be a selfish prick (another character defect), but he did fucking promise.

He told me I'd be fine on my own for a couple of hours, which kind of pissed me off because it was so condescending, but then I thought about it. It turns out that in addition to being ambitious and selfish, I'm also thin-skinned. In some ways, it can be liberating to be sober. It can also be a downer of the highest order to find out all the shit that is wrong with you.

So I put the brave face on it, another completely new experience, and I fucked off to the fair by myself. I do know how to drive. Got my license when I was sixteen, before everything went down with the drama teacher and the play and whatnot and I decided to go into seclusion. I just hadn't driven for a few years.

I took the old Buick that had been sitting off to the side of the house. Prudence had put insurance on it the week before, just in case we had an emergency and the truck was gone. No one had been brave enough to try and drive the car. No wonder. When Prudence's uncle crashed it last time, he screwed up the U-joint so the car drove like a suicidal steer. When I pulled out of the driveway and turned right, I saw my mom and Bobby sitting on the porch. I tried to wave, all cool-like, but the car headed straight for the ditch. I had to wrestle it to make the corner. It surprised them so much that Bobby nearly got up. I'm pretty sure my mom looked proud when I got the car back in my lane, but I couldn't slow down long enough to check. The whole drive was an epic battle to keep the car from plowing into a ditch or the median or the oncoming traffic. Good thing the fair was only about ten minutes away.

Once I got there, it was hard as hell to find a place to park and I couldn't make the parking attendants or assistants understand that I wasn't a regular fairgoer, that I was closer to a competitor.

"Support person," I told the big, pink-faced guy in the reflective vest.

"Huh?" he said.

"Almost like a competitor. But not quite. I need to park near the facility."

I didn't want to get sent on some long goddamn walk. My chicken grooming assistant's bag was heavy and another one of my defects is that I'm extremely lazy.

"Can I see your badge?"

I tried to keep my temper under control, even though a short fuse is another problem of mine.

"I don't have one," I said.

Then I made him wait for a few seconds while I repeated the serenity prayer to myself several times. I guess it worked because I calmed down before I called him a useless piece of shit.

Even so, the guy parked me as far as possible from the chicken exhibit hall. As a result my arms were about to fall off when I finally got to the gates and I didn't even get a break on my ticket price.

I'd never really seen a large-scale poultry operation before. Obviously, I'd read about those battery farms or whatever you call them where chickens have to live about ten to a cage and get their beaks cut off and are massively depressed before they get shipped off to KFC to be turned into family packs and strips. But even that foreshadowing didn't prepare me for the epic filth and stench of a chicken show barn. I can't comprehend how bad an actual factory farm would be. I mean, where none of the birds have been bathed recently, like all the ones here. These were the finest specimens the chicken world had to offer and still they reeked like a rancid pile of dead dogs on a hot day.

I found Sara standing near her frizzles. Her best hen was in one cage and the frizzle cockerel was down the row a bit in his own cage. I'd created these extremely cool signs for the cages based on the logo of that TV show, *So You Think You Can Dance,* only our signs read, *So You Think You're the Best Frizzle?* Over in the Polish non-bearded area, Alec Baldwin's sign looked like the one for *Inside the Actor's Studio,* which I thought was hilarious but no one got. I find that as I get healthier, I'm starting to leave a lot of people behind, intellectually or at least comedically.

You might wonder how I felt about the event in the first place because of my history and all. You seriously have no idea. Going into a crowd of people for me was like walking into a burning building wearing plastic pants. But since I'd been at Woefield, I'd been doing so much of it that I was getting used to the melting-pants feeling. After all, for the past little while Prudence had the place swarming with people from morning to night. Farmers coming by to give her advice, people who heard she had herbs and leafy greens for sale, her writing students, people helping get ready for the concert, and total random wanderers. Eustace told me that people don't care about me as much as I think they do and that going out in spite of my fear was the "rock and roll thing to do." He was trying to relate to me on my own level, which I appreciated even though his encouragement was somewhat lame. Truthfully, the fair was the place I was most likely to see people who'd been at the school the night of my big performance. But I was sick of hiding. So what if I'm the local pants-down drunk? If there was anything I'd learned since I'd been hanging with Eustace and going to those meetings, it was that I'm not the only one.

Anyway, when I was in the poultry barn, I resisted the urge to hold my nose and I made a big point of smiling at Sara when I saw her. One of the key principles of staying sober is helping others. Eustace told me that's how I could "get out of myself." Sounded like so much bullshit to me. I told him that I think about other people all day, every day, on my website and in my head and he said that talking trash about celebrities and musicians doesn't count and neither do paranoid revenge fantasies. Then he told me to look up all these quotes about gossip and character assassination in the Big Book and the Twelve by Twelve, which are like the bible and psalms of AA, even though it's not supposed to be a religious program or whatever. I hadn't quite gotten around to reading either of them because their nicknames freak me out a bit. The Big Book made me think of a very, very simple religion for reluctant readers or something.

Still, I tried the serenity prayer, as well as being helpful and thinking about other people, and Eustace was right. It worked. It was a relief to think about someone else for a while. For instance, when I saw Sara in the show barn she had this worried look on her face.

"I'm here," I told her, thinking that would calm her down from the pressure of the competition.

She looked from side to side, like she was about to steal something.

"It's rubbing off," she said, speaking through the side of her mouth.

"What's rubbing off?"

"The Magic Marker. On Alec. Even Bethany noticed."

"Don't these people have anything better to do than stare at your chicken's ass?" I asked.

"We cheated. I could go to hell."

"Come on Sara, don't you mean *we* could go to hell?" I said, trying to lighten things up.

She gave me a look and I realized that in her mind, my going to hell was a foregone conclusion.

The thing is, she wasn't kidding. She was always talking about hell and how she was going to end up there for one thing and another when the Rapture came. I don't know who filled her head with that bullshit, but if I find whoever it is I might take a break from controlling my anger defect of character and practicing "restraint of tongue and pen."

"You didn't cheat. You think women who wear lipstick are cheating? Elvis Presley put a sock in his underpants. What about women who get breast implants? What about them?"

A man next to us who was helping his kid write a sign to put on their little black bantam chicken's cage gave me a look. Judgmental prick.

"I'm talking about *reconstructive* breast surgery," I said, a little louder.

Sara took a step away from the kid and his father so they wouldn't overhear.

"Those people are cheating," she whispered. She looked stricken. "Just like us."

"We didn't cheat. We *enhanced*. Huge difference."

"We could get disqualified," she said.

"Don't worry. I'll take care of it. Where's Alec Baldwin?"

Her little face still white and pinched with worry, she led me down the row of cages, which ran the length of the long, narrow building, and over a couple of rows to where the larger birds were housed.

The back and sides of Alec Baldwin's cage were still draped with a sheet so that only the front was open. Earl stood in front of the cage beside a girl about Sara's age. The kid's stare was a little bit fixed and her mouth hung open slightly.

"Hi, Sara!" she said, breaking into this big smile when she saw us.

"Hi, Bethany," said Sara.

"Mr. Lymer came by. He wanted to know why there's still a sheet on your cage."

Sara looked at me. I looked at Earl. Earl looked up into the rafters.

"Tell Mr. Lymer the bird's kind of high strung," I said. "We're acclimatizing him slowly or whatever."

"Ha, ha! Acclimatizing," said Bethany. "I never knew that word before."

"Yeah. It's a big one. I bet it's new to Earl, too. Look, Bethany, we've got to do some personal grooming with Alec. So you should probably find your parents. Or check on your own birds. Okay?"

"I thought I saw some white on his feathers," said Bethany, who seems like she might be one of those savants you hear about who are able to memorize the New York City subway system, only her uncanny ability was detecting pigment changes in chicken feathers.

"God, no. Sara would never bring a bird with illegal white feathers to a show."

Bethany stared at me, mouth slightly ajar. "Did you just take the Lord's name?"

"Yes, but then I gave it back to him," I said.

I turned to Earl. "Can you help Bethany find her . . . people?"

"Jesus," he muttered. Which caused Bethany to look at him, equally shocked.

"You just took the Lord's name too!" she said, breathlessly.

In answer, he sighed and stumped off down the row of cages toward the front door and she followed.

"Keep a watch on things," I told Sara. "I'm going in."

I looked from side to side and then reached in and pulled out Alec. He went to jab his beak into my wrist, but I gave him a little squeeze to remind him who was boss. I handed him to Sara, who arranged him so that his head was tucked under her armpit. I could see the white ends on his feathers where the black marker had worn off.

"Shit," I said.

"We should have pulled them," said Sara. "That's the only cure for white feathers."

"I was worried it would make his ass feathering look less full," I said. "So let's pull them now."

"He'll get a bald spot."

"Let me talk to him," I said.

She turned the rooster to face me. His eyes were round and shiny and totally unconcerned under his big head of white feathers.

"Buddy," I said, "this is your fault."

Alec Baldwin blinked in that crazy, upside-down eyelid way chickens do.

"We need to take him outside," I told her.

She nodded and we walked fast back the way we'd come, out the front door and around the narrow alley between the poultry shed and the next building. People were everywhere, man. It was super stressful. Like being in *The Bourne Identity* or something.

Once we were out of sight in the passageway between the two buildings, I told Sara to turn him around again and hold him tight.

I got the tweezers ready.

I pulled out the first white feather and Alec gave a muffled squawk and tried to flap his wings, but Sara held him so he couldn't.

"It's okay, buddy," I said, and went in to pluck another of the offending white feathers.

I saw somebody walking past the gap between the buildings pause and I realized that from a distance what we were doing probably looked suspicious.

"Is your bird all right, little girl?" I asked loudly. Then I whispered, "Hold him so people don't think I'm doing something weird to you."

"My bird's okay!" Sara shouted. She's a pretty cool little cat, even if she does think about hell too much.

The dude who'd paused kept going.

I put my arm out to shield us from view and looked real close at Alec's rear end.

"It definitely looks plucked. Just one feather and it's less full."

"What are we going to do?"

She sounded like she was about to cry.

"We're going to put a little more marker on the white ones instead of pulling them. No one will notice."

I took the Magic Marker out of my pocket and removed the cap. The smell of the ink filled my nose. I'd just reblacked the white feathers when I heard him.

"You damned pervert!" he said.

EARL

The kid belonged to a pair of them Bible thumpers from out Cassidy way. I seen them or their type before, holding signs outside the liquor store and the doctor's office. Car crashes and dead babies. They like to get in other people's business, those ones.

They're part of that crowd parks their minivans at eight o'clock Sunday morning outside that New Church of Christ off the highway. Parking lot's still full at five. I guess they must serve lunch at that place. Either that or the whole lot of them are tough as hell about going without food. Enough righteous god anger will do that.

Oh, thank you so much, said the lady, who had on a pink dress and them sandals that showed her nylons poking out at the toes. It was hot as a Florida whore's snatch out, even though it was only early summer. You'd think she'd have left off the pantyhose. But I ain't been to church for a long time and things might have got more conservative since then.

The man nodded at me and called me sir by way of saying hello. He was in a suit. Him and his wife were standing in front of a cage of Rhode Island Reds. Nice-looking birds.

The kid introduced me. She said, This is Earl, he's Sara's friend.

The lady leaned in close and asked, How is Sara? She sounded kind of whispery, like we were sharing a big secret.

I told her Sara was fine. Them type of people appreciate cheerfulness.

The lady said, Ooooh, like that was a new one on her.

The man said, Poor kid. No guidance.

He was wrong there. Little Sara has some guidance. It's just piss-poor guidance for the most part.

I nodded and headed to the concession booth to get a coffee. I was never much for crowds and I don't care for heat and the fair had a good bit of both. I bought a Styrofoam cup of what looked like piss water for a buck and was putting my sugars in there when the first one come up and asked me if it was true.

I didn't have the first goddamn idea what he was talking about or who the hell he was. So I said, Sure, it's true. People like it when you tell them what they want.

Merle Clemente is your brother? he said. Holy shit, man, that's unreal.

Took me by surprise. I spilled my damned coffee all over the little counter and down my clean work pants.

He tried to help me, and started taking swipes at my pants.

I told him, Jesus Christ, just leave it.

Once I got her mopped up a bit, I gave the guy a look and damned if he wasn't one of them longhairs like to pretend they're farmers. Throwbacks to the hippie days, is what I call them. Merle used to call them New Grassers. New gassers is more like it, all the hot air they spout.

He was saying, An original member of the High Lonesome Boys. Living right here in Cedar. I can't believe it.

I didn't know whether to shit or brush my hair. Lost. I was lost for words.

I said, 'Scuse me, and went to get another coffee. He stayed right with me. Let me, he said. Just a young guy, long hair, wearing a plaid flannel work shirt, like mine only new and put on for show.

He said he would like nothing more than to buy a coffee for the missing Clemente brother.

That stopped me.

Finally I told him I wasn't the missing one. The one that was missing wasn't ever coming back.

He looked confused behind that little beard of his, probably only three days old.

Sorry man, I didn't mean to . . .

I said, 'Scuse me, again. I got somewhere to be.

I was nearly past him when I heard him say to the little girl he was with, her all dolled up like a goddamn pilgrim or something, They aren't going to believe this on the folk music listserv. Scoop of the century! Hey, did you bring your BlackBerry?

Like he was talking in French.

Sara

I bet if we hadn't cheated none of it would have happened. God makes people pay for their sins. It's one of his main rules and leaders are more affected by rules than other people.

Seth says that sometimes being a leader is about knowing which rules to ignore. But he doesn't have a very good moral compass. Neither does my dad, which is probably why everything went so wrong.

My dad had been drinking, which he doesn't normally, and he seemed upset, which wasn't surprising at all. Sometimes he pushes my mom around but mostly he just says mean things, except when he's throwing food. But when me and Seth were hiding Alec Baldwin's white feathers my dad came right up to us and pushed Seth. Seth swore at him, but that wasn't very unusual because Seth swears about everything. I can't repeat what he said because I am in enough trouble with God already.

Seth also said, "Watch the [bleep]ing chicken!"

And then my dad asked what Seth was doing out here with his daughter, which was me.

And Seth said, "Take it easy dude. I'm just helping."

Then my dad tried to take a swing at Seth and he missed and kind of fell over.

People started coming out of the poultry barn and over from the sheep barn, which was next door. You could tell they were sheep people because they were leading sheep.

My dad was crying and Seth went to help him up, and my dad tried to punch him again but he only hit the back of Seth's leg. That made Seth fall over, so they were both on the ground.

And Seth said, "Why does this [bleep] always happen to me?"

And my dad cried some more.

That's when Mr. Lymer came down the aisle between the two buildings. He was with Tommy Bristol, who is a Junior Poultry judge. Tommy's seventeen. Everyone says he's someone to watch.

"What's going on out here?" asked Mr. Lymer.

Tommy Bristol just stood to the side. He's quite dignified. I saw Bethany and Mr. and Mrs. Blaine watching, too. Bethany was holding her rooster, Mr. Red, who weighs almost ten pounds, which is a lot. Maybe too much for a competitive bird.

"Just a misunderstanding," said Seth. He sounded really upset. He also used some more swear words and Mrs. Blaine put her hands over Bethany's ears. A couple of the sheep people laughed.

"He's a pervert! He's inappropriately interested in my daughter," said my dad. Which was kind of strange because he never really cared who was interested in me before.

"I am not!" Seth screamed. "I was helping with her chicken. Doing service work." Then he added some more swears and said something about some guy named Axe Rose. I don't know why.

I was going to tell them that we were just working with Alec Baldwin, but I didn't want to confess about the cheating, and before I could say anything my stomach started to hurt a lot.

"Helping how?" said Mr. Lymer.

I saw Tommy notice the ink marker lying on the ground. I could tell he knew what it was for. Before anyone else saw it, he leaned down and picked up the pen and put it in his pocket.

"He was helping with her sign," said Tommy. "I saw him."

"That's right," said Seth. He picked himself up. "I'm in graphics! Among other things."

My dad was still sitting on the ground, in the weeds. He was leaning against the side of the building crying but not making any noise.

"Sir?" said Mr. Lymer. "Are you okay?"

Then I didn't hear anything else because the pain in my stomach all of a sudden got a lot worse.

Prudence

I was in a booth looking at charts of grass growth cycles when I saw the ambulance drive slowly through the crowd with its lights flashing. The strobes were hard to see, because the sun was bright and glinting off the shiny surfaces of tractors and amusement rides.

I have no idea how I knew the paramedics were there for one of us. The options were endless. Someone might have been choking on a corndog or a 4-H'er might have been trampled by a stampede of heifers tired of being paraded around the small arena like passive and overweight debutantes. But the intuitive part of me knew. Perhaps Earl had keeled over from some fresh indignation or Seth had slipped away from Eustace and gotten drunk and been beaten half to death by a tractor salesmen for an offhand but highly offensive comment.

I didn't even think to worry about Sara.

When I walked over to the poultry barn, I could see a small knot of people standing around the gap between the chicken barn and the next building. I pushed my way through the small crowd and headed down the narrow alleyway formed by the two buildings. Sara lay on the stretcher surrounded by people. The ambulance attendant, a spiky-haired, muscular young aboriginal man, was bent over, talking to her. I suppose he was really talking at her, because she didn't seem to be responding.

"Sara?" I said, "Sara?"

Before I could reach her, Seth reached out and touched my arm.

"They said we should meet them at the hospital," he said. "You should, anyway. She asked me to stay and show her birds."

"But—" I didn't finish the sentence.

"They don't know what's wrong with her. It's her stomach."

That's when I saw the tall, red-faced man standing off to the side. I thought I recognized him, although his face was so screwed up with emotion that it was hard to tell.

"Is that . . . ?"

"Her dad. Yeah. He saw me talking to her and kind of flipped out. Then she got sick. He'll meet you at the hospital."

Earl put an arm around my shoulder and pulled me so I wouldn't get in the paramedics' way as they carried Sara on the stretcher to the waiting ambulance.

Seth

Eustace still hadn't arrived and I was worried as hell about the kid. I was supposed to show the chickens but I'd just been assaulted by the kid's father and I was basically shitting bricks, if you want to know the truth. The weird thing though? I forgot to be paranoid about who knew what happened with me and the drama teacher. Which is kind of screwed up, I know. Like maybe I'm destined to go through life with one epic fuckup supplanting the next one. It'll get so I can't worry about anything that happens because something worse is definitely coming. There was a certain relief in the thought.

Anyway, back to the chicken show. I might have been helping Sara train the birds, but that didn't mean I knew what I was doing. I just got a kick out of the whole idea. I know nothing about competitive poultry and showing them off to their best advantage. So I was seriously considering making a run for it when a kid no more than four feet tall, wearing a nearly knee-length blue T-shirt printed with the silhouette of a chicken and some lettering that I couldn't read because it was created in a font that looked like chicken tracks, told me I was up next.

"I'm sorry?"

She consulted her piece of paper.

"Spratt. Frizzle hen. Number twenty-four."

"But where do I—?"

"Take your bird and wait by the judging table," she said.

I pulled the hen out of the cage. She was a limp little thing with all the personality of a used fabric softener sheet. Sara might have told me her name, but I couldn't remember it because most of my attention had been on Alec Baldwin and overcoming his shortcomings. Plus, I think I have brain damage from blackout drinking. I really do.

I stood there holding the hen with all the other contestants, not one of whom was probably more than twelve. Most were younger. I felt like the fair's prize asshole. The older kids, the Sr. Poultry Fanciers, were acting as assistant judges or watching the proceedings.

"Are you allowed to compete?" asked this one little girl. Her T-shirt said she was on the Nanoose Ninnies team.

I was about to say that (1) I hoped I couldn't compete, so as to spare myself further humiliation, and (2) her team name should mention chickens in case people thought she was simply a twit, when a voice interrupted.

"Mr. Lymer said he could."

I turned. It was Bethany, Sara's friend. She was hanging onto a red chicken the size of an overweight toddler.

"Sara's sick," Bethany said, to no one in particular.

"That's right. But she'll be better soon," I told her.

"Poor Sara."

I nodded.

"She has a bad home life. But God still loves her," continued Bethany.

"Yeah. That's true."

Then the two of us watched a boy show off a small gleaming-white rooster with a spray of black feathers for a tail. The announcer said it was a Japanese cockerel. The boy tried to push it along the piece of shavings-sprinkled plywood that was the runway. Two judges sat across the table from the kid and his bird. They watched as the little rooster took a step, crapped, took another step and crapped again.

"He's kind of nervous," said the boy. A fringe of hair hung almost to his nose. "He doesn't normally poop that much." The kid had on black skateboarding shoes, one of which was tapping the dirt a mile a minute.

The judges nodded. I got the feeling they didn't approve of birds with nervous stomachs. That made me think of Sara again. I was so nervous I felt a little like the Japanese cockerel. At least during the thing with the drama teacher I'd been wasted. This sobriety business was hard going.

A young guy walked up to me.

"You're up next," he said.

I felt my stomach do a long, slow flop, releasing a wave of acid into my throat.

"Don't worry. They'll go easy on you. Since you're an amateur."

I looked at him more closely.

"Thanks, dude," I said.

"Oh, and I think you dropped this earlier." He reached into his jeans pocket and pulled out the marker we'd been using to hide Alec Baldwin's white feathers.

I felt my face get hot.

"Yeah, we were just . . . writing something."

"Sure you were," he said. "I scratched that bird's entry for you."

"Oh, right. Thanks," I said.

When it was my turn, I put Sara's frizzle on the show table.

I'd heard Sara give the little talk about her birds' breeding, feathers, wattle and beak enough times that I could repeat it, more or less verbatim. The little dishrag performed pretty well. She walked the length of the runway with hardly any prodding from my piece of doweling, which was good, because if I'd had to move her too much, I might have fallen over. The table had been set up for small kids and I had to crouch way down so that I was pretty much squatting in front of the judges, looking every inch the tool.

When it was over, the older judge, a girl in her early twenties with a nose ring and spiky black hair, kind of cute if you're into young poultry judges, said, "Tell Sara she's done a nice job with her hen."

"Good work," said the other judge, a grim-looking kid with patchy facial hair.

I picked up the hen and as we left the judging area, I heard clapping. It was Eustace. He was standing there with, get this, my parents. Well, my mom, anyway. I barely recognized her out of her usual habitat. She had on her jean pantsuit with the Bedazzled seams, big old smile on her face. Bobby was beside her and the two of them were holding take-out Tim Horton's. Bobby had some Timbit remnants in his 'stache.

Fucking Hallmark never wrote anything for how I felt then. When Metallica and the rest of the metal community pitched in to pay for Acrassicauda, the Iraqi heavy metal band, to move to the US is the only thing that comes close. And maybe the late-breaking success of Anvil. I had a toasty heart, especially after I got called back to pick up first prize for Miss Frizz. Ah, never mind. You know what I'm saying.

EARL

The lady doctor told us the kid was okay and give us a look like we just drove the new tractor into the creek. Prudence told her that the kid's parents was indisposed but the lady doctor still had that sourpuss look on her face.

Prudence used her cell phone to call the kid's mom and I could hear the crying all the way over where I was sitting out in the waiting room. That woman is a one-trick pony if I ever seen one.

Then this other doctor, a young feller, come sidling over to me and asked if it was true.

I told him I had no idea. And then he asked me if I was really a Clemente brother. I told him I was, because we were in a hospital and he's a doctor and I was raised to respect the medical profession.

He told me he's always admired the High Lonesome Boys and what they did for bluegrass. And I said, Oh yeah, the way you do when you want to finish up a conversation. I was starting to feel some pain in my stomach from people bringing up my personal history every five minutes.

The doctor told me he played a bit of mandolin and I said I could just imagine. I didn't mean it, of course. He looked like the last guy you'd see playing mandolin. Then he said how he can't believe the missing Clemente brother was right here in his emergency room. That's when I shot him a look, doctor or no doctor, and told him what I told the other guy. That I wasn't missing because I was standing right there. He said he understood, but he didn't, because no one, not even bluegrass music crazies, know the whole story.

That's when Prudence came hurrying over. She had a hold of that phone of hers like it was a radioactive turd that'd blow up if she let go of it. Which is exactly how I'd hold one of them little bastards if anyone tried to make me use one. Regular phones is bad enough.

She started shouting at me, saying, He called! He called!

And I told her I didn't know who the hell he is and I more than likely didn't care. And she says, His manager called and he's coming.

I still wasn't catching her drift but the doctor was. His eyes went all monkey-bright and he said, Are you talking about who I think you're talking about? And she said she was talking about Merle Clemente coming to the First Annual Woefield Farm Music Festival and that the High Lonesome Boys were getting back together.

Prudence and that doctor grabbed each other's hands and started jumping up and down like a couple of goddamn Mexican beans. Jesus Christ. I heard Rex Murphy on *Cross Country Checkup* say the medical system in this country is in a crisis. I can tell you why: Them medical bastards has their minds on other things.

Finally Prudence stopped jumping and turned around and said, Isn't this great, Earl? and Aren't you excited?

And all of a sudden, I felt like I might have some of what the kid had and I needed to sit down.

Sara

One of the best things about the day before the concert was all the volunteers who came to help us get set up. The Blaines came and they brought Bethany. They were going to spread the Word of God with CDs of inspirational music from their church and sell tickets, but first they helped to paint the ticket booth. Seth's mom and her boyfriend walked over, although all they did was drink beer on the porch and talk about how their house looked different from this angle. Some of Prudence's writers came too, and they helped a lot after Reporter Travis finished giving them their writing lesson. Travis missed quite a bit of the second part of the day because of having to go to bed for the headache that he got after teaching. Prudence said it was very nice of Travis to help her out like that, but after he was gone she muttered that if all Brady did was write a single sentence with the words "man root" in it, Travis should count himself lucky. Prudence teaches lots of people writing now, not just the Mighty Pens. I think she's getting quite tough because of it.

I listened to part of Travis's writing lesson, even though it meant I had to take a break from helping to move my chickens behind Earl's cabin so they wouldn't get stressed during the concert and to make room for the truck to bring amplifiers and equipment and stuff. I thought the part where Travis asked the writers to explore their senses was interesting, even though that big lady, Portia, said good sense wasn't exactly anyone's strong suit. The mean girl and her mom came to the Pens' lesson again. I'm not a writer or anything, but the girl's mom looked really depressed. I guess I'd look depressed too, if I had a terrible daughter who was unpleasant to those who are younger and less fortunate.

I thought Seth's music that he played outside made everyone have more energy, even though after three songs Earl said if Seth didn't turn off that you-know-what racket he was going to take a hammer to the boom box. Megadeth is surprisingly more catchy than you'd think. I think I might like heavy metal.

The only person it didn't make go faster was Prudence and that's because I don't think anyone could go faster than her. She is extremely active and energetic for her age. It was pretty hot and sunny, but as usual she didn't even sweat.

When everyone was outside putting up signs for camping and the ticket booth and putting the equipment on the bandstand I tried not to show how excited I was because then everyone would get all worried and ask me how I was feeling and I don't like that. It's hard to feel like a leader when people treat you like a sick person. I knew the concert was going to be one of the best days of my life.

Prudence

The day of the concert, people started arriving at eight o'clock in the morning. Locals. Out of towners. The level of interest was extremely gratifying, and we'd sold a lot of tickets considering the concert was only announced five or so weeks before. The reunion of the Clemente brothers was big news for bluegrass fans.

The place was already busy with volunteers, including Bethany and her parents and the Mighty Pens, who came back after the previous day's lesson, though we lost them early on when one of Marvin's feet got run over as he helped move the ticket booth. Marvin said the pain was so excruciating that he might have to go home, but I got them talking about how one might describe a pain so indescribable and before I knew it, they'd all abandoned their posts and headed off to do another writing exercise. Which was a relief in a lot of ways, because Verna had dragged Laureen out of bed to help and Laureen's constant complaining about how lame country music is and how she didn't think she could stand a whole day and night of listening to it and how it was almost as bad as writing was getting on everyone's nerves. Her mother said Laureen was practicing "contempt prior to investigation" and that if she, Verna, could go to Al-Anon every Tuesday when she'd rather be watching her daytime shows on TV, then Laureen could participate in her recovery by helping with the sobriety festival.

I had to tell them it was a bluegrass festival, not a sobriety festival, and we were holding it as a sort of family reunion for our hired man, Earl.

"Bluegrass?" asked Laureen.

"It's one of the oldest musical traditions in North America," said Brady. "It originated in the—"

"Hillbilly suck music," said Laureen.

"This isn't a sober concert?" asked Verna. She was already in a bad mood because her feet got run over too. I think at this point Travis had already hurt his back and was in bed waiting for the spasm to stop.

"Well, not really," I said.

That's when the large panel truck with the words "Mobile Liquor Sales" painted on the side pulled up into the yard and the driver leaned out and asked where he should set up.

I'd been relieved to find that it's possible to hire an independent contractor to run a beer garden at your event rather than get the permits and kegs and so forth yourself. I'm increasingly in favor of delegating. I have Travis to thank for putting me onto the alcohol sales and so much more. I really don't know how I'd have put the event together without Travis's help and expertise. That said, the presence of alcohol at a place that many people thought was a treatment center was a source of some confusion.

"What kind of a treatment center is this?" Verna wanted to know.

"A cool one," said Laureen. It was nice to hear her finally sound positive about something.

Seth was also upset. He said he felt that the beer garden was going to undermine his sobriety and that he'd have to speak to Eustace about it. Again, delegation in all things is a byword with me.

That's when Phyllis Snelling, the banker, drove up. That was also when I realized that I hadn't yet had a chance to tell her that we'd changed the overall idea of the place and its mandate from treatment center to farm/bluegrass festival site. There'd been so much going on in the weeks leading up to the concert. Between all of the activity and the arrival of campers, things were hectic but in no way unmanageable. I wouldn't want to give anyone the wrong impression.

Seth

One of the key concepts in early recovery is staying away from "sticky" places and "slippery" people. Actually, I might have that reversed. When I first heard it, I laughed because it sounded so porny, if you know what I mean. Or like metal lyrics.

But that's not what the recovery people mean. Well, maybe it is, come to think of it. But they're also talking parties, bars, piss-ups and drug fests of any description. You'd think that as a person who stays at home most of the time with a kid, an old man and a girl who barely drinks, I'd be safe. Well, you'd be wrong, especially when beer gardens started popping up all over the property.

Even Eustace thought the beer garden was highly uncool. He actually listened for a few minutes while I bitched about it. Normally he tells me to try and "keep it positive" because he says I've got a tendency to be negative. Eustace is a good-looking guy and more or less has his shit together so it's easy for him to be positive. If I looked like Brad Pitt and George Clooney with a bit of Christian Bale around the eyes, I'd be positive too.

For a supposedly upbeat guy, he wasn't saying much to Prudence, who was ignoring him right back. It got on my nerves, the two of them. I was dealing with some serious issues and all they could do was pretend not to have the hots for each other. At one point I brought out the Big Book and started reading it out loud but Eustace told me I was supposed to practice "attraction rather than promotion," whatever the fuck that meant, and that I should stop getting on people's nerves.

That gave me a severe resentment in my ass, to be honest. I had to go to my room and listen to Queensrÿche's "Silent Lucidity" to calm down. I followed that up with some "Fade to Black," which always centers me.

Anyway, I was just about to go back outside to help when Prudence started letting people into the house. If the drinking and douchery had been contained in the beer garden, that would have been bad enough, but this was a highly unwelcome twist.

When I went downstairs, I found a guy with long hair leaning over the sink. Dude was actually *washing his hair* in the kitchen sink.

"What the fuck, man?" I told him. "Party's outside."

He had the dish-soap bottle in his hand. Some of that non-toxic, biodegradable stuff made out of recycled mosquito spit that Prudence insists on. It does nothing to get dishes clean and it sure as hell wasn't going to help with the gnarly set of snakes and ladders on the guy's head. He turned to me and, still rinsing, said, "She told us we could."

I assumed he was talking about Sara.

"Man. She's just a little kid. She doesn't know the rules. Campers, festival attendees, whatever you want to call yourselves, stay outside. This is a private residence."

He finally pulled his hair, which made mine look all neat and trimmed by comparison, out of the basin and wrapped it in a dish towel.

"It wasn't a little kid. It was the girl, lady, whatever, that runs this place. The nice-looking one." He nodded all thoughtfully and squeezed water out of the end of his hair onto the linoleum.

"She seeing anyone?" he asked.

I ignored the question, choosing radical restraint of tongue and pen.

"Dude, she misspoke. No one is allowed in the house."

"What are we supposed to do about water?" he said. "Are there any lakes nearby?"

"There's a hose on the side of the house. Campers can use that. Jesus, what do you hippies do when you camp out at Burning Man or whatever?"

Then I got worried that he might actually start talking to me about camping, so I herded him outside before he could. This was threatening to get even worse than Woodstock. Instead of hippies doing drugs and wallowing in mud pits, we'd have them doing drugs and dying of thirst in the dust bowl of our field. Just then another thought occurred to me. I went to Travis's room to check, and then ran outside to find Prudence.

She was talking to a short-haired woman who looked like a prison guard on her day off. The conversation looked pretty intense, but I had to get her attention.

"Excuse me, Prudence. I have to talk to you."

"Can it wait?"

"I don't think so."

She turned to me. Her hair, which is normally so neat and shiny, like a little cap, was a bit messed up. That seemed like a bad sign.

I pulled her a few feet away from the prison lady.

"Toilets," I said. "Where are the toilets?"

Prudence was all, "Seth, please. Stop joking around. The toilet is where it always is."

"No man, I mean for the crowd. The campers. The audience. The four hundred plus people who bought tickets to see the music."

She turned white. I knew I'd scored a big save then. Or had at least pointed out the net was empty.

"Oh my god," she said.

"Did you forget to order any?"

But good old Prudence. She's like a twenty-four-year-old girl, going on three-star general in the military. No hesitation at all.

"Please excuse me, Phyllis," she said to the lady, who was staring all around her at the people, the ticket booth and the bandstand, like she'd woken up on another planet. "I'll just be a minute." Prudence pulled me by the arm until we were almost on the porch stairs.

As we stood there, two more trucks with campers on the back rumbled into the yard and headed uncertainly toward the eight or ten that were already parked in the field, like lost buffalo looking for the rest of the herd.

"Can you find us some toilets?" she asked. "I'm kind of busy."

"How am I going to find outhouses on a Saturday morning? I don't have a lot of connections in the portapotty business."

"Seth—"

"Oh, okay. Just don't let anyone into the beer garden until I find some or there'll be piss all over everything."

"We can let people go in the house."

"You're joking, right?"

"No, Seth. This is a farm. I can't have people using it as a toilet." Her face grew thoughtful. "Well, maybe I can. I'm not entirely sure what kind of fertilizer is best for grass."

Then, almost without pausing, she pivoted and strode over, sandals slapping against the bottoms of her dirty feet, to continue her conversation with the fierce-looking lady.

"As I was saying, Phyllis, our focus has changed somewhat," I heard her say, before they moved out of my earshot.

That's when I remembered my buddy Corey. I mean, we were friends before I dropped out of school. He called me a bunch of times afterward, tried to keep in touch or whatever, but I didn't want to talk. I remembered my mom telling me he was driving a truck for some septic company.

I went to go and find a phone book, just as two gleaming gray tour buses pulled up the driveway. My first thought on seeing them was at least they probably had their own toilets.

Earl

I was trying to stay the hell out of the way, but when I saw the first shithouse fall off the truck, I thought, goddamn it, I'm going to have to get involved. No way around it.

That feller in the orange shirt with the palm trees on it, the one Prudence was teaching how to write, told Seth to pick it up, the shitter, I mean. And Seth told him no way, he wasn't handling no toxic waste accident. For once, I had to agree with the little bastard. I guess I can't call him Chubnuts no more since he's skinny all the way down.

Then the guy driving the truck started telling us how he took the units off a construction worksite and his boss didn't know and he could get fired if one got busted and on and on.

And Seth told him how much he appreciated it and the guy said, Man, I never thought this is what you'd ask for when you finally came out of hiding.

From what I could see, them shitters was well used. A couple of falls off a truck wouldn't make a hell of a lot of difference.

So I said, Jesus Christ, and pulled a few guys together as well as that big lady from the writing group, the one with the shoulders and the bad attitude, and we got it standing upright again.

Then we helped the truck driver, who was some friend of Seth's with the same long, greasy hair and scary bastards on his T-shirt, to get the other five crappers off the truck. If we hadn't been so rushed, we might not of set them up right in front of the house the way we did, but there was already a lineup of people waiting to use them. That was about the time when I noticed Merle's big bus parked over to the side of the house. I'm not a vain man, but I didn't want to be wrassling plastic shithouses the first time my brother laid eyes on me after fifty plus years. I apologized to Travis the reporter for swearing at him the way I had. My nerves was on edge. It was too bad about his hand. Getting it slammed in the door of that last shithouse was bad luck. It's a good thing Travis was holding onto his microphone or it would have been a hell of a lot worse.

I headed back to my cabin after that. The smell of them toilets mixed up with the reek of the rendering plant down the way started making my stomach kick up a fuss. I had half a mind to ask the kid for a dose of whatever it is she takes.

Sara

I don't think it was a very good idea to put the bathrooms so close to the house. But in one way it was good, because Prudence gave me the job of closing and opening the doors because two of the latches got broken when the potties fell off the truck. She is paying me twenty dollars an hour, which the guy who stole the toilets from his job site told Seth is practically a union wage, which is what I hope to get when I grow up. Anyway, because the potties were so close to the house, I could sit on the porch and watch to see if anyone wanted to use them. I sent people to the ones with the handles that worked first. If those ones were busy, I told them to go in one of the broken ones and when they were inside, I put a piece of wood through the latch and hung one of the "Occupied" signs I made on it. The sign's pretty nice for a toilet. I used metallic ink. When the person was done, they had to knock and I'd let them out.

Seth said it was a job with "plenty of room for error" and he was right. I don't think anyone with less maturity than me could have done it. When Bethany came over from where she was handing out Rapture pamphlets at the ticket booth with her parents, I said she could help, but I wouldn't leave her in charge by herself because sometimes she forgets what she's doing. At first I made some mistakes, like when I forgot to tell this girl that I was going to lock her in and when she heard the wood go through the latch, she screamed. But I explained what was happening and she calmed down.

One guy gave me money when he came out. He was dressed sort of fancy, almost like a cowboy. He said that ours was the first bluegrass festival he'd ever been to with a bathroom attendant. I looked over at Bethany so he wouldn't forget to give her money. He corrected himself and said two bathroom attendants and gave her a tip, too.

It was pretty busy working at the potties. There were strange people everywhere and they seemed really happy, like maybe they were on drugs or something. Not to be mean, but you don't usually see people that happy just walking around. Some of the people looked like farmers and some of them looked like the people you see in music videos, like they were young and had old clothes and interesting haircuts. Some were old and some were more Prudence's age and younger. They sat all over the place in little groups with their lawn chairs and they played guitars and banjos and harmonicas and other instruments, such as mandolins, which are like guitars. And while they did that, some of the professional musicians started setting up on the bandstand so they could do "sound checks," which didn't sound very good. The sound checks were annoying because the musicians would just start a song and then quit almost right away. Quite a few of the musicians came up and complained to Seth about different things, like "artist accommodations" and "backstage facilities" and stuff like that. I think they complained to Seth because he kind of looks like a musician and Reporter Travis was busy fixing equipment and cables and other things.

It was all pretty fun, especially when Prudence asked me and Bethany to sell muffins until the concessions were ready. Prudence made them at about three in the morning the night before, so they were really fresh. She also hired a truck to sell hot dogs and hamburgers and another one to sell pierogies and other food like that but they weren't due to start until one o'clock. When they showed up, they started arguing over who got to park where and they told Prudence she shouldn't have hired them both and they threatened to leave until she said they could park across from one another and promised to announce both their names between the acts.

Because there was no other food while the concession stands were getting set up, people didn't seem to mind spending three dollars on a muffin and most bought one from me as soon as they came out of the bathroom.

Then the mean girls from the store showed up and everything stopped being fun.

Prudence

The day was spectacular. Warm, but not stifling. Soft blue skies, silky breezes. Maybe that's why Phyllis was so reasonable. She didn't threaten me with fraud charges or anything. But she said she was disappointed and was going to have to report the change in our status to her manager. I reassured her that even though we aren't a treatment facility anymore, we are still in business.

"Doing what?" she asked, looking around.

"Well, first we're putting on a bluegrass festival. According to my projections, that should bring in enough to get us up and running. Financially speaking."

Phyllis smiled wryly.

"Prudence, I don't want to tell you the dire financial situation of most arts organizations I deal with. I can promise you putting on small concerts is no way to make money."

"But we're different. We've got a secret weapon."

She looked hot and a little uncomfortable in her boxy suit and I had to resist the urge to find someone to get her something to drink.

"Our foreman. Earl."

"I know Earl," she said. "He's lived around here a long time. He doesn't get out much."

"His last name's Clemente."

She stared, waiting.

"His brother is *Merle* Clemente."

She squinted a bit. Perspiration shone at her temples.

"Is he a curler on the national team?"

"No. Merle Clemente is a world-famous bluegrass musician. He performed at the Oscars a few years ago? After that black and white movie came out?"

Phyllis was clearly not a music or movie fan. No matter. I knew I could convince her.

"Our foreman Earl is Merle Clemente's brother. They had a band called the High Lonesome Boys in the early fifties."

She showed no sign of recognition.

"It's a legendary bluegrass band, especially the early lineup. And this"—I waved an arm around the farm, which was now packed with people and campers and RVs, as well as a steady trickle of backpackers coming in on foot and bicycles—"is going to be their reunion. I've been taking calls about this from all over North America. I even got a call from a bluegrass fan magazine in Japan. We have a reporter staying here to document the whole thing. It's a very big deal."

"Have you got a permit?" she asked, doubtfully.

"Of course!" I said. I could see she was impressed and once again I was so glad that Travis told me how to secure the permits quickly.

"Come and see me Monday, please," said Phyllis.

"Absolutely. I think you're going to be amazed. This concert is going to put us firmly in the black. And when it's done, we'll get farming. I hope you saw my raised beds over there. We're doing well at the local farmers' market with our specialty greens and I've got lots of writing students."

"I still don't understand how a treatment center can just turn into a music festival overnight."

I could see Eustace over by the bandstand. He was talking to Seth.

"I think the key is to remain flexible," I said. "Adaptable. And to marshal your human resources effectively."

"If you say so," she said. She'd just walked away when Seth came up. He also got his feet run over when we moved the ticket booth, so he was walking kind of gingerly. I'd had a moment of worrying that some of the people who got mashed feet would decide to file workers' comp claims against me, but Marvin, the business guy in the Mighty Pens, said volunteers have no rights. So that was a relief!

Seth came up and was starting to speak to me when I noticed out of the corner of my eye that Eustace was now talking to a girl. She was slim and blonde and, from a distance, looked as though she might be attractive. I didn't like to see that, but jealousy is never an acceptable response to competition.

"Prudence!" said Seth, raising his voice near to a yell. "Did you hear anything I said?"

"I'm sorry. Who's that over there?"

He shot an irritated glance in Eustace's direction.

"I don't know. Look, I think we have a problem."

I saw the girl walk away and felt myself take a deep breath. Then Eustace looked over and caught me staring. He waved. I waved back.

It was all very awkward.

"Earl won't leave his cabin," said Seth. "And your main attraction said a reunion is the whole reason he's here."

"Main attraction," I repeated, distracted. I had to tear my gaze away from Eustace. I've never apologized to anyone and I wasn't going to start now.

"Merle Clemente! The whole reason all these people have paid forty dollars to be here."

That caught my attention.

"What do you mean? Merle is here? Why didn't anyone tell me?"

"You've been talking to the prison guard woman so I kept everyone away from you. Mr. Clemente's mandolin player just came over and told me that they're not sure this is going to 'work out.' I guess Merle's offended no one's welcomed him yet."

"What? No one has gone to see him yet? What about Earl?"

"I don't know, Prudence. I'm too busy trying to ignore the goddamn beer tent you installed in my face and the toilets that keep falling every which way and stinking up the whole neighborhood. Not to mention the campers. Where did you get those people, man? They're worse than the people in that Woodstock movie. You know, the one with the guy with the miser parents and Liev Schreiber as a drag queen with a gun and a strap-on? I had no idea the bluegrass scene was so sketchy. Give me metal any day. Did you know I found one of them in the kitchen washing his dreadlocks?"

I took another deep breath. Seth was right. I had to focus. As a farmer/concert promoter, I couldn't afford to be distracted.

"Let me speak to Mr. Clemente. I'll get things sorted out."

"What about Earl? What are you going to do about him? Someone told me that he won't come out of his cabin."

"Can you go talk to him?" I asked.

I cast one more little glance toward the now empty place where Eustace had been standing, then I went to talk to Mr. Clemente.

SETH

I have no idea why Prudence sent me to talk to Earl. It's not like the guy likes me. He barely tolerates me. I may be in a program now and working on my issues and getting better at talking about my feelings and well-versed in my many, many defects and all that, but my focus has been mostly on my own feelings. I have no skills with anyone else's.

It didn't help having Travis and all the other reporter types trying to get background on Earl and asking me what I thought the reunion meant for the future of bluegrass. I was like, dude, I've basically been in my room since the end of eleventh grade. All I know about bluegrass is that it gives me a wicked headache. At least, I thought it did. I wasn't too familiar with the genre, to be honest.

Anyway, as a newly sober guy, being put in charge of getting two mulish bluegrass legends on the same stage was too much pressure. Think about it. I was being asked to overcome a family feud that was twice as old as I was. It was like sending me to patch things up between David Lee Roth and Sammy Hagar the night before *5150* was released.

I made the reporters wait outside the cabin. Earl's a very solitary guy, which I understand better than probably anyone. He spends a lot of time alone and I sort of figured strangers would upset him. He had the sheep for companionship, but I wasn't sure she counted. It was the first time I'd been in his cabin, and the first time I'd visited him alone. Shitting bricks pretty much describes my feelings.

I could have used my sponsor right about then. Considering that he's supposed to be my go-to guy, Eustace can be a bit of a selfish prick.

There had been times I'd called him late at night when I couldn't sleep and he totally screened my ass. I know he did. What is that? They never did that shit in the old days with Bob and Bill and those other old guys who started AA. Those dudes would have gotten up and out of bed and walked on bare feet over two miles of broken glass to help out a fellow sufferer and been glad about it. They were on the job. Not like sponsors of today. I could have gotten loaded on one of those nights. Fact: Three a.m. is the hour when the most people die. It's true. It's the hour of death. If a sponsor isn't available at three, he's really not available at all.

Anyway, when I went into his log cabin Earl was sitting in his old lady chair, watching Oprah. I shit you not. Oprah. The day of his big comeback, the day he sees his estranged country music star brother for the first time in like a hundred and fifty years, the day he makes hillbilly music history, there he was, watching daytime TV. Looking completely unconcerned. Dressed in his usual old green work shirt and green pants. I don't think he'd even shaved. I had to hand it to him. He was a cool mother.

"Hey, Earl," I said.

He didn't answer me.

"So it looks like this concert thing is really happening," I said.

Oprah was turned on so loud that the old TV was almost shaking. I doubt Earl had any idea how busy it was outside. His cabin faces away from the rest of the farm and his flowery curtains were closed. It was kind of cozy in his place, actually. If I ever decided to go into seclusion again, I might try for a place like his.

"Quite a few people here," I told him.

He didn't turn to look at me. I spotted his banjo, or what I supposed was a banjo. It had a country music look to it.

"That your banjo?" I asked. I felt like a total ass, but I'm not exactly a family therapist and you have to give me credit for trying. I have no idea how Prudence gets everyone to do what she wants. It's like an evil genius skill of hers or something. "Earl, are you up for this?"

Nothing.

I took a few more steps into the little joint, which smelled like coffee and damp wool but was pretty neat and everything. I wondered if Earl had started letting Bertie come inside. Anything was possible. I took a few more steps and sat in an easy chair covered in some chintz pattern, firm but surprisingly comfortable.

"Your brother's here."

At this he made a sniffing noise. He wasn't crying or anything. It was more like the kind of sniff a person gives before wiping his nose with his sleeve. A snot sniff, if you will.

"Right," I said. "I thought so." Then I sat back and watched Oprah give one of her staffers a thousand bucks just to show she could.

Earl

Now I wouldn't go around saying this to just anyone, but the truth is Seth reminds me of Pride in some ways. Pride was a handsomer man. No doubt about that. And he had some talent on him, which is different from Chubnuts.

But they was both bad drinkers. And one thing I know about bad drinkers is that they can't help it. At least, not the way you and me can.

Merle never could understand that. He never saw the sickness. He just figured Pride was trying to bring him down. I think he's one of them annihilists you hear about. From what I hear, a lot of them annihilists run major companies, like the oil companies and big stores on the highway. Merle's like that. Can only get his head around something for how it's about him.

I was sitting there trying to think my way through things and Seth was trying to be quiet for once, and I remembered that I hadn't seen him hitting the sauce for a while. So I asked him how it was going with the not drinking.

He looked at me funny. He didn't have on his sunglasses. In fact, he was only wearing those outside lately, I noticed. I guess that wasn't the question he was expecting. He told me he was geting used to it.

I asked him how that was working out for him. I musta said it the wrong way, because his forehead got all suspicious under that damned bandana he keeps wrapped around his head like he thinks his brains will leak out if he takes it off. Can't blame him for wondering. I ain't been that friendly since he got here. He said it was going okay, he guessed.

I told him I heard that wasn't too easy to do, sobering up, and he allowed that was so.

We set like that for a while and let that sink in.

Then he asked me how long since I last seen my brother. I thought about not answering, because sometimes that's easier. But then I told him since I was seventeen or thereabouts.

And he said a hundred and twenty years was a long time and then said sorry, he was just joking.

I said I'd be ready to play when they were ready for me. He said that was good.

The real open-type conversations ain't easy for no one.

Then he came out of left field and asked me if I missed my brother. He meant Merle.

That stopped me. I had to think on that for a while. I told him not Merle so much. It was my middle brother that I missed. He said he didn't know I had another brother. So I told him a bit about Pride, how he reminded me of Pride in some ways. He wanted to know how.

I said they both got to drinking and carrying on but how people liked both of them. I told him that he and Pride both had that way about them.

He asked if I really thought he had a way about him. I looked at him then, and remembered that he wasn't much more than a kid in a lot of ways. Like Pride had been.

I told him sure, stay off the sauce and you'll do okay.

He asked what happened to Pride and I told him how Merle turned him loose from the band and he went downhill and didn't make her back up.

He said Jesus and sorry and I said, me too.

After that, he didn't say another word until I was ready.

SARA

The girls from the big school, the ones who hang around outside the store and were mean to Bethany that time, found us when we were trying to put new toilet paper rolls in the bathrooms. The bathrooms smelled pretty bad, especially after a few people had used them, so we had to take turns and hold our noses.

When I came out of the second potty, the big girls were standing around Bethany. Bethany was holding her extra toilet rolls tight, and squishing them to her chest. Her cheeks had bright red spots on them.

"Hey, turd face," said one of the biggest girls. Her hood was pulled over her head and her shirt had little skulls on it. Which was sort of funny because she wasn't very bony. "You got any money?"

We had lots of money, because we sold a lot of muffins to people coming out of the outhouses. The money was in my backpack, which I was wearing. But I wasn't going to tell them.

Bethany shook her head. She looked really scared, which I don't blame her for because those girls are bad. They have no leadership qualities. Or maybe they do, but only the criminal kind.

"Come on, retard. I saw you selling those muffins. Where's the money?"

The three girls were standing really close to Bethany. Part of me wanted to go back in the portapotty and hide. I'm really sick of people being mean and angry. And my stomach hurt and I hoped I wouldn't have to go back to the hospital.

"Leave her alone," I said. My voice sounded kind of weird and low, like a scary movie. I barely even could tell it was my voice.

Bethany stared at me. The big girls stared at me.

The biggest one, the one who called Bethany the R-word, put her hand out.

"Hand it over or the retard dies," she said. All her friends laughed, like that was really funny.

"Bethany, go find Prudence," I said.

Before Bethany could leave, one of the girls grabbed her finger and kind of twisted it. Bethany started crying, which I didn't blame her. I put my hands in fists so they couldn't get my fingers and break them.

"Give me the money," said the big girl. She put her face right in mine so I could smell her breath, which smelled like cigarettes and like she just woke up.

"No," I said. "The money's for the farm."

The girl, whose face was fat and white, smiled, but not in a nice way.

"Then I guess it's into the shitter for you," she said and grabbed me and squished me under her armpit and started to drag me toward the outhouses. I was probably starting to suffocate when a voice said to put me down or let me go. I couldn't tell exactly what it said because I was kind of smothered.

I couldn't hear what happened next because my face was all smushed into the girl's shirt with the skulls on it that smelled like sweat. When she let me go, she pushed me away and I nearly fell down, but someone caught me. Someone tall.

I looked up and saw a man in a really nice gray suit. He had a suntan and wore a big, white hat. He was old but extremely fancy.

"This one of yours?" he asked someone. That's when I saw Earl standing near us. He wasn't tall or fancy. He was just Earl and he had whiskers and no suntan. But I was really glad to see him. Seth was with him and Prudence too. We were all there.

"Yup," said Earl.

"And these other little fillies?" asked the man in the hat.

"It's time they were leaving," said Earl.

"Hillbillies," said one of the girls, slouching away toward the drive-way.

"Smells like piss around here anyway," said another one.

When they were nearly past the house I heard one of them whisper, "Is that guy famous?"

"Shut up. Old people can't be famous," said the one with the skull shirt.

And then it was just me and Bethany and Prudence and Seth and Earl and the man with the fancy hat who turned out to be Earl's brother, the one I saw on TV. Plus all the people who wanted to write about Earl and his brother. And quite a few other people, like maybe twenty or so, who just happened to be wandering around and wanted to see what was going on and a few who wanted to use the bathrooms or buy muffins.

It's funny how you can be all alone and in danger and then a minute later feel totally safe, like you've never been lonely before.

PRUDENCE

Merle had tremendous star quality. Of course he wasn't a young man, but he leaked charisma. As soon as he and Earl met it was as though an electrical current ran through the crowd. Merle had a far more pronounced American accent than Earl, whose accent is an odd mix of what I had begun to recognize as small-town Canadian and grumpy old man of indeterminate heritage.

"Earl," said Merle. He tipped his hat slightly. His legs were long and thin and slightly bowed. There was white piping on his suit and his tan seemed to glow against the light gray of his suit.

"Merle," said Earl.

Someone took a photo when the two of them shook hands and a big black man in Merle's entourage, whom I later found out was the band's chef, frowned and the young reporter put the camera away. I thought that was a nice touch.

They weren't saying anything so I took the opportunity to take control of the situation.

"This is wonderful. Just wonderful. I know you two have a lot to catch up on. Including what time you'd like to go onstage tonight and what songs you'll perform."

I put a hand on each of their arms and managed to swing them around so they were facing Merle's gray motor home with the blacked-out windows.

"You'll both want to duck in there and relax and have a visit before the show."

Earl and Merle allowed me to steer them but they still weren't speaking.

"Merle, if you have any good concert clothes you could lend Earl, that would be fantastic."

Earl stopped up short. "I ain't wearing no special outfit."

Merle shook his head. "You never did want to get with the act."

"That is SO interesting!" I said loudly enough to distract them. "I bet you two have a lot of old memories to talk about."

Grudgingly, Earl allowed me to get him moving again.

"Goddamn it," he muttered.

I stopped at the steps of the bus and slowly Merle climbed up. He went inside and disappeared.

Earl looked at me, his small eyes bright and shiny.

"Thank you," I said. "Thank you for doing this for us." Earl grunted and said he goddamn hoped so.

Then he stepped inside and the screen door slammed shut behind them.

When I got back to the performing area, the first band was up onstage, playing a song. Brady was acting as MC and doing a fine job. In addition to his pornographic writing abilities, he really does bring a wide array of skills to the table.

The band consisted of two men in bolo ties and muttonchops and a woman in a full-length denim skirt. They played and people in front of the bandstand danced in the afternoon sun. That high thin music sounded amazing drifting down to the flat rocky ground like it belonged. Every so often the three musicians would crowd around the big microphone, singing harmonies and solos about leaving and loving and taking a load off their minds.

In the crowd hippies twirled and some country-looking older people, locals, maybe, danced in pairs, turning in tight circles together. At the edges of the crowd people had pulled up lawn chairs with umbrellas stuck in them. There were old people and kids.

I stood back and marveled at the scene. I had a feeling this was just the beginning.

When the song ended I felt the hand on my shoulder. I knew whose it was.

"You aren't ever going to apologize, are you?" he said.

I put my hand over his and patted it.

"No. It's just not my thing."

"You're a woman of great certainty," he said. "And you grow a nice, if small, radish."

"Thank you."

"Can you dance?"

"Of course," I said, even though I can't really. I think enthusiasm counts for a lot in dancing and in life.

The band moved into a slower song. The music journalists who weren't hanging around outside the bus trying to overhear Earl and Merle's conversation snapped pictures of the crowd, which was expanding around us, everyone giving everyone else just a little elbow room.

Eustace wasn't a very good dancer either.

SETH

I think for me the best part was when Merle and his band got up on that little bandstand and the crowd went wild and I thought, fuck, this is really something here and it's kind of cool that I'm actually seeing it. I wondered how much I'd missed up to this point, which they say is something that happens to people who are newly sober. You know, you start to wake up and find that life's not complete shit. Most of it is, but not all.

I was standing there watching, waiting for Earl and Merle to go onstage, and wondering how it felt to grow up with rhyming names, when my mom walked up to me. She was back in the Bedazzled jean pantsuit.

"You look good, honey," she said.

"Thanks. I feel okay."

"I'm glad I made the right decision."

"What do you mean?"

She took a deep pull on her smoke and the tip flared.

"Had to get you out of the house, babe. That shit with the drama teacher wasn't worth throwing away your whole life."

"Nothing happened with the drama teacher," I said.

"Bullshit," she said, and then went into a coughing jag. "Okay. I got to go meet Bobby in the beer garden."

"Okay, Ma," I said.

Then my buddy Corey came up.

"Hey man," he said.

And I thanked him for hooking us up with the toilets.

"Just glad you're out and about. Hey, you still doing your websites?"

"I don't know. I'm not as into blogging right now."

"Really? I thought Raging Metal was pretty good."

"You went on there?"

"All the time, dude. I'm Red Bull. I commented and everything."

"That was you? Why didn't you tell me?"

"You were doing your recluse thing. Anyway, glad you're out. You want to hit the beer garden?"

"Nah. I'm not doing that right now."

"Just like Steve Tyler. Right on," he said and stayed standing beside me.

The band took their positions and there was this pause and some instrument tuning and then some respectful head bowing when Merle climbed onstage, followed by Earl. Earl looked like he wished he was anywhere else. I recognized the signs. It nearly killed me that he hadn't even changed his clothes. I'm talking summer long johns poking out from green pants, grizzled old whiskers, his small selection of head hairs not even combed. The difference between him and that band was almost painful, you know, but it was real. Have you ever seen in magazines a regular person getting an autograph from one of the Bigs, a Pitt-Jolie or maybe a Depp? How you get this clear visual proof that life isn't fair? It's harsh but it's also invigorating or something. The reality of it. I can't explain it, except to say that when Earl got up onstage I felt kind of torn up for him.

But then something happened. He walked over and picked up his banjo and he looked a little better. I'd seen the man handle a hammer. He was no natural with the implements, I can assure you. But he looked good with that banjo. It added a whole other dimension to him. People started to clap. Even the ones who didn't know the family history. They sensed something going down. And they clapped more and more and they all stood and that applause rolled over everything.

Merle waited until people quieted down, paused, then said, "I'd like to introduce my brother, Earl. He lives in these parts."

Every local in the crowd went mental, yelling their heads off.

Then the music started.

I'd liked the first few bands okay. And I walked past some of the bluegrass workshops and they were cool, too. Some of the people could play and some couldn't. That music has a way of growing on you. But the truth is that nothing prepared me for Earl and his brother.

Earl kicked it off. He stood stock still a little way apart from the rest of the band. I swear to god, if Corey hadn't been standing beside me when I heard the first notes, I might have fallen over. Earl played like a demon. Seriously. He was like some old style music version of Joe Satriani. His fingers flew and he was using that special technique all the music journalists kept talking about. After a few bars Merle leaned into the microphone and started to sing. Dude had a voice. You know. Hairs rising on the back of the neck kind of voice that was raw and sweet at the same time. Earl moved up to his microphone and started to sing along and his voice put the whole thing into the stratosphere. Magic. The rest of the band joined in, tight like they'd been playing three shows a day for twenty years. And one of them was this youngish girl, like maybe my age, and they gave her a little space and she did this fiddle solo. I swear to Christ she was the most rock and roll thing I ever saw. The music journalist near us from the Japanese bluegrass magazine kept saying, "Holy shit. Holy shit. Holy shit," only because of his accent it sounded like a prayer. The writer from the *Newgrass Review* was literally crying. And Reporter Travis was sort of crying and laughing and doing this compulsive thing with his hand, like he was conducting. And when the song was over, so was I, sort of. And I wanted that fiddle girl's number.

I'm telling you, it was worth sobering up just to have not missed that.

Earl

It didn't feel half bad to get up there and play. I was just glad I didn't make a damned fool of myself. But I can also tell you I never got the same charge out of being onstage that Merle and Pride got. I don't give a shit if people like me or not and that's the truth.

After the set and the encore and once we got through the whole damned herd of people, reporters and bluegrass fans and young folks in old-timey outfits, Merle asked me to come back to what he called his office, which was the living room in the big motor home. With the sliders out, the damned thing was bigger than my cabin.

Once we were seated and I turned down a drink, 'cause I never did drink after Pride, Merle asked me if I felt it too, when we played.

I thought about playing dumb, but you know, we was getting to be old and there's only so many goddamn games you can play before you run out of time. I told him it was good to get up onstage with him and his band. He asked if I wanted to do a reunion tour around some of the bigger festivals. Maybe go to Nashville. He said his manager had been getting offers from promoters and organizers ever since word got out about the Woefield festival.

He said it was like I never left the band and that a person could hear the family connection when we played. I said that was true in some ways, even though it wasn't. Not really.

Then he asked again if I wanted to come on the road with them.

I sat for a minute or two and looked out the window at the dark. I could see fires burning at the campsites along the field and headlights sliding by from cars leaving. There was another act playing. I know we should have gone last so we could have kept people around drinking beer for longer, but I told Prudence I wasn't going to play in the goddamn dark and I wasn't missing my bedtime or I'd be dragging around here for a week. Truth is, I wasn't going to sleep worth a damn after all the excitement and I knew it as well as anyone. That got me thinking of Merle on the road all these years. Never going to bed on time. He might have a big RV bus instead of the Oldsmobile, but that didn't mean he wasn't on the road all the same. Only person I ever saw who loved being on the road all the time was Pride and that's cause he liked to leave a town behind once he'd been there, especially if he got to drinking in it.

I told Merle I didn't think I'd be leaving, unless Prudence sold the farm. He asked what was keeping me here and I said it was what I was used to. Then he pulled a check out of his pocket and slid it across the table to me. He said it was proceeds from our folks' old place. He'd sold the property a few years back when times were tight and nobody was listening to bluegrass much, but he held onto my share for me because he knew I'd surface sooner or later. I felt a sting in my heart then, thinking about where we grew up. And then it was gone. I can only give a good goddamn about one place at a time and might as well give a shit about one with some young people on it, even if they are pains in the ass worse than I've ever known, except little Sara, who's bossy but a good girl no matter how you look on it.

Merle got a funny look on his face when I told him I had to stay around to make sure things didn't fall apart. But he didn't say nothing, either. I told him Prudence has a hell of a lot of energy. Kind of reminds me of our old mother. A real domino, if you want to know. I told him Prudence would make a go of it, if anyone would give her half a chance. I figured with the money from the concert and if I bought a bigger share in the place, she just might have a shot.

So that's it really. The big reunion between the remaining Clemente brothers. My oldest sister died nearly ten years ago and Luanne a year after that, so me and Merle was the remaining Clementes, period. For all his fooling around, Merle never had no kids of his own.

All said and done, it wasn't something I regret. I just wish Pride'd been with us.

Sara

The rest of the night was extremely fun. Bethany's parents wanted to leave when the music started, but she really liked it and sort of started dancing, which I'd never seen before. Bethany has a lot of rhythm, at least that's what Seth said when he saw her. Her parents started smiling even though you could tell they didn't want to and her mom said to her dad that she must get her moves from him and he squeezed her mom's bottom and she giggled and it was really nice. Bethany's pretty lucky in some ways.

There were a lot of people who got sort of frisky because of the music. I saw Dr. Eustace and Prudence in his truck, but I didn't want to look too close and get a bad opinion of them. It's important to give people the benefit of the doubt even if they don't deserve it.

It was also very fun when I saw Seth dance with one of the girl musicians. Seth has almost as much rhythm as Bethany!

Later, after she got out of the truck with Eustace, I heard Prudence tell the bank lady that the concert and a new investor meant she was going to be able to get "up to date." I don't know what that means. Then they started talking about "intensive grass farming," which I know about from a lecture we had from a visiting 4-H speaker because it involves chickens. Chickens have a role to play in many kinds of farming, including grass. That's something a lot of people don't know.

I was very surprised when the mean girl who comes for writing lessons with her mom came over and told me she was sorry about her friends and they were sort of douche bags and I shouldn't take it personally. I don't know what a douche bag is, but it was nice of her to say. Those writing lessons really seem to be helping her with her personality.

All in all, I heard a lot of things and enjoyed myself. I even remembered to take my phone call with my mom and she said she's going to stay in Winnipeg with her sister and won't be coming home until the end of the summer. She said she talked it over with Prudence, and me and my chickens will be staying at the farm for the time being. Then she cried, but only for about half the time she normally does. Maybe she's feeling better.

My dad showed up at the concert. Prudence hired him to drive impaired people home and he seemed to like having something to do. Maybe he will become a taxi driver, like Prudence's friend Hugh. My dad told me he was sorry about all the yelling and throwing things and inappropriate behavior. He said he's left his construction job and is going to look for a new job and that he was sorry I had to be a "witness to his personal breakdown." I said that was okay, that everybody gets mad sometimes. I didn't say that most people don't stay mad for most of another person's life. He asked what my plans were, like I was an adult. That made me kind of sad.

I said I was staying at the farm because I like it and my stomach doesn't hurt when I'm with my chickens. He said he understood and he was going to try and get set up for when I was ready to spend time together and we'd "revisit the subject in the fall." I said he could come and see the chickens whenever he wanted. I even said he could come to the next poultry show, as long as he doesn't get in any fights. He swore then, but to himself, and before he could say anything else his walkie-talkie went and he had to go drive another person home.

It was good talking to him and also good to see him leave.

I went to visit Earl in his cabin to see if he'd teach me to play the banjo or the mandolin, whichever is easiest. When I got to his porch, Travis and Seth and Prudence and Eustace were already sitting there, up on the porch with Bertie. And Earl was saying, "Goddamn it, I don't want to talk to no goddamn reporter or be in no book." But they all just laughed. And so did I. Because he didn't mean it. He almost never means what he says.

Acknowledgments

I would like to thank all the people who dream of growing their own food and those who actually do it. Thanks to my mom, my brothers, Bill Juby, Stephanie Dubinsky, Greg McDiarmid, Susan Nielsen and Hilary McMahon for reading and rereading the manuscript; John and Shirley Alcock-White for giving me a tour of their little patch of abundance and regaling me with tales of sustainability; Megan McDiarmid for telling me about the apples sold at the market outside the Bronx Zoo; and Jeremy C. from the computer department at London Drugs for saving my life, or at least this manuscript. Finally, an extra special thanks to my editors, Iris Tupholme and Jeanette Perez.